Something had sl[...]
loneliness, the worst kind, the deep-in-the-
gut realization that I had been lonely before her without knowing it, but now would
never forget it.

I don't know how we got into each other's
arms, but I was stroking her hair, shushing
her sobs, wondering what would happen
next between us. It didn't seem possible
that either of us could undo the suspicions,
the bitterness, could usay the words that
had cut so deeply

Then the glass shattered. The sound of the
shot seemed to hit me a split second
later . . . .

The
First
Directive

Joseph D. McNamara

FAWCETT GOLD MEDAL • NEW YORK

Library of Congress Catalog Card Number: 84-4984

ISBN 0-449-12863-6

This edition published by arrangement with Crown Publishers, Inc.

Manufactured in the United States of America

First Ballantine Books Edition: January 1986

ACKNOWLEDGMENTS

With appreciation to Rochelle for her editing and photography and to Don for his early laughter. I thank Bob Cochnar for his encouragement and advice. I appreciate Bobby Miller's help and salesmanship. Jim Wade has my gratitude for his insights and for making me work harder than I intended.

One

BINI WAS SENIOR INVESTIGATOR IN THE SQUAD. THE SIGN on his desk read, "Our day begins when yours has ended." Homicide Squad humor. We worked in Northern California's technological wonderland—the Silicon Valley. Nearby, hundreds of corporations used tiny silicon chips to create microelectronic miracles destined to improve everyone's lifestyle whether they liked it or not.

But, at 0730 hours on Thursday mornings, we gathered to ponder those whose lifestyles had ceased to exist. The police department didn't respond to all cases with similar enthusiasm. Some of the dead were more equal than others. My team got the unequal. I waited for Lieutenant Foley to stick us with the dirtiest and most routine case on his list.

He stood at the distant end of the room, attempting to rise above the noise. "O.K. Listen up, men. It's time to set priorities, allocate resources, and exchange information relative to current cases."

The conversation of twenty detectives continued unabated. Nervously, our lieutenant fingered his silver 187 belt buckle. Section 187 of the California Penal Code justified our existence. It specifies the various illegal methods of taking a human life in the Golden State. The buckle, purchased to make him one of the boys when he took command a year and a half ago, had been a noticeable failure. He appeared wearing it on a Tuesday. By Wednesday, all other such ornaments sported by members of the squad had vanished from view. Now he rubbed the buckle like a genie's lamp, wishing in vain that it would bring forth respectful attention to his words.

The meeting droned on for an hour. Foley finally ended it. "O.K., men. That's it. Remember, anyone needing more information or some advice, feel free to come and see me." That got a few smiles, but people were already beginning to move back to their desks.

I was puzzled. There had been a couple of fatal wino knife fights, the kind usually dumped on us, but Foley had assigned them to other investigators.

"Fraleigh! You and your team. In my office. Right now!" he boomed. People hovered momentarily, wondering along with us, What is he up to now?

From the other side of the room, Bini wisecracked, "Are those guys getting another award, Lieutenant?" Foley's dislike for us was always good for a laugh.

Obediently, we trudged into his office. My two assistants, Paul English and the Block, thought it amusing to crowd in front of me and take the only seats, while I stood.

"I have a new case for you. A sixteen-year-old girl is missing under suspicious circumstances." Foley leaned back in his chair, enjoying our amazement. "Here's the file." He pushed the case folder across the desk. I made no move to take it. A snapshot of the girl slid out of the file and toppled off the desk to land at my feet. I didn't look at it.

"It's probably going to be a big one," Foley said into the silence.

"A big one? You haven't even spelled out enough to

make it a legitimate missing persons case, yet. And when did we get transferred out of Homicide to Missing Persons? Was I so engrossed in one of those important homicides you assigned us that I missed the orders?''

Foley couldn't quite keep the venom out of his voice. "Now, now, Fraleigh," he baited me, "we can't be too careful, can we? After all, remember how disturbed you were that we didn't pursue the Tricia Greene case sooner?''

"Tricia Greene?'' I snarled, incredulous that Foley would ever dare mention *that* case. I started toward him.

"Fraleigh!'' His voice went high and thin.

Paul English got up. Reaching for the case file, he obstructed my passage behind the desk. I took a deep breath.

"You . . . you were going to hit me.'' Foley's voice was still high.

"Hit you? I?'' English asked in his well-modulated, uncoplike voice.

"Not you. You know I didn't mean you. I meant Fraleigh. You saw it. We're going to the captain. You're a witness, too,'' he accused the Block.

The Block just sat there looking murderously at him. It wasn't anything personal. He looked at everyone like that, but Foley faltered.

Anger replaced alarm on his face. "I warn you, I'm going to be watching all of you closely on this case.''

Paul picked up the case file, which was just as well, because my hands were trembling. Tricia Greene . . . There might have been lower life forms than Foley, but I doubted it.

"We'll talk to the kid's father today and begin looking for her tomorrow,'' I told Foley disrespectfully over my shoulder, leaving his office.

English, a wise-ass, waited in mock deference, waiting to be dismissed. Walking away, I heard Foley saying, "You can go now, men," and English's camp reply, "Thank you, sir."

Back at my desk, I started through the file. Lisa Stone was beautiful, I conceded. There were two pictures of her, both professionally produced. A formal portrait in a pink lace dress enhanced the color in her cheeks and her honey-blond hair. I studied the delicate features and smiling eyes. She had a glow of youthful health and spirit. Somehow a sense of character flowed out of the picture.

The other picture was quite different. Her eyes were just as blue and the pure white Hollywood smile just as dazzling, but this time, she was looking over her shoulder, and her face was overshadowed by a shapely, little blue-jean-clad rump, which she had cocked at the camera.

I scribbled what statistics there were into the case bio sheet slots. Victim: Stone, Lisa; Height: 5'6"; Weight: 109 pounds; Race: Caucasian; Age: 16; Sex: Female. Decidedly, I thought. I would have to supervise English especially closely on this one. For a cop, he had a marked indifference toward the law in general and a complete disregard for statutory rape laws in particular.

I glanced at my subordinates. SOP was that each of us maintained our own copy of the case file. Paul English, a Robert Redford look-alike and a cop only by accident, was gazing dreamily out the window. I wondered if he had even opened the file. The Block, 265 pounds, five feet nine, looked like an ex-pug bouncer in a Grade-B movie. He was intently reading the papers, his sausage-size fingers slowly moving across each line, leaving smudged sweat marks as a trail of his progress.

Since Foley had dumped them on me, their on-duty antics had left me little time to think about the cases we worked. Not that they took much thought. Foley saw to it that we got the dregs. At best, Mom and Pop homicides requiring a strong stomach more than any deductive ability.

Suddenly, the Block looked up. "What's the big deal over Tricia Greene?" he questioned English.

A sharp pain cut through the lower section of my guts like someone had fouled me with a punch below the waist.

"You were still in uniform then, but the case has tortured Fraleigh's conscience for the past couple of years," English replied.

"Paul, shut the fuck up! That's an order!" I told him.

Relentlessly, he continued. "She was responsible for Fraleigh committing the unforgivable organizational sin. Tricia—"

The phone rang and English picked it up. I turned back to the Lisa Stone case file.

All questions over the assignment were answered by the third document in the file. It was a copy of a telegram from Lt. Gov. Fred Casey, in Sacramento, to the mayor of our fair city. He politely asked if local authorities could be of assistance to his longtime friend and associate, Adolph Stone, who, it seemed, was missing one daughter, named Lisa. Mr. Stone, being new in town, apparently hadn't yet had time to establish his civic-mindedness and good character by making hefty campaign contributions to the right local people, so had resorted to his old buddy, the lieutenant governor.

The telegram explained it all. No-balls Foley, in the face of that kind of political juice, had quickly put three homicide dicks on the case, making it top priority. It should routinely have gone to Missing Persons, but Foley wouldn't dream of taking a chance of offending some politico. As much as I hated to admit it, he had covered himself in case any police brass were alert enough to question the assignment. He would shrug, "Well, you know that team. Not much you can use them for anyway," and get away with it.

Carefully rendering unto the bureaucracy its due, I wrote "Thursday," the date, and "0850 hours" in the appropriate spaces of form 812 D-S Witness-Interview. Preparing to be bored by the standard parent lamentation on why his daughter just couldn't have run away to be a Moonie, Krishna, teenage addict, hooker, etc., I called the Stone residence expecting the butler to answer.

"Hello."

"This is Sergeant Fraleigh, Homicide. May I speak to Mr. Adolph Stone, please?"

"This is Adolph Stone. Thank God you called! I heard from them again on the telephone."

I hit the button on my phone recorder. "Them?" It had just become a case. "Could you tell me about the call, Mr. Stone?"

"There were two calls from this person and one from Lisa. This last call is very frightening. He said we don't have much time left to comply with his directions if we want to see Lisa again."

"What instructions did he give you, sir?"

"To wait for another call tomorrow. I'm sure this has to do with that madman Phillips and his Moral Reaffirmation Commune."

I stayed away from that for the time being. "Were any demands made for money?" I asked Stone.

"Yes. Well, no, not really. What I mean is that they must be after money."

"When did your daughter call?"

"At six A.M. I'm afraid I was half asleep. I had a terrible night's sleep, as you can imagine. But it *was* Lisa. I'm sure of it."

"As near as you can, sir, please repeat her exact words."

"Yes." He hesitated. "Well, she whispered that she was frightened. When I asked where she was, the connection was broken. I'm afraid that's all, but ever since she has been involved with this commune, I've been afraid of something like this."

The commune again. I couldn't put my finger on all the things bothering me, but it seemed to me that he was not the typical distraught parent by a long shot.

I wanted to see Stone. The telephone hides expressions, shifting eyes, nervous hands, and other signs of stress.

"Mr. Stone, I'd like to bring two investigators with me and take a full statement from you. Can we come over now?"

Incredibly, there was a pause of some thirty seconds before he answered, "Yes, of course. Do you have the address?"

Assuring him that we did and were on the way, I asked him to start preparing a list of Lisa's friends who might know something of her whereabouts.

TWO

VARIOUS ECONOMY MOVES BY THE CITY MEANT THAT IT
was now a major challenge to sign out a car with a reasonable chance of completing a short journey. We shopped
for about fifteen minutes and found a Ford that looked
moderately capable. Then I argued with the garage foreman about getting the car. He was adamant that we
couldn't have it without condescending to the point of explaining why. Catching the Block's eye, I nodded toward
the foreman.

The Block rumbled over, growling, "What's da mad-
der?"

Shrugging, the foreman handed me the sign-out clipboard
and walked away. No one argued with the Block. And no
one was quite sure how he got the nickname. Some said it
was from his football days, when legend has it that being
blocked by him was tantamount to sitting out the rest of the
season. Others claim that his father had thought he looked
like a block of concrete. Younger members of the department thought that it was his real name. Even I had trouble

remembering that his paychecks were made out to Arnold Schulster.

Spitefully, I tossed the clipboard, unsigned, onto a bench, knowing that an unsigned vehicle would cause anguish during the rest of the day for the petty dictator controlling vehicle use.

I drove. I hated driving, but with these two as partners there was no choice. The Block drove at an even sixty on freeways, through downtown crowded shopping areas, empty lots, fire lanes, play streets, anywhere. It was totally terrifying. Reportedly, when asked by a member of the Accident Review Board why he had hit so many pedestrians, the Block replied simply, "They keep getting in my way."

English, on the other hand, drove at moderate speeds, carefully observing traffic signs and regulations. The problem was he talked just as much when he drove as when he didn't. Of course, as he spoke, he looked you right in the eye, narrowly missing schoolchildren, handicapped persons, and elderly pedestrians. He was even more terrifying than the Block.

"How come you got right on this, Fraleigh? From what you said to Foley I figured you put this one way back on the list," the Block said as we rolled out of the police parking lot.

"What flea-brain Foley didn't find out was that the kid's old man got a ransom call. It's a snatch job if half of what Stone told me on the phone is true," I said, turning the corner smartly and cutting off a cabdriver before he could get ahead of me.

"You sound like you harbor some doubts as to the man's veracity," Paul English observed.

" 'Veracity,' " the Block snorted. "You're not at Stanford now, sonny; you're supposed to be a cop."

I swallowed a sigh. They were at it early today. Paul had

returned from Vietnam, a mental basket case. He had been enrolled in some kind of rehabilitation program at Stanford where he managed to get an honor's degree in classics, something the Block and other dicks never forgot.

"Doth thou think Adolph Stone speaketh with forked tongue?" The twinkle in Paul's brown eyes showed he was enjoying his impact on the Block.

"Maybe. Do you ever remember a relative getting a ransom call and not being sure whether or not they asked for money? Another thing, for some reason, Stone wants us to focus on a guy named Phillips, who runs the Moral Reaffirmation movement. Did you ever hear of them?"

Instead of answers, I got a question from the Block. "You're not going to tell Foley, are you?"

"Tell him what?"

"You know, you're supposed to tell him it's a kidnapping so the team can take over."

"Block, dammit! Foley and his special kidnap team couldn't catch the flu," I said, easing through the intersection on the amber signal.

"That's another red light you ran, Fraleigh," the Block chuckled, a sound resembling a truck changing gears.

"But the real answer to Fraleigh's haste, my dear Block," Paul interrupted, "is the tragic case of Tricia Greene."

"Knock it off, Paul!" I warned.

But English continued his monologue. As usual, I tried and failed to blot him out. "Fraleigh, your problem with Foley and the department is symptomatic of modern society, a state of anomie brought on by the dominance of large organizations. You're a bureaucratic Don Quixote, pitifully tilting at the inevitable inanities common to bureaucracies. Max Weber, the German theorist who wrote around the turn of the century, was the first to describe people like you. Yet, at the same time, you're not unlike Victor Hugo's Inspector Javert.''

English, in the front seat, never took his eyes off me as he delivered his analysis. Periodically checking the rearview mirror, I observed the Block sitting impassively. The game was to ignore English, never allowing him the pleasure of a reaction.

The Block had an unfair advantage over me. He didn't have normal human reactions to begin with. The mirror reflected a gorillalike image: huge head, covered with grizzly fuzz, sunken beady eyes, no visible neck, enormous arms and chest.

Our trip to Stone's affluent neighborhood took us through some of the less advantaged ones. The hot August sun had already sent the temperature above ninety. Here in the black section of town, it seemed even hotter. I wondered why Stone had said the connection was broken. That was a movie line, not real life, where people hung up.

Paul drifted away from organizational analysis. He was now saying something relative to Malthusian theory. I tried to guess how he would eventually work it around to quirks in my character. My mind wandered, attempting to recall what he had said about how Malthus's concepts applied more to Southern than Northern California. But he had already moved on, quoting Cesare Lombroso, the father of criminology, whose work on body measurements and criminals, according to English, probably explained the Block's antisocial actions.

Unfazed by the Block's total lack of response, English speculated on the similarity of Jeremy Bentham's utilitarian philosophy and the Nabokovian behavioral model explaining child sodomy in *Lolita*. I was fascinated now. He had the Block going. Some reference to the Block and child molesting might well provoke a battle between the two.

Checking the rearview mirror again, I saw that the Block's eyes were staring ahead, unblinking.

Shifting my glance forward, trying to disengage my thoughts from the ramblings of English's hyperactive, disturbed intellect, I was shocked to see us hurtling toward the rear of a tractor-trailer whose air brakes were working, but not its brake lights. I stood on the Ford's crummy brakes, sending us sprawling forward. We screeched to a halt after tapping the truck just hard enough to snap our heads back.

Three young black men were standing on the sidewalk. Our noisy stop had momentarily diverted their attention from hanging around the corner and spitting, a favorite recreational activity in the area.

I wanted to get us out of there. This little stretch of boulevard had produced more than its fair share of homicides. One from the riots came back to me uncomfortably. A motorist had died almost in the exact spot, and race relations were still tense this summer.

The largest of the heavily muscled men drifted up to us. The truck in front blared its horn at whatever was blocking its way. The leader reached the car and, putting his hands under the top of Paul's open window, said, "Hello, motherfucker."

Throwing the gear into reverse, I looked in the rearview mirror and cursed. A home-delivery milk truck was right on our bumper. It in turn was hemmed in by a Chrysler, behind which was a long line of traffic. No one was going anywhere. The scared face of the white, gray-haired milkman appearing in my rearview mirror showed that he appreciated the seriousness of our predicament.

Almost simultaneously with his "friendly greeting," the black man flexed his huge muscles and began to rock the car. In the background, a crowd of about thirty young people abandoned the basketball courts and slowly moved toward us to see what was going on. Things were happening in seconds, but somehow the whole situation was frozen in slow motion. My mind refused to accept what English said in response to the opening dialogue. "Hello, disadvantaged blacks," he said, smiling, as if we were exchanging greetings before a tennis doubles match.

Once more looking at the rearview mirror, I watched in horror as the Block pulled a "verboten" 9mm pistol from a shoulder holster and leveled it unmoving at the black man's midsection, which was conveniently framed by the open window. Any second I expected the weapon's roar. My mind flashed to the Internal Affairs and grand jury investigations that would follow.

The young black, dumbfounded by English's comment, released the car and bent down to look in. His eyes widened as he took in the Block's apelike presence. They got twice as wide as they dropped down to confront the evil-looking muzzle of the 9mm. Wildly, he looked from me to the pleasantly smiling English.

"You motherfuckers ain't cops—you mob," he exclaimed, backing away. The other two went with him, and people who had been coming forward to see what was going on stopped in confusion.

My palms were wet and knuckles white as I gripped the steering wheel hard to keep my hands from shaking. The pain in my stomach was intense enough to cause a spasm of dizziness.

"Don't fuck with the coons, sonny," the Block snarled at English. "They cut the nuts off assholes like you." The fact that the Block had been shook up enough to make a speech made my stomach hurt even more.

I heard myself barking at English, "If you want to check out, why don't you have the guts to do it yourself and not take other people with you?" A hurt look appeared and vanished instantly in Paul's eyes.

English rambled on. He was now calmly linking the incident—blacks, slavery, or something—with the elimination of rank in the Chinese Communist army. I felt my sanity slipping.

We had barely touched the back of the truck. I didn't think we had any damage, and I knew damn well the truck didn't, but I got out to check just in case.

"Shit!" Looking down, I saw the remnants of our broken headlight in the street. It didn't seem possible. But now all those dumb reports had to be filled out.

We were adjacent to a large park. Something was trying to break through in my memory. Smelling the freshly cut grass, I looked across the park lawns to the top of the red brick Booker T. Washington Housing Project, just visible through the trees. My God! No wonder it had seemed familiar. Tricia Greene had died just two blocks from where we stood.

"Fraleigh! For Christ's sake, are you crazy? You keep staring at that crowd like you're daring them to take us on."

Startled, I saw that the Block had gotten out of the car. He was squeezing my arm hard enough to leave bruises. I realized the crowd had stopped. A couple of loudmouths were urging people to come back toward us.

"We should call the patrol sergeant to do an accident investigation. It's a police vehicle involved . . ." I said without conviction.

"I don't think that would be particularly wise under the circumstances, Fraleigh," English said. "The crowd isn't especially hostile now, but by the time we and the uniformed people clear the scene, we might have real trouble."

With as much dignity as possible, I hurried behind the wheel and followed the departing truck. Even so, we took a couple of rocks on the roof from the stronger throwing arms in the group.

A mile safely out of the neighborhood, I pulled into a diner, lying, "I'd like some coffee." I needed to calm down before facing Adolph Stone.

I left the Block and English at the counter and headed toward the rest rooms. The men's room had all the conveniences and charm of a cell at the county jail. Ignoring the sewerlike smell, I splashed cold water on my face and began to feel a little better. After a vain search for a towel or toilet paper, I gingerly took off my new sports jacket with wet fingers and hung it up. Safely out of staining range, I began to shake my head and hands like a wet dog.

The door opened and a gray-headed man in an Ideal Milk Company uniform looked at me curiously. It took me a moment to realize that it was the same guy who had been stuck behind us. Even when the traffic in front had cleared, he hadn't dared touch his horn. By then, he had probably been more frightened of us than of the blacks who had so hurriedly retreated.

His eyes, carefully avoiding my face, took in the magnum in its shoulder holster. I continued to shake dry. "Go on, you can take a leak," I reassured him. He did as neat an about-face as I'd seen since my involuntary servitude in the army many years before.

A couple of minutes later, impatient with the drying process, I put my jacket back on and left the rest room, hoping the salesman had been wrong about even water staining the fabric. The Block was at the counter with a heaping plate full of eggs, steak, hash brown potatoes, and two bottles of beer. It was five minutes to ten in the morning. I slid onto the stool next to English. He was trying to convince the fat waitress that it really wouldn't be too much trouble to fix him up with some freshly squeezed orange juice.

The milkman, sitting a couple of stools away, was studiously not looking at them, but the mirror behind the counter revealed him blinking furiously when he noticed me joining the party. Abruptly, he rose and exited the diner, pausing only long enough at the deserted cash register to deposit a five-dollar bill. I saw that he had hardly touched his omelet or coffee.

Three

THE LAST MILE TO STONE'S HOUSE WAS STRICTLY HIGH-rent district. We drove steadily upward in bright sunlight on long, wide streets. It was new construction for the new wealthy. A lot of the homes couldn't be seen from the immaculate streets. The electronic entrepreneurs, venture capitalists, developers, and their well-rewarded chief executives, attorneys, and bankers hid behind luscious palm, eucalyptus, and pine trees, as green as the money of their owners.

The foliage spared the golden people from the sights below of dark-skinned children playing amid rusted, abandoned autos and decaying shacks. The dirty side streets emptied into a main drag populated by taco, hamburger, chicken, and wiener emporiums crowded next to used-car lots and convenience stores that sold a lot of cold beer.

All of this was also out of sight, sound, and smell of Stone and his neighbors. But with a good pair of binoculars they could look over the tops of the palm trees and gaze with affection on their various electronic manufacturing plants stretching northward for almost forty miles to where huge passenger jet airliners moved continuously in and out of San Francisco International Airport. Stone and his neighbors were high enough so that the toxic chemicals seeping into the ground from the "clean" electronic industry didn't threaten their water supply.

If they looked early enough, San Francisco Bay's sparkling blue waters added to their pleasure. Later, the view would be marred by the wave of dirty yellow air moving relentlessly southward to settle over two million people in the valley, which, a decade earlier, had boasted of its crystal-clear air and lovely fruit orchards.

At night, a million lights blinked up at Stone and his peers. A warm distant glow. It was easy for them to be unconscious of the stark grubbiness in which we worked. For years, growth advocates had proudly predicted that the valley would become the Los Angeles of Northern California. Each year, as the congestion, smog, traffic, and crime came to more closely resemble that of the City of the Angels four hundred miles to the south, the public screamed in alarmed protest. Yet, the building continued.

We pulled into Stone's estate, moving upward in the circular driveway. I put the Ford close to a new Jaguar XJ6 two-seater parked about fifteen feet from the entrance. Our car had appeared shoddy before, but now, next to the Jag, almost as if in shame, it decided not to turn off.

We had passed a distinguished-looking Adolph Stone standing next to one of the two white pillars framing the entranceway to the huge, elegant house. English and the Block, never without a sense of theater, ignored my "Wait" and advanced on the house as I fumed helplessly at the backfiring Ford. Finally, abandoning the damn car, which was still sputtering, I followed them.

Stone, obviously in his mid-to-late fifties, silver-haired, and slim-dressed in expensive slacks, blazer, and loafers, wore a frown on his handsome face. Paul, dressed in a flashy Hawaiian sports shirt, moved quickly, preventing me from getting close enough to lend any dignity to our introduction.

"Hi, I'm Paul English," he greeted Stone, waltzing past him as if he were talking to a valet.

Stone looked bewildered. He turned from following English's progress through the open door into the huge living room and actually recoiled as the Block, only a couple of steps away, rumbled toward him. Not to be outdone by English, the Block managed an awesome burp, ignored Stone, entered the living room, and sank heavily into a luxurious couch.

What could I do? "Mr. Stone," I tried, "I'm Sergeant Fraleigh, and those were Officers English and Block."

Precisely at that time, the Ford gave a final explosion and became silent. Stone gazed at the oily smoke plume from the backfire for a moment before turning to me. Shaking his head from side to side, he asked, "Those two men are police officers?"

"Have you been able to put together the information about your daughter I asked for, Mr. Stone?" I asked, edging toward the living room. I wasn't going to get into a discussion with Stone about them, but I sure didn't want those two guys left unobserved in his house.

The living room was standard California, multimillionaire version. English was prowling around the vast open space, no doubt preparing to regale us later with learned descriptions of its contents and the true significance of the various art treasures he was now cataloging in memory. He paused to admire a huge grandfather clock. Its rich walnut wood encased a brass pendulum that swung back and forth with hypnotic rhythm. As Paul moved on, the clock chimed the hour with magnificent gongs. It must be nice to be rich enough to own your own Big Ben, I thought, listening to the echoes floating through the open room.

After complaining about how long we took to arrive, Stone forgot about the Block and English and began to speak emotionally about his daughter. "She's a very special child, Sergeant," he began. I leaned forward to catch his words. "Her mother, my first wife, died nine years ago, and it hasn't been easy bringing up a sensitive youngster like Lisa. She's a beautiful person. Not just physically; I mean she has special qualities of feeling and compassion for people. Along with her strong spirit, it's sometimes worrisome," he added.

English interjected, "Isn't this an original Remington sculpture, Mr. Stone?" I resisted an impulse to walk over and kick him in the groin. Many times I had told him not to interrupt a witness who was talking on target. Despite my citing chapter and verse from interrogation textbooks that one person did the questioning unless specific strategy dictated otherwise, English spoke whenever he felt like it. At times it was as if he were humoring me, allowing some police work to be done during our field trips to observe life's spectacles.

The Block sat motionless, sunk deep into the plush sofa, his beady eyes staring fixedly at Stone, who answered English, "Yes, that's one of his finer pieces from his adobe period."

"No, I believe this is a later work from his range period," know-it-all contradicted.

He was probably right, I thought, watching a frown flicker across Stone's face. Our host murmured something polite in loose agreement as a flurry of movement caught everyone's attention through the french doors. A group of slim and fit young people was laughing and conversing alongside a pool that wasn't quite as big or as impressive as the Hearst pool at San Simeon Castle. Still, the marble construction job must have put some decorator's kids through Harvard or Stanford.

I tried to bring Stone's attention back to his missing daughter as a blond twenty-three-year-old or so he-man opened the doors, carelessly dripping water over the expensive parquet floors. About six feet two and two hundred pounds, he had the graceful figure of a running back: large muscular shoulders, strong legs, and narrow waist. He moved with the ease of a powerful athlete, but he staggered once, and I didn't think it had anything to do with the wet floor.

He owned a golden tan and wore a mini-bikini swimsuit that left nothing to the imagination of the nubile twenty-year-old females around the pool. Being on duty, we had hardly looked at them, even the two exquisite brunettes and the ponytailed blond with a ten figure.

"This is my son, Eric," Stone explained. He told young Adonis, "These men are police officers. They're here about Lisa."

"Three more public officials to add to your stable, Father?" he drawled, moving forward to shake hands. The Block was first in line. Eric Stone started to extend his hand, and the Block leaned forward on the couch to receive it, apparently missing the insult young Stone had just thrown at us.

"Speaking of stables," he paused, eyeing the Block, "do I shake hands with it or throw a saddle on it?"

"Eric!" his father admonished sharply.

Still smiling, Eric turned to English, extending his hand, "Hello, officer of the law."

"Hi, indolent rich young man," returned English, making no move to shake hands.

Nervously, I watched the Block's reddening face. He had already had more than his share of stress today.

"I think you may have miscalculated, Father. These three look as if they may not jump through the hoops quite as obediently as you're accustomed to."

"Eric, for God's sake, shut up!" Stone was as close to losing his cool as he ever would be, I guessed. Eric only smiled in response to his father's unhappiness. Then he sank into an easy chair to better savor his old man's disapproval. Eric's bloodshot eyes were normal enough for someone popping out of the swimming pool. And his slightly running nose, which he now carelessly wiped on his hairy forearm, might also have come from energetic underwater swimming. That is, if you ignored the very red mucous membrane between his nostrils. In our business we didn't ignore such things.

Adolph Stone's withering look would have demolished an ordinary son. Either Eric was made of better stuff or he was so high that he was oblivious. In any event, we resumed our conversation under junior's overly bright eyes.

Without stating it specifically, Stone implied that his short, apparently hasty second marriage had been an effort to provide Lisa and Eric with a normal upbringing. It didn't seem to have helped Eric, but I was curious about Lisa. She had really hit it off with wife number two, he told us. Stone didn't elaborate on why he hadn't, but that would be an easy one. One of the names he had supplied us with as possibilities for Lisa to have contacted was Doris Learner of Rio Del Mar, his second wife, Lisa's stepmother and presumably her pal.

The girl was, as he had indicated, a different kind of kid. She had been into a lot of causes for someone her age. At the same time, Lisa had been a normal, fun-loving girl, who had discovered boys, with gusto, about a year ago. He closed up a little as I probed this area. Naturally, it was important to know if her sense of adventure and excitement included older men, hitchhiking, drugs, blind beach parties, etc. Stone, intentionally or not, wasn't giving away much on these issues. He did point out that Lisa's best friend, Judy Fortune, could help. The two had become buddies when

Lisa spent part of last summer at the beach in Rio Del Mar with her stepmother. Judy lived nearby with her parents. Being about the same age, the two had become close. Her address was also added to our list.

We picked Stone's brain on general information for another twenty minutes. Then I tried steering him gently toward the telephone conversations, which stood out like igloos in the tropics. But Stone was a man who gave orders, not followed them. He continued at his own pace, telling us that Lisa had departed Monday A.M., according to the servants. The surf was up, and she had loaded her board on top of the Triumph convertible Daddykins had provided on her sixteenth birthday.

He had arrived home late that evening, about 11:00 P.M., after a full day of business, which included a dinner meeting. He hadn't really been concerned until the next morning. He admitted thinking that she was home, so he never checked her room. He added that even if he had, Lisa often stayed overnight with friends. Her being gone wouldn't have been a big deal. She was only a few days from her seventeenth birthday, and he believed in allowing her appropriate freedom. He put it to us as if we were going to be critical.

Instead, I politely asked, "And the first phone call, Mr. Stone?"

It had been the anonymous call that first alarmed him. Early Tuesday morning, just as he was leaving to drive to a business meeting in Carmel, about 8:10 A.M., he had answered the phone. The caller, not too clearly, said that if he wanted to see his daughter in one piece, he'd better be ready for a call that night.

The man hung up before he could question him. Putting it down to a crank call, thinking Lisa was safely asleep, he had left the house. After starting his car, he turned the ignition off and went back to check her room. Seeing that it hadn't been slept in, he became concerned and, around nine o'clock, called his friend, Lt. Gov. Fred Casey, for advice. Casey had been unreachable, but had returned his call around 1:00 P.M., by which time Stone was "deeply worried."

Diplomatically, I refrained from inquiring why our distinguished businessman hadn't pursued such a mundane course of action as calling the cops. I suppose if you spend a fortune in campaign contributions, the ego demands at least a show of privilege in return. But more puzzling was his failure to call any of his daughter's friends to see if she had stayed over.

Lisa's call had awakened him this morning at 6:00 A.M., after a restless night. She had told him in a whisper that she was frightened, and the connection broke as he asked, "Where are you?" Under prodding he conceded that there had been some background noise. We pushed that around unprofitably for a few minutes. He just couldn't identify the sound.

"Sergeant Fraleigh, I don't mean to be presumptuous, but I really think your first stop should be Guy Phillips. This Moral Reaffirmation Guild he runs deserves much closer scrutiny from law enforcement."

"Don't forget your own conglomerate, Father. That would certainly be an interesting study for law enforcement." Young Stone had appeared almost asleep, but apparently had followed the conversation. "For example, Lisa might not be trying to reform the guild at all. She might have returned to the Booker T. Washington Project to try to amend for your pillages of that hapless community."

Adolph Stone rose and slowly approached his son. I was sure he meant to hit him, but the young man slid easily out of his chair and headed back toward the swimming pool.

Stone senior had a touch of the aristocrat about him.

Clearly he felt no need to explain or apologize for his son's conduct.

I pushed him a bit. "Your son mentioned the Washington Housing Project, Mr. Stone. I had a case there a couple of years ago. I'm curious. Do you really own that property?"

"No. We've never owned anything there. I seem to remember that we had some options years ago, but obviously, it's not the kind of property we're interested in. We're not philanthropists, Sergeant, we're businessmen. My son likes to stir up trouble. I can't really say why."

The girl's telephone plea and the two vague ransom calls called for a change of plans. It was possible that we had a hoax or prank, but I really didn't believe it. I didn't like her call ending abruptly. Stone was uncertain about the precise location of the Moral Reaffirmation Guild, so we would head over to Santa Cruz and check it out. We could get the MRG location while checking out her surfing buddies, stepmom, and girl friend Judy.

A sense of urgency had developed as Stone spun his tale. We might have a dead kid and a live father with clout who didn't particularly like us. It made sense to try to find her immediately, especially with Foley gunning for us. Then too, it was the first interesting case we'd had in months. I assured Stone we would get right on it and let him know as soon as we had any information.

Four

WE HEADED BACK INTO THE VALLEY. THE DAY'S SUPPLY OF smog had arrived and wiped out the horizon. Since we had not scheduled ourselves for the trip out of the county, I telephoned Gladys, our secretary. She was unhappy that I interrupted her lunch. The squad detectives estimated that it lasted from about 11:45 A.M. until 4:15 P.M., when she judiciously stopped out of fear of ruining her appetite for dinner.

It was important to make the official notification of where we were going, even at the risk of offending our gargantuan secretary. No one else bothered. On the other hand, no one else had the same loving relationship with Foley.

Grudgingly, she made a note of my call. I started to mention the broken headlight, but she interrupted me. In her own sweet, authoritarian way, she instructed me to call the office at 1700 hours, on orders from Lieutenant Foley, who desired an update on our progress.

"I'm putting you down as notified," she told me.

I hung up without confirming. That and not signing out our vehicle this morning was my way of striking back at the overregimented world we live in. It wasn't much, but better than nothing.

Then I called Raoul Chavez, one of the dicks who was always good for a favor. He bitched a little, but finally agreed to contact the telephone company to get a trap set on Stone's phone. The trap would trace incoming calls for us if the callers stayed on the line long enough. Stone had hooked his own recorder up, so we would have a tape of any future calls. If we didn't find Lisa in Santa Cruz, we'd have to call in the kidnap team and the FBI. Stone's house would be bugged from end to end by the time the experts finished stumbling over one another.

We drove west through an endless sea of new condominiums put up by fast-buck artists, who joined the Rotary and spread enough charity and political bucks around to keep from being lynched for highway robbery.

There had been a bad accident at Hamilton and Bascom. A weathered motorcycle officer was in the intersection directing traffic to let the ambulance and tow cars get in and out. Noticing our car, the way experienced cops do, he held the cross traffic, giving us the sly wink bike cops reserve for such occasions.

As he waved us through the intersection, English was cautioning me that I resembled Ibsen's Dr. Stockman in *An Enemy of the People* and that the eventual outcome was likely to be the same. I wondered what the uniformed cop's reaction would have been to that had he somehow been able to eavesdrop on our conversation.

Not getting a rise out of me, Paul decided to work on the Block. "I say, Block, didn't you think it rather transparent the way Adolph Stone stonewalled Fraleigh's line of questioning about the Washington Housing Project?"

"Screw you and the housing project. If I never go back there, it will be too soon. And one more crack from his son about me, and the old man wouldna had to worry about that punk sniffing any more coke. He'd be paying the bills to have his face put together again."

"I know you jest." Paul smiled happily.

"You two guys are queer about a housing project. Leave me out. You investigate the housing project. I'll get Stone's daughter back while you're getting yourselves sliced up in colored town." With that, the Block leaned back and took a little snooze.

I had only half listened to them, making the loop onto Highway 17, heading west through the Santa Cruz Mountains to the sea.

It was curious. For almost two years, I had tried to erase Tricia Greene and the Washington Housing Project from my mind. Then Foley brings it up out of the blue. Going to interview Stone, we almost get into a brawl a block from the project, and incredibly, Eric Stone implies that his father is involved with the project.

Against my will, I found myself remembering the afternoon I had rolled on the call. It had come over the air as I was returning to headquarters.

"A jumper or accidental fall," the dispatcher had said.

Everyday stuff. But it hadn't turned out that way.

There wasn't much of eight-year-old Tricia Greene to look at when I got to the scene, and what there was, was gory. Three marked cruisers were already present. A field-training officer was dutifully monitoring the performance of a young, blond female officer who had a nice ass and a very white face. That was understandable. The body had met the pavement headfirst, after a descent of some eight stories from the roof of a building in the Booker T. Washington Housing Project. The blond's shiny brass nameplate read T. BRUNO.

It was being routinely handled as a homicide crime scene. The female rookie had roped off the area around the body and was canvassing the crowd for witnesses to the fall or for someone who could identify the body.

My stomach didn't feel much better than the rookie's, but I squatted down next to the remains, looking for nothing in particular. Death as we saw it was always so undignified. The least we could do was to pay our respects to the victims by being interested. Then too, the photographs and neatly typed lab reports never totally captured the reality necessary for a homicide investigator.

A heavy-shouldered black man dressed in work clothes brushed by the uniformed officer and got right down next to me. "Oh, Lord, it be Trish," he moaned, slumping down in a half faint. We managed to lift his heavy form away from the body, which still hadn't been cleared for removal by the coroner.

The man turned out to be Lionel Greene, the victim's father. Returning home from his job as a telephone lineman, he had seen the crowd. His shock and grief seemed sincere, and it had taken a few minutes to get even his name from him. Nevertheless, when a child dies by violence, the parents are the first suspects. It was time to inform the mother that her daughter was dead. Then ask questions that only she could answer.

I took a reluctant T. Bruno with me. Greene stumblingly led us to his apartment in another high-rise building. A slender, pretty black woman in her early thirties opened the door. She backed away from us as we half carried her husband into the room. His sobs brought her hand up to her mouth in a gesture of pain.

"No!" she screamed. "I doesn't want to know. Don't y'all tell me nothing!" Mrs. Greene sank to her knees, crossed herself, and began wailing prayers. Across the immaculately clean living room, a framed photograph graced an end table. It was a picture of Tricia with her parents. She stood, happy and smiling, in a stark-white Communion dress. You could sense the pride of her parents, standing protectively on each side of their child.

Lionel Greene reached out a hand in an ineffectual gesture of comfort, but his own sorrow was too deep. I had brought the female officer along because they were usually good in situations like this, but I was a couple of years early. The kid's face was even whiter, and her eyes were moist.

I had a pain in my stomach. I didn't know it then, but it was going to get a lot worse in the weeks ahead. "Mrs. Greene, do you have any idea how this might have happened? Did Tricia come home from school today?"

Both mother and father stopped sobbing and stared at me. "You mean you didn't know? You ain't been looking for her and the others?" Lionel Greene's soft accent had been born a thousand miles away in Alabama or Georgia. "We reported Trish missing four days ago. She be the fourth little one done gone from this project in the last six months."

Something didn't add up. The city was over a million people. It was impossible for cops to follow every lost-child report. But four kids from the same housing development within six months? We should have known about them, especially since the Atlanta cases. Every large police department had begun to pay more attention to missing persons reports on children, including us. A new special order required the Homicide Squad to be notified when a child under fourteen had been missing for more than forty-eight hours. A pattern of four kids missing would have been of special interest to us. I hadn't seen any reports.

They saw the doubt in my face. The mother's anguish turned to hate. "If she was white, you would have known about her," she yelled, hammering my chest with her closed fist. Her husband gently stopped her, but his eyes on me were accusing, anything but gentle.

There was no point in trying to question them. I left my card. Bruno and I rode down in the rickety, urine-smelling elevator by ourselves. We had almost reached the ground floor when she asked, "Sergeant, was what she said right? You know, about if the child had been white, we would have known about her?"

Four kids from a white neighborhood? After a moment, I answered, "Yeah."

By the time the elevator bounced to a stop, she was crying softly. "The poor child and that poor woman."

I wanted to say something reassuring. I watched her, neat as a pin in the blue uniform, wiping away tears before she got out in public again. I noticed that she was wearing a wedding ring. Unless she was married to a cop, it wouldn't be on her finger much longer. Not that the divorce rate for men was anything to crow about. Women, on the other hand, typically divorced within two years of taking the job. It hadn't been like that in the old days. No one expected a woman to be a cop then. It had been mostly matron duty. Now they worked the street. Dealt with the garbage, picked up the DOAs, tried to cope with the things they saw, just like men did. No wonder when they came home, the baker, accountant, banker, or executive they had married couldn't understand.

Returning to the scene, I was relieved to see that Barney Fuller's forensic tech team was handling the case. We used two teams in homicide. You could always depend on Barney for a professional job. The other team . . . well, on one case they had classified deep red stains near the body as fresh blood, probably type O. We hadn't nominated them for any award when the state lab reports identified the scrapings as originating from a raspberry ice Popsicle sold by street vendors.

"Barney, watch this one. The kid was reported missing four days ago."

His raised eyebrows rebuked me. Barney was so goddamned thorough that occasionally we got on him for being slow.

"Thanks, Fraleigh. I'll try not to leave any limbs behind us when we leave."

I ignored his sarcasm. "Spot anything interesting yet?"

He paused before answering. Most dicks wouldn't get a word out of him until the last comma in his written report was checked and rechecked. But we had worked together enough through the years to develop mutual respect.

"Look at this, Fraleigh." He pointed to the child's tiny right hand clenched in a tight fist.

I tried to remember. Did rigor mortis set in that quickly in jumper cases?

"It's not rigor mortis. It looks to me like a cadaveric spasm. I won't be certain until I hear what the coroner has to say," he added guardedly. "But remember that cadaveric spasm means that any object held in the deceased's hand at the time of death will remain firmly grasped and require even more force to break the grip than if rigor mortis had been prevalent."

"So what did the kid have in her hand, Barney?"

"Here, look." He held up a transparent envelope holding a couple of dark hairs. Then triumphantly displayed another envelope containing a number of fibers. After deliberately putting them back into his closely protected evidence bag, he showed me a third envelope containing what I assumed were some dried blood scrapings.

"In addition, I took several smears from the subject's rectum. It's hard to be certain, of course, considering the damage to the body from the fall, but it's quite possible that it was semen. And look at this." He dipped into his gruesome bag to produce two glass slides sealed together.

I glanced down at the glass slides holding a cloudy smeared whitish substance with a single black hair starkly visible by contrast. "You're right, of course," Barney told me, although I had said nothing. "It's quite possibly a pubic hair."

I looked up at the rooftop, now overflowing with bright floodlights used by the tech crew evidence gatherers and photographers. "If she grabbed something in a spasm, that meant she did it on the roof, not after she hit the pavement. That means she was killed up there, not by the fall."

"Not necessarily," he said.

I thought I detected a trace of smugness in his voice as he continued. "After all, she could have been killed somewhere in the building, then the body hurled from the roof."

"After she had been sodomized?"

"Now, Fraleigh, you know I won't commit myself until the lab analysis is complete."

"Any wounds, Barney?"

He was considerably more reluctant to answer. "With a fall like this, numerous lacerations and the presence of punctures are to be expected."

"What killed her?"

"Only the autopsy can answer that."

"Between the two of us, Barney, if you had to bet, it would be the stab wounds and not the fall, right?"

"Neither." This time, there was no mistaking the smugness. "You didn't ask about the marks on her throat. She may well have been strangled. On the other hand, this child has been abused. We need to proceed slowly and carefully."

So we had a sexual assault homicide. On a child. It belonged to me, and I didn't like the feel of it. The Greenes' anguish, the anger and hate I had seen on their faces, had sent a chill through me. And what they said about the four missing kids being reported to the police didn't sound good. Besides which, Raoul Chavez and I were by our lonesomes. The third slot on the team had been vacant for two months since Phil Matsukawa had been made sergeant and gone to patrol.

The next day, I went to Lieutenant Henderson, the squad commander, for help. He was a tough old pro. In a couple of months, he was retiring after thirty years of service, but no one watching him work would have guessed it. I was pleasantly surprised when he agreed to let me have Bini for the duration of the case. Bini, in his early fifties, fat, red-faced, and slightly alcoholic, was easily the most popular dick in the squad. He was also the best investigator and had broken me in years ago when I was first assigned to investigation.

Raoul and Bini pulled chairs up to my desk, and we went over what we had so far. I briefed them on the meeting with Mr. and Mrs. Greene and summarized Barney Fuller's comments.

"You know, Fraleigh, you ought to go into the hospital and let them take a look at the ulcer you got. You have plenty of sick time coming. Let someone else handle this case," Bini said.

For a moment I wondered if I had made a mistake in asking for him. Had his drinking finally gotten out of control? But his eyes were clear and sharp. I was in no mood for his odd sense of humor.

"Listen, Bini, the department never knew you drank until you made the mistake of showing up sober one day, so let's stop the nonsense and get on with the case. We have a lot of work to do, and the brass will be on us as soon as the media put the heat to them."

"I mean it, Champ."

I had been boxing when I broke in under Bini. He had always called me Champ. His use of the term now reminded me of how close we had been. I paid more attention to what he was trying to tell me.

"You ought not to work cases on kids. It gets to you. Furthermore, not everyone appreciates your charm the way I do. You got a lot of enemies around this joint, and this case is a bummer. I can sense it. They'll love to see you take a fall.''

For a fleeting second, I thought of grabbing it, of not having to go back into the decaying housing project, not having to speak to Tricia's parents again. . . .

''Bini, I want you to go through the Sexual Assault Squad records.''

''Round up the usual suspects?''

''Right. And not just child molesters. If you see any other likelies, pull their files, too, even though they may not have messed with kids before. And set up a meet with the Sex Squad dicks a couple of days from now. We should have some good info for them to chew on by then. One other item, Bini''—he could find out anything, I thought—''check with Missing Persons. I can't really believe what the Greenes said about three other kids reported missing, but we need to know for sure whether other kids are involved.''

''O.K., Champ.'' Bini waddled out, all business. Fortunately, he had gotten off the counseling kick.

''Raoul, I want you to survey the housing project. You know, did they see the kid with anyone? Have they seen any suspicious strangers hanging around? Oh, yeah, see if they know about any other kids supposed to be missing.''

I sought out Barney Fuller in his lair. It was too early to be consulting him, but instead of greeting me with scowls, Barney was beaming.

''Got it all wrapped up, Barney?''

''Not quite. However, I think you will be happy to see that we have some goodies for you.''

''Yeah?''

''First, although the autopsy isn't complete, the coroner agrees that the cause of death, as I suspected, will turn out to be strangulation. Second, preliminary analysis indicates that the victim was dead when tossed from the room, and judging from postmortem lividity, death had occurred two or three hours before the body hit the pavement."

"Room? What room? When did we figure out that she hadn't come off the roof?"

"I personally reviewed every piece of evidence the technicians took from the roof. There was nothing. I went over it again this morning. Nothing. I'm prepared to state that the victim could not have been hurled from that roof without some trace evidence being present. Ergo, she must have been thrown from a room in the building."

"It's unlike you to be so prompt, Barney. Now tell me who did it."

"We do have to leave a little work for you sworn officers. Otherwise, they couldn't do all those television shows on cops. But if you find us the right male Negro, possibly five feet seven or eight, mid-twenties, who owns a straight razor, I will help you convict the son of a bitch."

" 'Son of a bitch,' Barney? You usually speak of 'suspects.' "

"I don't always have your objectivity, Fraleigh. This child was held prisoner for several days. When you read the report, you'll understand my reference to a straight razor and what happened to her during that period."

My stomach hurt. "When will you have the report for me?"

"It's in the typewriter. You'll have it on your desk first thing tomorrow morning."

"It seems to me that you're pretty optimistic."

Barney rubbed his hands together. "Fibers, Fraleigh. We picked up fibers from a carpet and two different pieces of clothing. You find the suspect and the place of confinement, and I'll match his fibers to those found on the child's body. As a special bonus, we'll find fibers from her clothing on his."

"Is it that sure proof as evidence?"

"Yes. Before the Second World War, clothing tended to be all cotton or wool material, mass produced. It was virtually impossible to differentiate one thread or fiber from another. But with our electron scanning microscope, we can isolate the synthetic fibers now used by their shape, cross-sectional characteristics, and chemical constituents. It was testimony on fiber evidence that convicted the killer in the Atlanta child murders."

Barney was a small man, about five six. As he stood there in his white lab coat, he was mentally on the witness stand.

"Didn't they criticize the electron microscope for destroying the fiber itself?"

"Ah"—his eyes glinted from behind plain metal spectacles—"I see that you do read, unlike many of your peers. It's true that the neutron activation bombardment of the fiber necessary for comparing it destroys the fiber. We, however, are using microspectrophotometry, an experimental ultraviolet-light process developed by the Royal Canadian Mounted Police. It provides fiber measurements so exact that I could testify with authority that the material is almost certainly the same."

"I don't like my cases coming down to testimony that something is almost certain."

His face dropped a little. Barney loved innovative solutions. "Of course, we also have this, look!" He led me to a microscope. "I lifted this latent from a toy compact in the victim's pocket. It was shiny metal and left a beauty of a print."

I looked down at the print. "It's a whorl, right, Barney?"

"I'm glad at least you didn't insult me by asking if I was sure that it wasn't hers." Excitedly, he edged me away from the microscope, putting his eye to it. "I'm about to make your day. You see, due to the complete circuit formed by the ridge in the center of this impression, the pattern looks like a central pocket loop-type whorl, but if you look more carefully, you can see that the left, or inner, delta is located on the recurring ridge. This spoils the recurve. Thus, it will be classified as a loop with twenty-one ridge counts referenced to a central pocket loop-type whorl with an inner tracing.''

"Yeah. That's what I said—a whorl.''

"Don't put me on, Fraleigh.'' He stood back from the microscope. "You know as well as I that it's a highly unusual pattern. Identification will be a snap. Just go out and collect the body belonging to the print. Even the nerds in the Fingerprint Section should be able to move quickly on a print like this.''

Barney had unsuccessfully tried to have the Fingerprint Section put under his control a couple of years ago. But I wasn't interested in bureaucratic wars. "The state Department of Justice has all registered sex offenders on file in their computer. We should be able to get an ID on this within ten days.''

"Ten days? Not with this print. I predict they'll match it within four hours.''

"Unless he's not a registered sex offender.''

Barney smiled at my fantasy.

"Remember the case last year, Barney. The rape murder of the woman in her bedroom. The guy was an out-of-state sex parolee. He slipped through the cracks. He wasn't on file in Sacramento.''

"No''—he smiled sweetly—"but your fingerprint technicians had his prints and missed him for four weeks, as I recall.''

"Can you send this over the facsimile equipment?''

"Of course I can. That is, if the department ever gets around to repairing it.''

"I'll have to find someone to drive it up to Sacramento. I don't think we want this character walking around any longer than necessary. Thanks, Barney.''

It was an investigator's dream. The odds were a million to

one that the killer's prints wouldn't be on file as a registered sex offender. We would tie him to it with his fingerprint, semen, blood, hair, and fiber analysis. Despite what I said to Barney, I knew the value of fiber analysis testimony when it was supported by other evidence. The knowledge that the child had been thrown from a room was also important. It was probable that we would be able to link the suspect to the apartment in some way, and Barney would no doubt get his additional fiber evidence.

Other events were moving as quickly as the investigation. The Greenes were respected members of their community. Their priest called an evening meeting of prayerful protest over the lack of police service in the neighborhood. Tricia's murder served as a catalyst, bringing black people's rage to a boil. The meeting didn't focus just on the lack of action on the missing children. Speakers raised long-held grievances against the city government in general, as well as past police shootings and brutality cases. The crowd was particularly incensed over steep rent increases in the housing project and eviction of families unable to pay. Mr. and Mrs. Greene sat in silent grief.

The evening after the prayer meeting, their church held a candlelight procession to the city hall in memory of the children. The mayor refused to attend, issuing a statement instead: "Although I have sympathy for the parents, I have full confidence in the police department." The police chief was quoted as "having concern that Communist agitators might be at work in the black community."

Constant media coverage of the events and rumors flooding the "black community" increased tensions. One rumor in particular bothered me. Word was spreading that police were dragging their feet in the investigation of the missing children because they had been molested and killed by a white policeman. Like most destructive rumors, a germ of truth lived behind it. A couple of years before, a white state patrolman had molested a twelve-year-old black girl in his patrol car. There hadn't been enough evidence to prosecute. A deal had been made. He resigned, left the area, and sought psychiatric help. It hadn't gone down well with the girl's parents or the community. Now word was spreading that he had been seen in the project, talking to children.

But that wasn't what finally ignited the riot. A year before, in an experiment of "government partnership with the private sector," the city had sold the housing project to a private corporation. The company got enormous tax write-offs and the promise of federal development money. The theory was that these benefits would be passed on to residents in the form of lower rents and improved facilities. Protests from residents and community leaders were dismissed. Several months later, the corporation quietly started raising rents. A number of families defaulted. Court orders were obtained by the corporation. One by one, the families were being evicted. A police officer was always assigned to preserve the peace while the court order was being executed.

At 1330 hours on day three after Tricia Greene's death, a cop on eviction duty shot and killed a seventeen-year-old boy in the same building from which Tricia's body had been thrown.

Young Louis Bryant had been full of hate when movers arrived to evict his family. He had armed himself with a butcher knife and defied the movers. He was screaming incoherently about Tricia Greene and the missing children and white man's justice. The officer, gun in hand, tried to talk him into dropping the weapon. When he lunged forward, slashing with the knife, the cop fired one shot. The boy died.

And that was it. All hell broke loose. Disorder spread to the streets. In the next three days, eleven people died. Four were white motorists dragged from their cars and beaten to death after unsuspectingly driving into the area. A police officer was killed by a sniper, never apprehended. A black child was killed when run over by a car out of control after its white operator had been hit in the face by a rock. A black store owner and his customer were shot to death by two white men cruising the area in a pickup truck. They were never identified. Three other black men were killed by police bullets in incidents connected with looting and arson of retail stores.

More than one hundred people were injured. A cloud of black smoke, marking the demise of just about every store and business within five square miles, hung over the neighborhood. The cloud of racial allegations hanging over the police department seemed to rob it of its ability to halt the disturbance. The riot would peter out only after there was nothing left to destroy.

In the meantime, the investigation was going well. Raoul had returned from the housing project with very interesting information. He had interviewed the mother of Felicia Frank, the first child reported missing six months ago.

"She swears that she not only gave all the information on her daughter to the beat officer, but even named a suspect. A Rodney Lark. She claims that he's been in trouble over kids before, and they've chased him away from the playground a couple of times. The beat officer was Clint Malgren. I worked with him years ago. I can't believe he didn't include the suspect information on the report."

"He did include it. Rodney Lewis, aka Rodney Lark, is one of the folders I brought down with me," Bini said.

"Why didn't Malgren follow up, Raoul?" I asked.

"He got rear-ended in his patrol car about five months ago. He's on disability. But if you really want to hear something, listen to this." Raoul's eyes shone. "The suspect's aunt occupies the top-floor apartment in the building that Tricia Greene came down from."

"What?"

"He's right, Fraleigh," Bini cut in. "I think Lark is our boy. He was busted five years ago for attempted rape of an eighteen-year-old female. Location? You guessed it—the Washington Housing Project."

Bini paused for a genteel belch. The sweetish mouthwash smell didn't cover whatever booze he had had for lunch. "While Lark is out on bail for the two-sixty-one charge, he takes a kid out of the playground and forces oral copulation. The victim's older brother was home on leave from the marines. He caught Lark and almost killed him. In any event, they let Lark cop to two-eighty-eight c, but the courts declared him a mentally disordered sex offender and shipped him to the state mental hospital for sex offenders at Atascadero. He got back about seven months ago—'cured.' "

Seven months ago. Just a month before little Felicia Frank disappeared. "Cured? Too bad those fucking doctors at Atascadero don't have to investigate the cases their 'cured' patients give us. Wait until you hear Barney Fuller's report on what this animal did with a straight razor."

"Take it easy, Fraleigh. This is just another case," Bini counseled, his whiskey-softened voice at its most low-key pitch.

"Yeah, just another case." I thought for a moment. "The facsimile equipment is out of order, but Barney got a beautiful latent. Let's take it to our fingerprint people and have them compare it with Lark's. When they match it, we can get an arrest warrant and search warrants for his pad and his aunt's. I bet we can make him on one-eighty-sevens for all four kids. It's almost like he was asking to be caught."

"That's not unusual for these people," Bini said.

"Yeah, I know. But we should have nailed him six months ago when the first kid was reported missing."

Bini glanced away from me, looking out the window.

"Well, Bini, how about filling me in on the saga of the missing Missing Persons reports?"

"Why not leave well enough alone, Champ?"

"Give, Bini."

"All right, you guessed it. The reports were never circulated. Missing Persons got a new lieutenant about a year ago. He blew it. Stuck them in his desk, that's all."

His face didn't go with the story. "You're full of shit, Bini. I've seen dozens of reports on missing kids since the department put out the new special order. Tell me why those four reports didn't go out. I want to know. All of it."

"I ain't from Internal Affairs," he protested.

"No, but you're still a policeman, a cop, Bini. I know your memory. You spoke to the lieutenant. Give it to me verbatim. I'll take the responsibility."

"You take on more than you ought to, Champ. O.K., verbatim. I asked the lieutenant about the reports. He smiled at me and said—verbatim: 'You've been around long enough to know that I have to be selective. I can't clog up the organization with paper every time some little nigger or spic kid doesn't come home for dinner.' "

Raoul's face had gone blank. Bini's softly spoken words echoed around us. I sucked in air like I had been hit. The terrible descriptions in Fuller's reports kept floating through my head. Three children had probably been tortured and murdered unnecessarily. Eleven people had died in the riot. It was beyond belief.

"Who was the lieutenant?" I asked hoarsely.

"Aloysius Foley," Bini answered.

The following day the riot was still in full swing when our fingerprint people confirmed that the latent print on the compact belonged to Lark. I stuck a copy of their report in the bulging case folder. We hadn't even needed it to obtain the arrest and search warrants sitting uselessly on top of my desk. All police personnel had been ordered to stay out of the riot area until further notice. The burning ghetto was encircled and isolated. The phone rang.

"Fraleigh."

"This is Officer Gentile on the front desk. There's a guy here by the name of Lark, Rodney Lark. He's got his lawyer with him, and they want to talk to someone about the Tricia Greene case."

"Send him up! No, wait a minute. Someone will be right down to escort them."

Bini and Raoul were all ears. "Lark and his lawyer are at the front desk, Raoul. Bring them up. I don't want them to change their minds and vanish on us."

We led Lark and his attorney into the interrogation room. Lark was clean-cut—the all-American look. His lawyer, considerably darker in skin than his client, wore rumpled clothes and thick spectacles. His voice lacked Perry Mason clarity. It was thick and coarse. "Gentlemen, let me inform you that my client, against my advice, is here to confess certain crimes to you."

"Wait a minute, Counselor." I didn't want any shyster tricks like a confession that would be ruled inadmissible because we hadn't conformed to some technical court ruling. "First I'd like to inform you that the tape recorder you see on the table is recording the conversation." I didn't see the need to inform them that the hidden mike was also recording the conversation. We had broken a number of cases by conspicuously turning off the table tape recorder. It was amazing how often the suspect would then spill everything. It wouldn't be necessary this time. We already had Lark cold.

Despite that, I gave him the Miranda warnings.

"I just couldn't stand to see any more of this burning, shooting, and killing. I came to tell you what I did to the children." His voice was clear and educated. Unlike his attorney's speech, Lark's had none of the street in it.

"Once more, for the record," his lawyer said, "I advise you to make no statements to the police."

"Shut up, you fool." Lark barely glanced at him.

Almost as contemptuously, he said to us, "I left clues from the start. I don't want to do these things to children. Why didn't you pay attention?"

We let Lark talk. He took three hours. He had taken all four children. He told us in detail what he had done to them, usually showing no emotion. But a few times, he suddenly wept into his hands. Then he would just resume his talk. He was enjoying himself. At one point, when he was describing the razor and Tricia Greene, I left him with Raoul and Bini and the recorder, and went into the john, where I puked without even looking around to see if anyone was watching.

Bini's eyes studied my face when I returned. Lark was almost finished. He was describing the locations where he had buried the bodies of the first three children.

"Rodney, what made you throw Tricia from the window instead of burying her like the others?" I asked.

"I had to do something to get you pigs to pay attention. I even sent you a letter about my concern for Felicia, and you did nothing."

"A letter? Where did you send it, Rodney?" Bini asked, ever so gently.

"I telephoned your so-called Information Desk three times. They really don't like to give information, you know?" he challenged.

"The letter?" Bini encouraged him.

"Yes," he drawled. Several times during his narration, I had wanted to smash that supercilious look off his face. Instead, I waited once again with Bini and Raoul for his answer.

"I wrote, as directed by the Information Desk, to the Missing Persons Unit. I was quite angry, you know. I wanted to know what they were doing about finding the little darling."

I got up and stretched. Lark's lawyer watched me.

"Did you sign the letter?" Bini asked.

"Of course!" Lark was indignant.

"With your own name, Rodney?" Bini was persistent.

"You fellows are really slow, aren't you? I suspect that it's the civil service mentality. I suppose one can't expect much from people willing to work in these shabby, unclean surroundings," he sighed. "Yes, I didn't put a return address, but I signed my name."

Bini and Raoul took Lark to the county jail after booking him on four counts of murder. We would consult with the D.A. tomorrow to see what other charges he wanted to add. The shadows were deep in the squad room. It was 2015 hours. I slumped at my desk, head in hands. The office was deserted.

Lark was a psychopath. He was capable of lying without even being aware of it. Yet, I was sure that he had told the truth about a letter. It was too bizarre a thing to make up and totally in keeping with his enormous egotism. Six months ago, a registered sex offender, using his own name, had sent a letter to the police department asking about a missing child. Nothing had been done. Two other children had died painfully, and the fourth had to be hurled eight stories to the pavement to get our attention. I was glad the mayor had complete faith in the police department, because I didn't.

I started. Bini had grasped my shoulder. Raoul stood behind him. "Come on, Champ, we don't want you sitting in the dark. We're going out to eat and get drunk," Bini ordered. We did.

But I didn't feel any better the next day. The riot had finally ended. I drove through the area on the way to work, awed by the burned-out destruction. I got to my desk and began to type a memorandum describing the case. It would be sent through the chain of command to the police chief. I didn't spare Lieutenant Foley, but in quoting him on "nigger and spic kids . . . and clogging the organization with paper," I made it appear that he had said it to me, not Bini.

Bini leaned over my shoulder, reading the memo. Silently he pointed out a couple of typos. I finished it with the conclusion that "irresponsible behavior on the part of the Missing Persons Unit commander led to three unnecessary deaths of children and was instrumental in causing a riot." I signed it and asked Bini to make a copy.

On the spur of the moment, I stuck the copy in the envelope, not the original. Let them worry about that for a while.

"Drop that in the captain's In basket for me, will you, Bini?"

"I don't help my friends self-destruct, Champ," he answered, and left for an extended lunch.

I dropped the envelope in the captain's basket myself. It was 1115 hours on a Friday morning. All day I waited. I was cleaning up a lot of paper work on the case and even stayed an extra couple of hours. There was no reaction. I was off duty Saturday and Sunday, but on standby. My telephone and pager were silent—until 1815 hours Sunday evening.

The phone rang.

I picked it up on the second ring. "Fraleigh."

"Fraleigh, Charlie Spetale. I'm watch commander tonight. I just got an official notification for you. You're to report to the Town and Country Motel, Hotel Circle, San Diego, 0900 hours tomorrow. It's a Federal Department of Justice course on terrorism for local police. You lodge at the hotel. Tickets for PSA flight 762, 0700 hours, are to be picked up at the counter. It's a two-month course, all expenses paid by the feds."

"Terrorism?"

"That's what it says, pal."

"Charlie, isn't it kind of unusual, getting a notification this soon before a course?"

"Yeah, but I guess you know more about this than I do, pal. I'm putting you down as notified 1820 hours, O.K.?"

"Yeah. Thanks, Charlie."

I got back two months later from my mandatory training course, one of the police administration's favorite techniques for burying employees too hot to handle. There had been too much heat to send Rodney Lark back to Atascadero, so his lawyer copped him out to two charges of murder one. It was understood that Lark would be sent for psychiatric evaluation upon admission to the state correctional system. In a couple of months, they would declare him insane, and he would be quietly shipped to a mental hospital so the doctors could "cure" him again.

Lieutenant Henderson had retired. We had a new boss—Foley. Bini and Raoul had been moved to another team. The Block and Paul English, two unusual characters to say the least, were assigned to me. Squad veterans concluded that the personnel changes represented the police hierarchy's response to my memo. The kinds of cases Foley had been assigning to my team made clear what his response was to the memo. I wondered more and more who had killed my memo. Who was Foley's silent protector? One thing was for sure. It was someone with lots of clout.

Five

Now, NEARING SANTA CRUZ, I KNEW THE RECESSION was still in full swing when I saw a couple of American cars among the Mercedeses, Porsches, BMWs, and Jags. But the ride had been cool, serene, and uneventful. The first sniff of ocean air as we entered Santa Cruz wasn't bad at all.

Neither Paul nor I cared much about lunch, but the rumblings from the Block's stomach threatened to shake our crummy Ford apart, so we pulled onto the Santa Cruz Pier. English and I settled for clam chowder at Stagnaros. I had a buttered piece of sourdough bread with mine, while he remained virtuous. The Block had a whole loaf of sourdough bread with his soup, three more bottles of beer, and an open-faced crab sandwich smothered with french fries. It quieted his stomach momentarily.

The young girl waiting on us simply couldn't keep her eyes off English. She didn't quite succeed with her hands, either, giving him a friendly pat on the shoulder as he kiddingly asked if she was studying for a career in films. Had I tried a line like that, she would have hit me with a bowl of chowder, but you would have thought English was Neil Simon the way she giggled and rolled her eyes.

I took advantage of her sexual arousal to flash the picture of Lisa Stone, something that apparently never occurred to English. I hoped he wasn't offended by my bringing some police work into our day at the seashore.

With real regret she admitted that she didn't recognize the girl.

"I'll keep my eyes out for her. Like, you know, these surfing kids are all over. Why don't you check back with me," she said, eyeing English.

Gallantly, he acknowledged that he would.

The waitress wasn't quite accurate about the surfers being all over. Most of them gathered along East Cliff Drive, opposite the now rarely used St. Joseph's Seminary. Maybe it was new gods being worshiped, I thought, watching the tan-faced youngsters, male and female, climb up and down the cliff. It was all rubber-suit stuff, the temperature of the Pacific never getting much higher than fifty degrees, even in the August heat. For Northern California, the ocean was to look at, not bathe in, unless you wanted to wrap yourself in one of the body-clinging rubber outfits. I never had, but no doubt Paul English, who talked of sky diving, wind surfing, and auto demolition derby experiences, had done this as well.

When the exact configuration of the moon, stars, wind, and tides were in place, English was one of the most skilled investigators I've ever seen. The conditions must have been just right because he led the Block and me to a shabby-looking mini-bus parked on a bluff overlooking the sea. Its amateur blue paint job was yielding to the moist salt air by the second.

The surfers, treading back and forth like so many soldier ants, would have been an impossible interview challenge for either the Block or myself, but English had rapport; that was clear. For me, it was difficult even getting their sexes straight. Clad in rubber suits as they were, you had to rely on other than usual indices to determine boy or girl. Hair length and style didn't work here, nor did heaviness of build. They were all slim from hours of water life. Rear ends and breasts were of some help, but in more than a couple of cases, I passed rather than guess.

Starting a conversation with them would have been tough, but Paul had no difficulty. He had apparently identified the head honcho, or surf-guru, or whatever, and within five minutes had him talking easily to us inside the smelly bus. At least, I assumed he was talking easily, because most of the conversation was unintelligible to me. They were jazzing each other about entering a tunnel and getting blown out like a freight train, power slicing, and digging rails. Also there seemed to be a discussion over the advantages of dovetail foam twins over round tails and quiver boards. I managed to control my excitement over it all.

Duane Fisher, the guy holding court, was about thirty-five or so, clad in ragged, faded blue-jean shorts, sandals, dark glasses, and a sickly looking two-day growth of blond fuzz on his chin, which matched the blond fuzz on his scrawny chest. He hadn't needed any announcement that we were cops, but Paul's success in breaking through seemed to be related to convincing him we weren't narcs. So much dope had been smoked in the bus that the aroma of the walls could give you a mild high if you let your imagination work. I didn't.

The Block had been staring hungrily at the beer can languishing in our host's hand.

"Beer?" He blatantly offered a bribe to the Block, who accepted instantly.

I must have been less frightening. The offer to me was only a nod and raised eyebrows. It's always important to put the subject at ease, besides which, it was hot as hell, so I accepted.

He climbed over a sitting youth, who was either stoned out of his head or comatose, and got two beers out of a small refrigerator running off a generator. I watched him closely to make sure the cans had not been opened or taken from a special batch reserved for cops and other unusual visitors.

Sitting on a hardwood fold-down bench, I had a clear view out the bus's front windows of surfers some two hundred feet or so down from the cliff. The surf was up, and awesome waves were breaking about three hundred yards out into the ocean. The jutting cliff provided the right topography to produce these monster breakers. It was fascinating to watch. For one thing, the skilled surfers had the grace of ballet dancers. Just as you were sure they were about to be crushed to death by the tons of breaking water, they would master the wave, standing on their boards, and for two or three minutes race horizontally, staying ahead of the breaking wave as it moved toward the shore.

It took them about fifteen or twenty minutes to get out past the breakers, but it would have taken two weeks if they hadn't had their boards secured to their ankles by a three-foot strip of rope. When the wave caught them head-on, its force made it impossible to hold the board, which untied would have ended up half a mile away. After watching the board jerk away from them by the wave's force, only to snap back when the three-feet slack of rope was used up, I looked down at the guru's ankles. Sure enough, there was deep scar tissue on both ankles where the rope had burned skin as it halted the runaway board. I didn't like to think of Lisa's pretty ankles looking like that. Then again, maybe she had more than that to worry about right now.

I tuned back in on the conversation. Our interview subject was a bum who lived off welfare and food stamps, with some grifting from the young kids who still lived at home and had money to contribute for his grass and/or the privilege of gathering in his shadow. He regarded people like us, going to work every day and collecting a paycheck, as fools wasting our lives away. There were days when I agreed with him a lot more than I wanted to admit, especially since Foley had taken over the squad.

The highs of sex and dope combined with surfing for many of them, but not all. Lisa had been in the "not all" category. The guru was a character who took advantage of these kids and anyone else who was available. He didn't exactly project an image of someone who admired people with sensitivity toward others. Oddly enough, as he talked of Lisa, some respect crept into his voice. He had, of course, tried to bed her. She was a fox. Somehow she had put him off without the retaliation that such refusals usually brought from creeps like him.

He told how she used to spend hours reading to a blind woman whose boy had died from a broken neck as he tried to master the surfing down below. "None of these kids would have thought of doing something like that," he told us. It was laughable coming from him.

Our new friend didn't have much to contribute in helping us find Lisa, however. There was no big gang feud or narc crackdown right now that disturbed the tranquillity of the surfing community, he told us. It wasn't a lost point that he regarded the two as equally bad.

Paul nudged him a little more on Lisa, eliciting the information that she had been consulted by some of the kids, who saw her as someone with her head screwed on right.

Recently, a group he dismissed as child stealers had been recruiting in the area for the Moral Reaffirmation Guild. Our expert clearly disapproved of it.

He had gotten our attention when he told us that Lisa had counseled a couple of the kids against the movement. He heard she had gone to some of their meetings and argued with them. He couldn't help us on the location of their camp. It was someplace nearby in the mountains.

He did drop another little nugget for us: the name of one of the kids he heard Lisa had tried to steer away from the Moral Reaffirmers. It was Judy Fortune, the kid Stone had said was Lisa's best friend.

It was almost 1430 hours when we finished. Paul had done well. I almost told him that, but held off out of fear he would feel compelled to do something to cancel out his good work.

Six

THE FORD WAS HOT FROM THE SUN. THE BEER AND AFTER-
noon heat made me drowsy, creating a wild temptation to let
one of them drive. I rejected it, heading the car back onto
Highway 1 for the ten-minute drive southward to Rio Del
Mar.

My estimate of Stone's worth, or more precisely his financial worth, went up considerably when I saw the digs in-
habited by wife number two. The house was an expanded
Eichler. The outer entranceway led into a living area open to
the sky. It must have been hell during the rainy season, but
in the warmth of a sunny summer day it was very nice indeed. The area was filled with luscious greenery. Hanging
ferns, fuchsias, a couple of tropical-looking things that I
couldn't identify, and some miniature rosebushes hanging in
a sunny corner gave it a cool and pleasant touch. It was populated by furniture suitable for inside or outside, but done
cleverly enough so that you didn't realize that by removing a
couple of cushions here and there it was feasible to leave the
stuff out in the rain.

The house, with a magnificent view of the ocean, was deceptively large once you got inside, which we did. Our entrance into the atrium had been signaled by a gently ringing chime from a fancy, hanging-rope thing set in motion when we opened the half-door guarding the entrance. Now I touched the bell to the left of the formal, handsome wooden door. The bell set off some musical echoes inside that my tin ear couldn't name and my ego wouldn't permit asking English to identify.

It was all very Californiaish. I thought the house was probably put up for around fifty thousand dollars ten years ago, but a combination of inflation, housing shortages, population growth, and California insanity meant that now, with its beach location, it would go for a cool million-plus. I had to up my estimate of the construction costs by about thirty thousand dollars when a uniformed maid let us inside. I hadn't calculated on the full-length swimming pool and outdoor paved paradise we now gazed on through the sliding glass doors of the living room.

The other thing I hadn't calculated on was sunning herself next to the pool. The second Mrs. Stone, judging from what I could see, must have been a good thirty years younger than Adolph. I guessed with some daring because she was face-down on one of those inflated mats. What was visible belonged to a shapely young woman.

As the three of us approached her after being announced by the maid, I realized uneasily that our interview subject's face wasn't the only part of her anatomy about to be exposed to our full scrutiny when she got around to looking up at us. A skimpy piece of black cloth did only a partially successful job of covering her well-constructed rump. But the top half of a swimsuit was not in sight, nor were towels or other articles of clothing that could have been used to cover her breasts when she rose to talk to us.

The Block's curious, eager expression showed he too had made that observation. English's delighted grin, anticipating my discomfort on figuring out what the hell we did next, revealed that he also had been observant.

Doris Learner looked up, catching our facial expressions as she raised up on her arms. She laughed and, turning to me, asked, "Are you guys really cops? You look more like terrorists."

I didn't know what I looked like. Nothing like this had ever been covered in our training sessions on investigative procedures. There had been some archaic stuff warning about solo interviews with females, who might subsequently make complaints of a sexual nature. But somehow it didn't apply here.

I must have looked stupid trying not to stare at her well-endowed, naked upper half while wondering whether or not I should gallantly offer my sweaty sports jacket for shelter, or formally announce, "Ma'am, we're leaving until you get dressed."

English seized the initiative, plumping down in a pool chair, remarking, "Doris, we're here to ask if you can help us find Lisa Stone. Her father is worried about her."

You would have thought the two of them had been out discoing last night. The Block, too, had sat. Only I stood, with a face whose redness had nothing to do with the sun's rays. She seemed to be enjoying this immensely. The twinkle in her eyes gave a pretty good hint that she had staged the whole meeting.

But now the fun went out of her comely face as she asked, "Lisa? What's wrong? Has anything happened to her?"

Paul filled her in on what we knew so far. I sat down, resolutely pushing out of my mind any thoughts of trying to justify to the Internal Affairs Unit why we interviewed a half-nude, beautiful twenty-eight-year-old woman. Two things were apparent, besides the other two things that were apparent. Doris Learner was fond of Lisa and worried. They had become close during the brief period of the marriage.

"Lisa's a beautiful child, no, a beautiful person," she told us. "I remember once she was almost killed trying to defend a young girl from one of those tough gangs around the high school. They hadn't been bothering Lisa, but she just wouldn't, you know, stand around like the rest of the kids, who were afraid to get involved. The girl they were picking on was a new transfer from a poor family. They made her a target and were really pushing her around one day. Lisa tried to stop them, yelling they should be ashamed, but they wouldn't stop, and she tried pulling them off the girl. She had more courage than sense. They beat her unconscious."

She looked at us a little angrily. "Don't you see what kind of a person she is?"

There was no way of telling her that we disapproved of heroes. They increased our case load. Paul got her going again with a question of whether the gang might still harbor animosity against Lisa.

"No, some of them went to jail for other things, and the gang kind of broke up from what I understand. Lisa didn't let it end there; she actually helped the other girl, tutoring her after school until she caught up. Somehow she was able to give her some money to buy clothes without hurting the kid's pride. Lisa isn't rolling in money; her old man is stingy as hell."

She saw my raised eyebrows and look around the sumptuous surroundings. "I got this the hard way," she said. "Stone gave it up because he knew what the consequences would be if I talked during the divorce." She clamped her lips shut and stared defiantly at me.

We talked for a while longer without getting any further. A couple of times she gracefully dragged her fingers through the pool water and once ran them through her light brown hair, which was as nice as the rest of her. Twice I saw the maid pass by the picture window in the living room and glance out at us and shake her head. I couldn't blame her; I didn't want to believe this, either. Anyway, it was a chance to reject that old theory that I had never believed in, the one that went, after you get used to nudity, it was something you didn't really notice or find exciting.

The ex-Mrs. Stone, disregarding my rank and status as team leader, asked Paul to please come back and keep her informed. He gave her his card along with a smiling promise that he would be back to "brief" her.

She laughed and reached for a helping hand. As he helped her up, she unsteadily leaned into him. He, in turn, off-balance and in some danger of flopping into the pool, stuck out a hand to steady himself.

"Thank you," she giggled, the two of them leaning into each other.

The Block smiled benevolently over the scene. I turned to get the hell out of there.

The maid, who had been taking in the scene from the living room, walked into the interior of the house. I hoped she didn't moonlight on the side as a free-lance journalist.

I found myself thinking again about Adolph Stone. First, his initial report on Lisa sounds fishy as hell. He flashes political pull to get cops assigned to the case, but doesn't even call people who might have knowledge of her whereabouts. Eric Stone seems unconcerned about his sister's safety. Instead, he makes cracks about the old man having politicians in his pocket and just about accuses him of running a crooked business. Then Stone's ex-wife, bare-breasted Doris, slips and hints that she got plenty of dough in her divorce settlement in return for her silence on Stone's dealings. What more would we learn about this handsome, all-American tycoon as we looked for his daughter?

Seven

WE DROVE TWO BLOCKS TO JUDY FORTUNE'S HOUSE. THE green lawns were well kept by professional gardening services and the streets were mostly clean, but this was quite a few notches down from Adolph Stone's neighborhood. And it wasn't as pretentious as the one we had just left. Two streets inland made a multi-hundred-thousand-dollar difference in the Monopoly-game madness of California real estate. You didn't see any cars parked in the driveways, but at least children were allowed to play on the lawns. A couple of teenage boys were rushing the football season a bit, lazily tossing a regulation ball back and forth across the broad street.

Two little girls of about six played a very serious game of potsy in the safety of their driveway. A pleasantly cooling ocean breeze came through the open car windows. The sky was pure blue and the light was the special kind you only saw in seashore towns. I thought of Laura for the first time in at least a month. This was the kind of street we had dreamed of raising children on during those magic days six years ago. Six years. Bile rose in my throat and I started to

61

spit out the bitterness, then swallowed it. I would have spit on Stone's street.

I didn't allow myself to wonder what she was doing now, as I steered toward the Fortunes' large ranch-style house. Painted cheerful shades of blue, it eschewed the Spanish tile roofs of neighboring homes in favor of wooden shakes turned gray by the salt air.

Once again my frisky, fun-loving associates decided to get the jump on me by entering the residence first. They left the car before I could maneuver it to the curb. Large, round stone slabs made an attractive path up to the front entrance, which was nicely surrounded by well-maintained foundation plantings. Two eight-foot-tall stained-glass panels brilliantly caught the afternoon sun and I wanted to take a closer look. Instead, I followed the Block and English up the driveway toward an open garage. An impressive array of richly blooming rosebushes lined the driveway. Their heady scent filled my lungs. This would be an easy house to come home to.

The garage led into a huge, walnut-paneled, recreation room. By the time I got there, Don Fortune had involved my two partners in a game of Space Wars on his home computer.

The large room was packed with every kind of toy on the market. There was a bumper pool table, an electronic pachinko machine, a movie screen, television recording gizmos, stereo setups, tape decks, and phonograph equipment. Given the burglary rate, owning all that stuff would have made me nervous.

On the other hand, I noticed that Fortune guarded his treasures with one of the latest and most sophisticated alarm systems on the market. It employed both perimeter and intrusion sensors and utilized a combination of activators, glass breaking, door openings, sound vibrations, or light beam interruptions. Ironically, we had walked into the house through a carelessly open garage door. A brand-new Mercedes XL220 sedan stood next to a more mundane year-old Porsche coupe. In addition, a Toyota station wagon sat surrounded by three English racing bicycles going for around a grand apiece. The expensive alarm system appeared to be just one more toy rather than a reflection of concern about burglary.

The alarm control paraphernalia was next to a glass gun case containing about a dozen handguns, including a brace of collector's eighteenth-century dueling pistols. Prominently displayed on the rough-hewn timbers above were three graceful-looking, beautifully finished shotguns and a long-barrel collector's revolutionary war era rifle.

Doris Learner had told us she thought Don Fortune was a school bus driver. I asked him about it as casually as I could under the circumstances, after first apologizing to the Block and English for interfering with their turn at zapping space invaders. Fortune had welcomed them into the game, and I guess I was a real rat for causing a distraction, but then a policeman's lot is not a happy one.

Fortune confirmed that he indeed drove a bus for the Santa Cruz school system, which, he explained, was great because it gave him a chance to be home and play with the kids during the summer.

I hadn't seen any kids yet sharing in his play, but skipped that to ask him bluntly how he was able to afford all this on a bus driver's salary. It was crude to be so direct, but the noise from the Block and English cheering or moaning about the obliteration of various spaceships and missiles, combined with the noise of the machine itself, and Fortune's frequent praise for his two new playmates—"Hey, you're really picking it up" and "Boy, that was neat the way you read that diversion attack and zapped the red fleet"—didn't make it exactly a normal interview.

He answered that he was also an investor and, with profuse apologies to my colleagues, said, "Let me just interrupt a minute to show this guy something. Don't worry," he soothed them, "this has a memory. I'll bring it back to right where you were in the battle." Disregarding the Block's sigh of disappointment, Fortune tapped a few keys to bring a batch of unintelligible words and numbers onto the screen.

"You see, those are my investments—real estate, crop futures, oil exploration, and stock options. That's why I need this computer. It cost thirteen thousand bucks, but it's deductible as a business expense, and I couldn't really do without it."

Catching my skepticism, he added with a grin, "Well, O.K., I do enjoy the games, too, but I work hard. I deserve something for myself, right?"

"Sure," I told him, blatantly ignoring English and the Block's impatience to get back to war, "but where did you get the money in the first place to invest in all this stuff?"

"You don't know how to read the display, copper," he told me. "You didn't pick up the leverage factor."

"Leverage?"

"Sure, look." He massaged the keys again, and a whole new array of numbers, etc., appeared. I still couldn't make heads or tails of it.

"You get it?" he continued. "First you pick up one investment for nothing down, then you borrow on that; you see, that's leverage. Then you pick up other investments, always putting as little down as possible and using the credit line that you established. I owe over two million dollars right now," he finished, exuding pride.

"You mean they'll lend two million to a bus driver?" I asked.

"An investor," he corrected, unoffended by my question.

I saw that he did indeed wear the obligatory heavy gold chain of the California rich around his neck. It was surrounded by a mass of dark masculine chest hair and fit in nicely with the car and dark sunglasses. I guessed he was about my size and age. He would appeal to the gals, I supposed. Yet there was a curious lack of expression on his rugged face.

He switched back to the game material.

"Hey, you guys want to try this one?" he asked Paul and the Block. "We can all play."

Ostracized but undaunted, I roamed a bit. Looking out into the backyard, I observed two youngsters playing in a sandbox. It was sort of reassuring that they hadn't technicized that yet. A girl of about four, in what once must have been a pretty pink dress, was intently shoveling sand into a pail. A boy of about two picked up a handful of sand and threw it full in her face. She whacked him good on the head with her little shovel. Instantly, he bellowed, "Ma," set up a wail, and headed toward a rear entrance on the other side of the house.

Curious, I headed in that direction. Not surprisingly, it was the kitchen. My eyes didn't immediately adjust to the cool shadows of the room, which was shaded by an outdoor lattice covered with some kind of a vine.

A woman seated on a stool in the far corner of the kitchen said, "Come in, Sergeant Fraleigh," in a low, pleasant voice.

Moving a couple of steps nearer, I saw that she was breast-feeding a baby. Flustered, I mumbled, "Oh, I'm sorry, I'll come back in a while."

"For God's sake, come in," she ordered. "I haven't talked to an adult all day."

She had light brown hair that managed to look casual. But its fluffiness had been expertly shaped to frame her clean-cut features. Her overly large, almond-shaped eyes were green and smiling. At first, I thought she was without makeup. On closer inspection, I noticed that she wore just a touch of pink lipstick. Politely, I skipped my eyes downward past her maternal activity and saw that she wore appropriately faded jeans. There was no doubt in my mind that they were an expensive designer brand. Her legs were long, and shapely. Her feet were bare. You had to look close to see that she had colored her toenails with the same pink tint as her lips. Her feet, like her face, showed that she was an outdoors person. Her skin was a healthy brown, but she wasn't one of the tanning fanatics.

My eyes slid back up over the full, voluptuous body to meet her amused, self-possessed green eyes. Right about that time, the toddler, screaming at the top of his lungs, arrived in need of motherly comfort. "Sit down," she commanded, just about shoving me onto a stool. Throwing a towel over my shoulder, she deposited the baby on me. "Just tap him lightly, like so, until you get a burp," she directed, nimbly evading the tackle-hold the crying two-year-old was putting on her legs. She was holding her light blue blouse closed with her right hand. Reaching for the toddler she took her hand away from the blouse for an instant and I caught a glimpse of two well-shaped breasts lushly heavy with milk.

Little Don, as he turned out to be, got picked up and seated on the counter where Mommy nuzzled his face, nose to nose, and teased him with some baby talk that told him she wasn't going to let anyone hurt her little baby. In no time the tears were gone, he was giggling, and Mommy was correcting the odor that had assailed our noses when he entered the kitchen. All during the diaper-changing process, she continued her nonsense baby talk, to his delight.

I saw the Block, his fleet of spaceships no doubt annihilated, enter the room, see me burping the baby and the shapely mommy changing the diaper. He turned and left. A moment later, English duplicated the scouting expedition and silently returned to the game room. Without question, the scene would work itself into one of his automobile monologues as part of my continuing psychoanalysis.

With a last nose rub, she dispatched the toddler into the backyard and momentarily disappeared to do whatever had to be done with the diapers. I had no regrets over that. Despite my homicide-scene-hardened stomach, the smell had been getting to me.

Waiting for her return, I observed the toddler's arrival at the sandbox. His sister, still intent on her own building efforts, didn't look up. He, grabbing shovel and pail, resumed work. I noticed he didn't throw any more sand.

Mommy, it turned out, was Sandra Fortune, as she informed me after returning and serving me an unrequested bottle of Henry Weinhard's beer. Conscious of the need for good police public relations, I avoided giving offense by refusing it. Besides, it was still hot. Taking the baby back, she was quite close to me and smelled of the talcum powder used to dust baby Don's rump and a scented hand soap. Her femininity was hitting me in a way that I couldn't remember experiencing in a very long time.

It wasn't a come-on, but suddenly she was aware of her impact. For a second her deep green eyes widened, looking full into mine. Then she looked away. Both of us sat in embarrassed silence for a moment. She recovered first.

"You have some scars around your eyes and your nose looks like it was once broken. Did that happen to you as a policeman? Or were you a football player?"

She was looking at my shoulders. I squared them a little.

"I played some football in college, but the nose and scars came from boxing."

"Where did you go to college?"

"University of Pennsylvania. But I didn't finish there."

"Why not?"

"Er, Mrs. Fortune . . ."

But she was not to be denied. "The injuries to your face, is that normal or—"

"Or was I lousy?" She smiled but didn't withdraw the question. "The answer is yes, it's normal, and also that I wasn't good enough to kid myself for more than a couple of years."

"I wonder?" She gave me a dazzling smile and turned her attention to the baby.

It was childish, but my stomach tightened and I took a deep breath. I watched her trim figure as she gently cradled the baby in her arms and walked through the kitchen into a corridor. The designer jeans hugged her hips. I knew damn well that this wasn't sixteen-year-old Judy Fortune's mother. "He's asleep." She had returned sans baby.

I was some detective. I had been in this kitchen about twenty minutes without asking a question, burping a baby, drinking beer, getting aroused, and being pumped by the witness about my past.

"How did you know my name?" I finally got around to asking.

"My gadget maven," she replied, gesturing up at a speaker. "He's got the whole place wired like CBS. I turned it off when you came in the kitchen, but I heard you introducing yourself in the next room."

"What about all that leverage stuff?" I continued, determined to get back to earning my pay.

"Who knows? It sounds as crazy to me as it does to you. But he's been doing it for seven years now. Did you see that big house on the ocean when you came up the street? It just went for about a million three, and the gal who had it was a secretary for the Public Works Department. Was? Is, I should say, but she had picked it up around four years ago in one of those weird financing deals. Someday the bubble will burst, but we've been saying that for years, you know. I was brought up to save and be thrifty, but everyone doing that is poor now, and the people who went into hock up to their eyeballs are worth plenty.''

''We're not really into that stuff; I was just curious.'' I changed the subject. ''We did want to talk to Judy, though.''

''You're out of luck. She's camping with her friend Lisa.''

I felt a chill as the warmth of the kitchen spell suddenly dissipated.

''I don't know much about police departments, but isn't it a little heavy sending three police officers over a graffiti joke? Besides, Judy wasn't even with them,'' she said. ''What squad did you say you were from? Juvenile?''

I tried to think of something to say.

''You're strangely silent all of a sudden, or did you say Narcotics?'' she questioned, growing more apprehensive.

''I didn't say, Sandra.''

''What's wrong, Fraleigh?''

She was far too alert, I thought. Carefully, I told her, ''We're actually trying to find Lisa; her father's worried about her.''

I realized how badly I was handling this. What the hell was wrong with me?

''Her father never worried about anything except his lousy money,'' she commented with surprising bitterness. ''You're not from Missing Persons, either. There is something about you three. You're too grim.''

I had seen it before. People suddenly recoiling from us as they got a glimpse of what we did for a living. I chided myself for being bothered that this attractive, sexy woman had reacted that way. The interlude had been pleasant. She was intelligent as well as beautiful, and when she realized I had reacted to her she seemed pleased. I had been fighting to keep from feeling flattered that she was interested in me. As she had said, she hadn't talked to an adult all day, but still . . .

"What section of the police department do you work in?"

What could I say? I pleaded, "We don't have any evidence that anything has happened to them, but we need your help to make sure nothing does."

"What unit, Sergeant?"

There was only one answer: "Homicide."

Her mouth tightened. I noticed that her hands were clasping and unclasping. An anxious frown covered her brow above those striking green eyes.

"Where are the girls supposed to be camping?" I had taken out my notebook and waited to write.

She gave me an address a few miles south. It was a camping grounds used by a Sierra Club youth group. The weekend expedition was called a satellite experience, with the girls pairing off for day-long hikes and other activities, but returning for a 7:00 P.M. cookout and songfest.

"Mrs. Fortune, tell me when you last talked to the girls."

Her apprehension had increased with that question, but it had to be asked.

"Sergeant, is there anything you're not telling me?"

"No. Honestly, we're only following up on her father's report that she's missing."

She sighed. "I didn't actually speak to Lisa. Judy did. Lisa went straight to the Sierra Camp Monday evening, but Judy had a dental appointment Tuesday morning. She went to the camp that afternoon. I haven't heard from them since." Her big green eyes were watching me intently.

An evening summer fog off the ocean vanquished the bright warm sun, sending dampness and shadows into the kitchen. The shadows reminded me that it was almost time to call the office, but I strongly wanted to finish and leave.

"You're too young for Judy to be your daughter," I encouraged her.

"You're right. She's Don's by his first marriage. I've tried, but it's been very difficult for Judy to accept that her mother yielded custody, and of course, the sibling jealousy rejection syndrome when her father married me is also a problem.''

I understood her meaning, but she carried the explanation further. Her use of language was interesting.

''Lisa has been a dream come true. If one prescribed ideal therapy, it would have been peer-oriented, as with Lisa. She was able to pull Judy out of obsessive-compulsiveness and even delusional moods. Not that Lisa has ever been trained, but instinctively, she's the type of person who understands and reacts naturally in supportive modes. For example, the appeal of personality-altering groups is a natural phenomenon in sibling rejection cases like Judy's, yet Lisa's ability to influence her against them simply couldn't be achieved by an adult, given the rejection trauma. Lisa never criticized the Moral Reaffirmation Guild to Judy personally; she simply went to the meetings and asked questions of the organizers that revealed the flimsiness of their premises.''

''This camp they're at tonight, is it connected with the Moral Reaffirmation group?''

''No,'' she replied, ''but they do have a meeting place nearby, and I suspect Lisa had hoped to attend their meeting tonight with Judy and, once and for all, get her to reject them by a forced comparison with the wholesomeness of the Sierra experience.''

She rose. ''I'll have to get the children in. The fog has chilled things,'' she said with a shudder.

The fog and us three grim reapers, I thought as I asked, ''May I use your phone to call the office?''

''In there.'' She gestured to a nearby paneled den with a nifty-looking leather-topped desk.

The phone, of course, was push-button. What else in this house? As I waited to be put through to our leader, my eyes absorbed two framed scrolls displayed handsomely against the wood paneling. One signified that a Bachelor of Arts degree had been conferred upon the recipient by Columbia University, New York, upon graduation from Barnard College. The other indicated that a Doctor of Philosophy degree had been awarded by Stanford University. That one was dated six years ago. Both of them named the recipient as Sandra Jacoby.

Gladys answered with her mouth full. If I hadn't known what number I called, I would have been in trouble. "Fraleigh. Put Foley on," I ordered, enjoying my rudeness.

"Lieutenant Foley," our supersleuth answered. Persons all the way up to deputy chief simply gave their last name, but Foley had his own charming ways.

I identified myself and brought him more or less up to date, stressing that we had good information that the two girls would show up tonight at a seven-thirty meeting.

Bulldog Foley, in typical fashion, whined, "You can't. You know no overtime is allocated to you guys this week."

"You know that we don't put in for it on this kind of job," I mimicked him.

It was true. Despite their shortcomings, English and the Block never complained about us working overtime without compensation. Everyone knew it, but Foley resented it. He once made the mistake of telling me that it made him and the others look bad by comparison, and the Police Union Association didn't like it, either. His face had gotten very red when I told him what he and the rest of them could do.

"That's filthy and insubordination," he had stuttered. I repeated my suggestion, just to make sure he had gotten it right the first time, knowing full well that even he wasn't stupid enough to put down on paper that he was trying to discourage subordinates from donating free time in the so-called war against crime.

Not that the overtime policy wasn't a problem. Ironically, we had lost two cases because of it.

One of the most despicable, devious, dishonest, and

therefore most prosperous criminal lawyers in town had discovered our oddity and used it to his advantage. He had successfully defended two vice cops who thought they were entitled to franchise fees from massage parlors and call girl rings. In gratitude for their reinstatement to the force, they freely discussed the work habits of our team in a murder case where we had nailed a pimp who, in a drunken rage, beat one of the teenage girls in his stable to death for squandering a dollar fifty on a Hollywood fan magazine.

Three long days had been involved in grilling some questionable witnesses among the questionable folk who make up the prostitution scene: hookers, Johns, pimps, and assorted onlookers. The defense attorney had a field day with our witnesses, whose arrest records were as long as their arms.

We should have made the difference as upright guardians of the law. But the lawyer beat us. He had me on the stand and asked how many hours I had worked the first day. I told him, "Seventeen."

"And the second day?" he politely inquired.

"Sixteen," I had answered. At the time, I thought it was a dumb question that might be making us cops look good. I should have known better.

"And the third day, Officer?" He really had the jury's attention now.

"Eighteen."

"And how much of that was overtime, Officer?"

"None," I replied.

"I see, and your normal working day? How many hours?"

"Eight," I gave him back in my own loquacious style of testimony.

"So, in three days, you and your partners worked more overtime for nothing than you worked duty hours for pay."

The D.A. should have objected, since it was a statement,

not a question, but he looked as spellbound as the judge and jury by the line of questioning.

"How do you feel personally about prostitution, Officer?"

I had begun to smell what he was up to, but for the life of me, I couldn't think of an intelligent answer to the question.

The showman barrister leaped on the advantage, demanding, "Your Honor, I insist that you instruct the witness to answer the question."

It was about that time that the judge also discovered what he was up to. Fairly, he asked, "Did you understand the question, Officer?"

"Not really, Your Honor," I responded. But the damage had been done. The shyster had managed to plant a seed in the jury's mind that we were personally involved and had been out to get the pimp, who, it turned out, through the years, had made numerous complaints of police brutality. It was enough to create doubts of our objectivity in the minds of the jurors.

The pimp's attorney had called other witnesses, including one of his former cop-clients, to testify that police officers were entitled to and demanded time-and-a-half compensation for work over forty hours.

What could we say? That the department policy was insane or that we were too dedicated to insist on being paid for overtime?

Several other skilled witnesses had been hired to testify that the pimp had been a "street" minister and friend of the downtrodden. The D.A. had been overruled in trying to bring out that the extent of the ministry had apparently been shelling out ten bucks some years ago for one of those mail-order ordinations.

It had been an expensive legal production. To afford it, the pimps must have been doing almost as well as their lawyers.

At the annual department picnic the next week, the Block broke the cop-witness's jaw after he reportedly jostled him in the chow line. As it turned out, he and his codefendant soon left the department for greener pastures, as they say.

Yet, overtime was one of those Catch-22s for us. If we just dropped a case after eight hours because no overtime was available, we weren't dedicated. If we worked overtime without pay, we were fanatics who were personally involved and couldn't be believed on the stand.

So Foley had touched a nerve. I hadn't expected him to be concerned about the kids' safety, but now he reached into new areas of bureaucratic pettiness, saying, "Also, the garage complained that you didn't sign the car out this morning, in violation of Operational Order Sixteen."

"Goddammit," I blew up. "Do you care whether these kids are alive or dead, or about your fucking operational orders?"

"Fraleigh, I'm putting you on notice that from now on I'm recording this conversation for formal disciplinary procedures. And another thing, a milkman called in complaining that three gunmen left the scene of an accident this morning, and he gave your license plate."

"What?"

"What do you know about that, Fraleigh?"

Goddamn that milkman! "It was nothing. We tapped into the back of a trailer-truck and broke our headlight."

"Did you comply with department procedures and call a field supervisor to the scene?"

"No. The crowd would have had us for lunch and the field supervisor for dessert. It's only a broken headlight. I'll fill out all the accident reports when we get back tonight."

"You'll do nothing of the sort. I'm notifying Internal Affairs to begin an immediate investigation. And I'm giving you and your two subordinates a direct order to return the car to headquarters immediately and to cease all police work until 0800 hours tomorrow morning.''

"Just a minute, Lieutenant." Somehow I kept control, but my voice sounded choked. "I need clarification."

The bureaucratic rules of war mandate that no subordinate can ever be silenced if he insists that he is only asking for clarification. "You understood by my report that we consider these two girls to be in real danger because of the circumstances and threatening phone calls, right?"

"I heard your report," he said.

"And you're also aware that we have information as to where they will be in another two hours?" I pursued him. "And that we are willing to work the case without being compensated because of the imminent danger to these youngsters?"

"I repeat, I heard your report. Now what is it that you need clarified?"

The string had run out. Anyone less dumb and petty than this man would have had enough sense to back off such a nitwit, vindictive order, but he hadn't, which left me with no place to go other than disobeying a direct order.

"You're giving us an absolute order to return immediately to headquarters and not work on the case any further?"

"That is your order, Fraleigh. I put you on notice that under General Order A-Fifteen, a subordinate disobeying a direct order is subject to termination, and that will be my recommendation based on past problems with you."

"Can you tell me why, Lieutenant?" I crawled, because deep in the pit of my stomach, something told me that those two youngsters shouldn't be left the night in the camping grounds.

"Why?" He was gloating. "Because just this morning, you didn't think it was much of a case, that's why."

"That was before we spent all day on it. Now we're convinced that there is danger," I cut in.

"Department vehicle regulations must be adhered to, and a lieutenant doesn't have to explain an order to a sergeant. All I'm required to do is to make sure you understand it. Now the three of you get back here, do you understand?"

Once again, I hung up without confirming, but this time, it was even more of an empty gesture.

I had an audience. The Block, English, Don and Sandra Fortune, and even toddler Don and his tough older sister were standing listening to the call. Only the baby was missing.

"I don't understand. Your police department thinks my kid may be in danger, but you're not going to look for her because of some overtime or cars?" Don Fortune asked aggressively.

It was close. Foley had exceeded my kindling point. Ready to explode, I actually shifted my feet, poised to open Fortune up with a left-right combo. Accidentally or otherwise, English walked into my path, providing the necessary second that it took for me to realize that Fortune was the wrong target. After all, his kid was possibly in danger.

"You heard it," I snarled. "I'm not God. I have to follow orders. If you don't like it, write a nasty letter to the mayor."

The expression on Sandra Fortune's face, as she silently watched me, was a lot of different things adding up to something I couldn't read but sure didn't like. Maybe that was what made me give it a one more long-shot try. Without asking this time, I returned to the phone and dialed Stone's number. Perhaps a personal call from him might prevail upon Foley to reconsider his senseless order. Luck was riding another horse. All I got was the recorded message that he wouldn't be home for several hours and to please leave a message.

Hanging up, I told the group, "I called Stone, hoping he

could get that order rescinded. He's not home. I don't have any other cards to play."

No one disagreed. We walked toward the door.

Fortune spoke with none of his former game-playing humor. "I'll take care of this myself, since we can't depend on the law for anything more than parking tickets."

He was opening the gun case as we left.

We reached our vehicle at the curb just as Don Fortune screeched out of the garage in the Mercedes. The front door opened and Sandra Fortune stood looking at us. I walked slowly back up the path. Paul followed me. Her face was contorted.

"Don scares me when he's like this."

"Do you know where he's going?"

She didn't answer me right away. "No. He can be very unpredictable."

Her answer struck me as evasive, but there was nothing ambiguous about the worry in her face.

"Mrs. Fortune, here's my business card. You can call me anytime. Or call the local police and use my name. I suggest you do that tonight if you haven't heard from the girls by ten o'clock." I felt like two cents, knowing the great reception she'd get from the local gendarmes using my name. They might not tell her in so many words, but the fact that we had gone home without continuing the search would lead them to follow the tried and true police tactic of doing nothing unless something else occurred.

"I feel so helpless." She held my card in her fist.

I opened her fingers and took it back from her. "I'm writing my home number on the back. Remember, call me if you need help."

Suddenly, her eyes focused on me. She reached out and put her hand on my forearm. "Thank you. You really do care! I appreciate that."

It only made me feel worse. Paul and I walked back to the

car. I was convinced that something bad was going to happen. I would gladly have seen Foley in hell.

"Her karma involves you, Fraleigh. I saw it in her eyes." That was English's contribution as he took the wheel. I didn't care who drove. I simply sat in the front, or death, seat, as it was known to the highway patrol. The summer fog had closed in, and grayness covered our five miles north up US 1 to Highway 17 headed inland.

We were halfway up the mountain on the way to the valley when the sun burst forth, still brilliant at 6:15 P.M. Yet, almost instantly, the cathedrallike redwoods closed out the light, allowing only gloomy yellow shafts to penetrate as we drove over the mountain. English's silence, which should have been welcome, only increased the somber mood in the car.

Other teams talked about interviews, helping to bring things together by analyzing a number of impressions. But English's conversations rarely touched on police work, and the Block was nonverbal. Nevertheless, I did ask the Block what he thought of Don Fortune.

"He cheated" was his reply.

Mulling that one over while waiting to see if further elaboration would take place, or whether English would expand on it, I looked for the meaning, the true significance of the statement. Had the Block meant to imply that a man who cheated at computer games lacked basic character, or was he merely reporting an observed fact without any value judgment? Nothing more was forthcoming from either one, and our ride through the magnificent scenery was silent, matching the darkness falling over the huge trees.

It was almost 1900 hours when we returned to the nearly deserted Investigation Bureau. Foley had been playing for all the matches, and I wanted a little more feeling for what he had in mind next. His office was dark and the squad room deserted. I nodded meaningfully toward his door to Paul, who pulled a number of keys and slender tools from his pocket.

"The lieutenant probably forgot and locked his door, not realizing we couldn't get the written instructions he left for us," he said without cracking a smile.

The Block, I noticed, just happened to be in the outside corridor, reading the bulletin board, where he would immediately be aware of anyone approaching the squad office.

I sat in Foley's chair and played the tape recorder on his desk. As I suspected, the bastard had lied. He hadn't started the recording when he announced. He had recorded the entire conversation. I thought Paul's eyes got a little tired-looking as we played it all back. I motioned to him that we needed a copy, and while he sauntered off to the tape copying machine, I thought to myself that Foley had really blundered and cooked his goose this time. Somehow, I didn't feel good about it. Recollections of the enjoyable interlude in the Fortunes' kitchen came back, as well as the different things we had heard about Lisa all day. Against all of my training and instinct, I had developed admiration for the kid. I found myself praying that this wasn't another time when Foley's string of mistakes ran out at the expense of a victim.

We wrote up our reports. It had been an intense probing. Gradually, a picture of the youngster had emerged by the end of the day. She fought teenage gang thugs against the odds, read to a blind woman who had lost her son, counseled kids, and fought exploitative cults. We didn't come into contact with many such souls in our business.

But if her character seemed a little clearer, others were not. Her enigmatic father, for example, and her coke-sniffing brother—hardly the model family likely to produce an idealistic champion of underdogs. Her stepmother-pal, Mrs. Stone number two, interesting certainly, but not exactly a candidate for Mother of the Year. And what about Eric Stone's puzzling references to the Washington Housing

Project, shady politicians, and his father's demonstrated lack of scruples when it came to using them to get his way? These would not have been secrets to young Lisa. How had she handled it all? Was it somehow involved with her absence and the phone calls?

She also had relationships with Judy Fortune and her electric stepmother. How deep was she into the surfing community, with its drug and counterculture ethos?

And most interesting of all, the inconsistencies between what Sandra Fortune had told us and Adolph Stone's version. How was it possible that Stone had been unaware that Lisa was supposed to have been at the Sierra Camp when he was allegedly receiving ransom calls?

Glassy-eyed over the reports, I stared at the wall, overwhelmed by the feeling that had we stayed and finished our work, Lisa would have been sitting opposite me explaining away all the mysteries. It was almost 2300 hours when we finished. Despite Foley, we each had donated another eight hours to the city and the cause of decency.

Eight

I SLEPT FITFULLY, DREAMING OF BARE-BREASTED NYMPHS armed with laser-beam pistols. They soared back and forth on surfboards, roaring to one spaceship after another.

Tired and out of sorts, I headed downtown. I had a court appearance and wasn't all that sorry. Foley and the IA people would have been a little tough on my stomach so early in the day.

I retrieved the murder weapon for the trial (a seven-inch kitchen knife) from the property room and hurried over to the lab for the written analysis, which I was supposed to have picked up four days before. It profoundly noted that the stains on the weapon were human blood of the same type as the victim's.

It had been a uniform pinch. Two cops in a blue and white had screeched around the corner after being called by relatives of the sixteen-year-old female who had loved unwisely. Her vicious and not very bright boyfriend had stabbed her in a fit of anger and had thrown the knife under the car seat. Neither the cops nor the deputy district attorneys they consulted were willing to chance being on the wrong end of the Supreme Court's latest decision on whether or not they dared to take possession of the murder weapon. They called me. I wasted two hours getting a judge to sign a search warrant so that I could reach under the seat and take the weapon to the county lab.

Now six of us guardians of the law were impressively lined up when His Honor strode in to begin the morning festivities; at least the assistant D.A. hoped we were impressive. He had us all there to try to pressure a plea of voluntary manslaughter from the defendant, who was charged with murder one. The D.A. knew he had an airtight case for murder two, and a little reasonable hondling would save him a two-week trial and the state a lot of money. Thus the lineup of six cops.

That was the D.A.'s mistake. We could have told him that the kid wasn't smart enough to be impressed by any of his brilliant tactics, but he wouldn't have listened, so the six of us filed out and sat in the witness room. If we testified at all, only the arresting officer would be on the stand for more than two minutes. Through the years my mind had set up its own defense mechanism against the irrationalities of criminal court. I simply shut everything out until I was called. If someone had tapped me on the shoulder and asked what I was thinking during these sessions, I probably couldn't have given an answer.

The trial droned on. Around 1100 hours one of the other cops nudged me. I looked at the guy who had jabbed me. He nodded toward the courtroom door. English and the Block were standing there.

I knew. There wasn't anything about their expressions. They made no gestures. But I knew as surely as I knew I was sitting in a courtroom.

We went into the hall. Neither wanted to say anything. The Block avoided my eyes. English stared into them as if seeking some deep truth.

Finally, I demanded of English, "Well?"

He said, "Lisa," and stopped.

"Strain yourself, sound like a detective," I barked, but we both knew my anger was not at him.

"An old man who lives with his wife in the mountains, walking, probably illegally hunting small game, with his dog. The dog began to whine, excited. He went over, found the remains, called the sheriff. The deputies found her Sierra Club Camp pass."

"Who made the ID?"

"Old man Stone," he said.

I had to face the fact that I had been hoping that it wasn't really her. There had been so many through the years. This bright, pretty, animated kid whom we had learned about just yesterday—I hadn't wanted her to be another victim, another homicide case.

"Cause of death?" I questioned mechanically, shocked despite myself.

"Not sure." Paul was uneasy, evasive.

"Come on, Paul, neither one of us is a cherry. Spit it all out."

"The body had been dismembered," he answered, as I stared. "They still don't have it all. Remember, I haven't been there. This is what I got on the phone."

"Dismembered," I repeated stupidly. Ugly pictures of other such cases floated unbidden into my mind. I hoped that she had died quickly.

"When?" I asked.

"The old man found her this morning."

He looked away from my glare. He had answered a question not asked and he knew it.

"I know they're not big-city dicks like you, but they must have been able to tell you whether the body had been in the woods for days, or what."

"They had some information," he answered, so softly

that I had to move closer to hear. "Stone told them that she had been with the Fortune kid. When they checked with Mrs. Fortune, she told them about the Sierra Camp. The deputies went over to the camp. The counselor told them the two girls had been at the barbecue and songfest and were last seen going to their tent around ten o'clock. There's no trace of the other kid. Not only that—Don Fortune's shotgun was found, smashed, near the Moral Reaffirmation Camp, along with his bloody shirt with a tear like a shotgun blast would make. They have their hands full running all those crime scenes at once, but they think Fortune may have gone over the cliff into the surf. They're not even sure divers could get down in that area. It's one of those locations with the waves smashing into the rocks and cliff walls with all kinds of treacherous currents, but they won't even be thinking about that for a while."

Rage flooded over me. I had hardly heard his report on Don Fortune. All that I could think of was that the kids had been in camp last night. Foley's stupidity had called us back, and now one or both were dead. It was the Tricia Greene case all over again.

"Don Fortune, too," I mumbled dazedly. I went down the stairs, skipping the elevator, even though we were on the fifth floor. I was in a hurry. The Block's question, "What about your court testimony?", went unanswered.

The police building was adjacent to the courthouse. My head was pulsing—"Foley, Foley, Foley." I had no plan, but English and the Block hardly kept pace with me. My heart was pounding after running up the stairs in headquarters to the third floor. I wrenched Foley's door open. It slipped out of my hand, slamming loudly into the wall. Capt. Louis Robinson's homely, black face looked up at me from his seat behind Foley's desk.

"Sit down, Fraleigh," he said.

"Foley, where is he?" I asked, not in control of my voice or breathing.

"Quantico," he told me, "the FBI Academy, an investigation training course for local police."

"What?"

"Sit down. What's wrong with you, anyway?"

But Louis knew. He knew everything that went on, probably had played the tape and arranged Foley's absence. Everyone knew he ran the bureau, kept it going with his touch and skills, despite the fact that he was only a captain and two deputy chiefs were supposedly in command.

Turning, I walked numbly down the stairs and out of the building, wondering, What if Foley had been there? What would have happened?

Not for the first time, the thought came to me that we weren't that much different from those we hunted.

Nine

"DO YOU WANT ANOTHER MARTINI?" THE SLOVENLY BAR-
tender asked me.

"Martini? I never had a martini in my life."

"Jesus!" he said, moving down the bar, shaking his
head.

"Why the hell did he ask me if I wanted a martini?" I
asked the big ugly man sitting on the stool to my left.

"That's what you been drinking."

I looked at him more closely. It was the Block. "Where
are we?" I asked.

"Morty's."

There was a glass in front of the Block. "What are you
drinking?"

"Martinis. You kept ordering them, one after the other,
even though you know I drink beer," he accused.

"Oh." I searched my memory. No Morty's surfaced. In
the mirror behind the bar, I saw a disheveled, red-eyed
drunk sitting next to the Block. It slowly dawned on me that
I was looking at a reflection of myself. My God! Martinis.
How many, I wondered.

"Why are my eyes so red?"

"You were crying," the Block answered.

"Crying?" I tried to remember. Blank.

"What over?" I questioned.

"Who," he answered.

"Who?" Staring at him, I realized he was drunk. The Block drunk?

"What do you mean, who?"

"It wasn't a what you cried about, it was a who—you know, a person."

"I cried over a who?" Even drunk, I knew we sounded like vaudeville.

"Lisa—you cried over the kid. Then Tricia Greene. And Paul—you cried over him. That's when he left. You didn't cry over me."

Drunkenly, I studied him. Was he proud, disappointed, hurt? Should I try a few tears for his sake to cheer him up?

"Let's go. I don't drink in shit holes like this." I stood up. The room revolved and I started to fall over backward. The Block grabbed my jacket with one hand, easily holding me up.

"Let go of me, you prick," I threatened him.

After a minute, when he saw I wasn't going to fall, he released me.

The fat bartender was at the corner of the bar talking to a homely woman in her thirties with big tits.

"Anyone who'd serve someone in my condition ought to lose his license," I told him.

He started to say something, looked at the Block standing next to me, and shrugged.

We walked into the parking lot. It was dark. "What the hell time is it?"

"Almost two in the morning, closing time," he supplied.

"Where are we?"

"Fremont."

Good God! Fremont at two in the morning. I didn't even know they had a Fremont at two in the morning. "If there's no there, there in Oakland," I heard myself chuckling, "then what can you say about Fremont at two in the morning?"

But two in the morning? We had left the police building around noon. I couldn't remember anything in between.

The Block was walking—staggering. I followed. He never staggered. Other times I had seen him drink all day without staggering. I couldn't let him drive. But he was very strong. I realized that I needed strategy, so when we got near the car, I jumped, without warning, onto his back.

English had been sleeping in the front seat. He woke up to see the Block striding toward the car with me riding unsteadily on his shoulders.

"Put me down!" I ordered the Block. I studied Paul's face closely for any sign of derision, ready to crack down on insubordination. He was deadpan.

"That expressionless look on your face is disrespectful, English. Don't think you can fool me with that bullshit. Take me home, I've had enough of your insolence."

He drove soberly, winding through some dark side streets and getting to the freeway like he knew where he was going.

"Paul," I asked, "what was all that talk about the elimination of rank in the Chinese Communist army? You can't have an army without rank. Everyone knows that."

"It raises some fascinating questions about politics and organizational behavior," he replied calmly, as if we were all sane and sober.

"You see, when the Communists took over Mainland China in 1949, they were in a mess. Eight hundred million people, a yearly famine that starved millions to death, a fragmented country, many different dialects spoken, no economy, and so on. The one thing that had worked and had some stability was the Red Army. It was popular with the people and essential to the survival of the government and the country. Naturally, the Communist party leadership feared that the military might take over. So one thing they did was to eliminate rank to prevent any military heroes from developing. Mao and the other party leaders would be presented to the masses, not military people. It was ironic because Mao rose through his military accomplishments on the long march during the 1930s."

"Yeah, but what the hell does that have to do with those guys trying to turn over our car the other day?"

"I'll try to explain it. You see, there is an amazing similarity between the egalitarian political philosophy of the United States and the theory of the Communist party. In both, everyone is supposed to be equal, but in any tribe, society, culture, organization, or whatever you want to call it, there will be people who acquire more goodies than others."

"And that explains those kids trying to overturn our car?"

"In a way, yes. Eliminating rank didn't eliminate power and privilege; and eliminating slavery and passing laws against discrimination didn't give minorities equality, because they didn't have the positional status to get the same share of goodies as everyone else. The result is the Washington Housing Project, the high-density slum and disparate subculture with its own values. And the disinterested handling of the Tricia Greene case by our enlightened department."

"Where'd you learn all this stuff, Paul?" I asked.

"Stanford. It was part of my therapy when I came home from the war."

"I'm sorry it didn't work. Really, Paul, I mean it."

"I know," he said, his eyes flicking a glance at me.

Not too many people knew that Paul had been tortured in a North Vietnam prison camp after an escape attempt with another member of his marine platoon.

Three years into the Stanford program, he came in contact with a faculty psychologist even nuttier than he. They put their heads together on the murder of a professor. The local cops were stumbling along when these two amateur sleuths came up with the idea that a disgruntled student must have done it. Incredibly, it turned out that a disappointed doctoral candidate knocked off the professor when his dissertation had been turned down for the ninety-ninth time or something. Paul's mentor reached the brilliant conclusion that his ward had been turned on by helping the police solve the mystery.

I knew tears had been wetting my face as he talked. I turned to look at the Block in the back. His eyes were closed, but I thought I saw some moisture under his curiously delicate eyelashes. Then again, I could have been wrong; it could have been sweat.

"Stanford. I know someone else from Stanford, a Ph.D.," I said sleepily. Paul, pulling one of his old driving tricks, looked me full in the face with a troubled expression.

"Fraleigh . . ."

"Can't remember who, though," I got out before konking off.

They delivered me to my apartment and left. It was hardly a sight to warm the cockles of your heart. Yet, everything was in its place. The leather recliner that Laura had surprised me with on our first anniversary sat next to the end table with my supply of escape fiction. Paperback espionage junk. Two days after she had moved out I added the nineteen-inch color television set. It was my last refuge from loneliness, and I hated it for that very reason. But not enough to get rid of it.

Three of her watercolors remained on the walls. I remembered how I secretly hoped they were a sign that she might come back. A couple of years later it finally dawned on me that she wasn't when I heard that she had remarried. Mrs.

Mendoza cleaned with dedication above and beyond the line of duty for a once-a-week housekeeper, but the place had lacked a woman's touch for six years. There had certainly been female visitors from time to time, but that was what they were. Visitors. Not one had left a trace of her presence.

I stumbled to the closet and neatly hung my clothes next to my boxing and running gear. My fishing pole stood in the corner of the closet, silently reprimanding me for its inactivity over the past three months. I took my trusty magnum and, knowing I was still drunk, very carefully placed it in the drawer of the table next to my bed. On impulse I took the small jewelry box from the drawer. Opening it, I looked at the engagement and wedding rings that Laura had thrown in my lap that day as I sat in my chair listening to her anger.

What had it really been? What issues had been so important that they had destroyed our marriage? I had never really been able to articulate the cause. Oh, I knew it had to do with two strong people too stubborn to compromise on some things. But, no! It had been more than that. She had asked me to change for her in ways that eventually would have killed my self-respect. Inevitably, she would have stopped loving me.

The house near the ocean became the point of conflict. But it really had only been a symptom of deeper incompatability. In our house hunting, Laura had gradually pushed up into brackets where I knew my cop's salary was hopelessly inadequate. She was an artist who made a couple of hundred bucks a year. It didn't bother me, and I don't think she was concerned. I'm not even sure that she believed that someday her paintings would bring in real income. It was her basic attitude toward money that caused the break. Her father was a prominent surgeon in Philadelphia who apparently had gotten some good investment advice. His yearly income was prodigious, and neither he nor his wife had come from poverty by a long shot.

She was an only child and took wealth for granted. We had met a couple of times at the University of Pennsylvania when we were both students. Oddly enough, there hadn't been any sparks then. But four years later when we happened to spot each other in an art gallery near Ghirardelli Square, in San Francisco, it had been thunder and lightning. Within a year, we had married. At first, she had enjoyed the fact that I was a detective. Only when we got to house hunting and dreaming about the six beautiful children we would raise did I come to realize that she saw us living off her parents. Any little hobbies we might enjoy personally, like painting or detecting, were fine as long as they didn't interfere with the lifestyle she envisioned for us.

It had been hard for me to bring it up. I anticipated that she wouldn't be able to understand. She hadn't. Six months of misery had culminated when she tossed the rings in my lap and told me, "Put them next to your badge." The divorce itself had been a civilized thing. We hadn't even seen each other. Her father's lawyers had done well.

I put the jewelry away and staggered to the bathroom. Cleverly, I took three aspirins, then collapsed into bed.

Thus, when I woke at 1000 hours, instead of wishing I were dead, I just felt that I was. It was a bright and sunny Saturday morning, my day off. I hit the squad room by 1100. The Block and English, also on off days, were there by 1115. When Louis Robinson arrived at 1130 on his day off, he made a fourth for bridge, but somehow we didn't play.

"You alive, Fraleigh?" Louis asked.

I maintained a dignified silence, giving my eyeballs a silent command to be less red.

He was not to be denied. "Did you three bums get into any trouble yesterday afternoon?"

This time I gave him an honest silence, not having the slightest idea what the answer was.

"Well, off the record, for the record, you all signed out at 1700 hours yesterday, and officially, none of you is working today. Got it?" He paused.

"Stone called up here yesterday, raising all kinds of hell against you guys, screaming you let his daughter get whacked, and I backed you guys, so don't play games with me."

"You're already beginning to sound like Foley, Louis. Why don't you go for a jog around the levee or something to calm down?" I asked.

"All right, all right, I give up. I'll buy you lunch, but let's knock it off, O.K.?" our commander pleaded.

Louis was an old-time cop who remembered when rank meant something, so in the restaurant, he ordered a round of Bloody Marys with a command presence. It was O.K. with me as long as he was buying. The Block, I could see, was toying with the idea of asking for a beer but went along rather than say anything to Louis. English gave no sign of hearing the order. He and the waitress had locked their eyes in a deadly embrace. Apparently, she hadn't heard, either. After a couple of minutes, while we just sat there watching nature on a rampage, she turned with a flushed face asking, "Are you ready to order yet?"

"Yes, I think so, miss," Louis sighed. "Could you please bring us four Bloody Marys?"

"Is that O.K.?" she questioned Paul. He shrugged acceptance, and she wiggled off without asking me or the Block for consent. Louis had watched the whole thing with interest.

"How would you like to go through this every day, Louis?" I asked.

"No thanks, but don't feel sorry for yourself. You could have studied for promotion too, you know."

Almost before he had finished speaking, the buxom waitress, who looked about eighteen, three years under legal age to be working in a joint like this, was back with the order. Somehow she served us without once taking her eyes off Paul.

"Are you joining us?" I asked sweetly as she continued to gaze in adoration.

Her glare at me turned into an appreciative smile at Louis, who said, "Don't be such a grouch, Fraleigh. Some of us like solids along with our liquids, and the young lady was waiting for an order."

I knew what she'd been waiting for, and it wasn't any order, unless maybe an obscene one from Paul, but I remained silent. Offending people who control your food behind closed doors is hazardous.

She and Paul were having a giggle over his choice of salad dressing. Naturally that was what he ordered, a salad. Finally, she pinned him down to Russian dressing. After dutifully writing it down, she burst into uncontrollable laughter.

"Oh, my goodness, I forgot we have a salad bar. You get your own salad and dressing."

Paul and Louis found it equally amusing. The Block was eyeing her lecherously. Her laughter got a little nervous as she avoided him, turning to me.

"And you, sir?"

"Another Bloody Mary." I wasn't about to let someone in her disordered state mess around with anything going into my stomach.

As usual, trying to talk about a case with English and the Block around called for the utmost determination and concentration. A couple of times Louis lost his train of thought as he gaped at the Block demolishing two huge plates of spaghetti and meatballs, a loaf of bread, and six bottles of beer. The Block, being next to English, got great service, unlike the rest of our waitress's customers, who starved while she chatted with Paul. At one point Louis, describing the mess made of the crime scenes in the mountains and the inept questioning and release of Guy Phillips by deputy sheriffs, came to a complete stop, watching Paul rub the smiling waitress's rear end, left mostly bare by her skimpy costume.

Louis winced a bit when he got the bill, but had to admit the show had been spectacular.

"When are you going to let some other sergeant share these golden moments and get me a new team?" I asked on the way to the car.

He stopped. "Listen, Fraleigh, you guys are a real team, and you look out for one another. They'd do anything for you, and they know you're going to take care of them." Louis was serious.

"Louis, for God's sake . . ." I started, but gave up. The next thing he'd tell me what a prince Foley was.

During lunch Louis had disclosed that he put the weekend dick, Gregory Day, on checking names surfacing so far in the case through NCIC, the National Crime Information Center, run by the FBI; CJIC, County Justice Information Center; and CJIS, the Criminal Justice Information System, run by the California attorney general.

Day was known as the Zombie by the squad, but the name check was routine, so I made no objection. Besides, Louis had sprung for lunch and I was appreciative. The celery from my four Bloody Marys made me feel better. You can't beat nutrition.

Back in the squad room, the Zombie approached us with a message: Adolph Stone had called with the local address of the Moral Reaffirmation Guild recruiting office. It was somewhat of an odd location, mostly industrial. But then these organizations were a little odd themselves.

Something was bothering Louis about the message. He was a good cop, and I was interested to know what had him frowning down at the note. Detective Day was standing, waiting with his usual vacant-eyed enthusiasm. He was about five feet ten, 170 pounds, on the thin side, pale-faced in California, and as distinctive as a Coke bottle on an assembly line. I was tempted to tell him to get back to work and not stand there like a zombie, but Louis didn't like that kind of approach and might launch into a personnel courtesy lecture, which was no fun, even without a hangover.

Grabbing the case folder, Louis secured Stone's number. While he was dialing it, I looked at what the Zombie had produced in his name checks. It wasn't much, which led me to believe that he hadn't been killing himself with overexertion while we slaved over lunch. Not surprisingly, Duane Fisher, the surf-guru, had a couple of drug busts and a slew of Vehicle Code violations, including a year's suspension two years back for a hit-and-run conviction. If there had been any sex offenses, we would have taken another look at him. But this time around he looked clean, just another witness. I wasn't sorry. The surf scene would have proved an investigative nightmare.

There was a technique to name checking. Many of the folks we arrested were less than candid about their identities. Names themselves were meaningless until we could nail them down with other hard identification, such as fingerprints. With people like the guru, the approach was standard but not foolproof. In the middle of the interview, I had offhandedly asked for his driver's license. He hadn't wanted to produce it, but couldn't think of a way to get out of it. I had handed it back casually enough, but not before memorizing his DOB (date of birth), which would enable the computer to distinguish him from a lot of others with the same name. Of course, the license could be a phony.

Adolph Stone types presented a somewhat more delicate problem. For him, we had to go the other way around, checking name and address through the Department of Motor Vehicle's files for his DOB before we could query the criminal history files with any degree of accuracy. In reality, there was always some ambiguity unless we got fingerprint verification from NCIC in Washington and CJIS in Sacramento.

The trouble was, we only got those IDs three to six weeks after taking the prints from people under arrest. It was routine that each year, a half-dozen people arrested for minor charges gave phony names, got released, and disappeared before their true identities were determined showing that they were wanted for such mundane crimes as murder, robbery, kidnapping, and so forth. The television cops had it all over us, but then they operated on big budgets and unlimited technology, while we scrambled for the crumbs left over after the politicians took care of their favorite patronage charities.

If you had a suspect in mind, it was possible to pick up a latent print or two on the sly; then, provided they weren't too smudged, you could get an ID. But in most cases, unless you had some idea whose prints you had lifted, forget it. Even with those name checks, we took the identities with a grain of salt until we got around to confirming them with fingerprints. It is simply astonishing how many dishonest people there are making life difficult for us poor cops.

Louis hung the phone up. "No answer."

"Why don't the three of us take a run over to see if we can get morally reaffirmed?" I suggested.

"I don't know. We really know nothing about these people. And they can raise the First Amendment, religious stuff as soon as you flash the star."

"On the other hand, maybe one of them is a female, and Paul can smile her into orgasm. Then she'll tell us where the hatchet and saws are kept."

He ignored me. "We all seem to be getting rushed into looking at this only from the side of the MRG. I don't like feeling that Stone thinks he can direct this investigation."

"My goodness," I said, "if his friends in high office hear that kind of talk, our miserable little jobs will be gone."

Louis pulled out the phone book and, after a couple of minutes, said, "They're not even listed. Why all the mystery? Is anyone in today from Intelligence?"

"On a Saturday? Louis, let me explain how a civil service system works."

"Some other time. You want to go out there and question those people, don't you, Fraleigh? But why not wait until we have some more to take them on with?"

He was right. But the bitterness of the last time we delayed was still with me. Louis sensed that. It was probably why he agreed to let us go.

"Try not to let them know how hard we're going to be looking at them. And none of that crazy bullshit. Hear?"

"Yes, Captain. But you know these men will do anything for me—except act sane—and I have to take care of them."

He looked at me unsmiling as the three of us stood. The Zombie had lethargically returned to his desk without reacting to my snappy dialogue. He picked up the phone as we left.

Ten

THE AREA, IN THE CENTER OF THE CITY, HADN'T QUITE made up its mind what it wanted to be. Old truck-loading platforms were surrounded by some recently opened chic antique shops. A block away, one of those new garden-office parks sat on the edge of railroad tracks that still carried freight to the meat, canning, and machine tool businesses. They were mostly quiet at 1645 hours. It was almost time for us to stop working if we had been working and not on a day off.

We pulled in to what had been a loading platform. A not-too-classy set of wooden stairs had been placed against the platform. The loading-bay doors were down and had been painted over in what someone must have thought was modern-decor green. To the right of the doors was a small, glass-windowed office, which had once housed the foreman, bookkeeper, and time clock for a small shipping business. I looked twice to make sure we had the right location. Sure enough, some recent lettering on the window read "Self Awareness Through Moral Reaffirmation."

The Block and English were already halfway up the steps

when I got out of the car. About thirty yards to our right, a group of men paused in their halfhearted unloading of a furniture truck to look at us.

The Block's huge form obliterated my view of the office as he entered. Paul was a step behind him, but as usual, the two of them had left me about six paces behind. That's what saved us.

Stepping through the door a couple of seconds behind Paul, I caught a glimpse over the Block's shoulder of a heavily built man leaning against a desk some eight feet or so from me. He brought a pistol from behind his back and shot the Block at point-blank range. The flash and noise filled the room. Paul jumped forward behind the Block, who, incredibly, had lurched frontward, driving the heel of his hand viciously upward under the shooter's nose. Another shot went into the ceiling as the Block careened into him. Both of them went down in a heap. Too late, I caught a flurry of movement back to our left. Had I been only a step behind Paul, the man hiding behind the door would simply have squeezed the trigger of his shotgun and blown us away. Unable to get both of us, he instinctively smashed the butt into the back of Paul's head, dropping him like a sack of lead. Then he swung the gun stock at me, standing flat-footed and vulnerable. Just in time, I twisted my head away, taking the full blow on my shoulder. The force knocked me through the plate-glass window onto the loading platform.

Almost blacked out from the agonizing pain in my broken shoulder and sick from the sight of blood spurting from a deep slash in my left arm cut by a shard of glass from the broken window, I watched him step forward and deliberately raise the shotgun to his shoulder for my swan song. Had he fired from the hip, it would have been all over. I didn't remember pulling my gun as I sailed through the window, but I shot the gunman through the left eye before he had gotten the weapon above his hip. Somehow I had managed to keep my balance and landed on my knees. It was the kind of thing you pick up in the ring, being hurt and groggy, but forcing yourself to function.

Through the broken window, I saw the second gunman pick up the automatic he lost when the Block took him down. He turned toward me. I shot him twice in the chest. He bounced backward. Suddenly worried that he might be wearing a protective vest, I carefully put two rounds into his face.

Then I calmly walked to our car, started the motor, and told radio that we'd been shot, send ambulances and a fill immediately. At least, that's what I thought I did.

Eleven

AN OBNOXIOUS MAN WEARING GLASSES AND A WHITE COAT was talking to me. He was being stern with me. He looked like he was about twenty-two years old and wore a stethoscope around his neck like armor so that people wouldn't ask why a squirt like him was walking around in a white coat.

"You've been extraordinarily lucky. The tourniquet and thirteen pints of blood provided by your colleagues pulled you through. But it could easily have gone the other way."

"Did you screen their blood? Some of those guys lead dirty lives."

"I heard you had a strange sense of humor," he told me primly.

The door swung open. Louis Robinson said, "I thought I heard you talking. Christ, are you lucky."

"They ought to get you a bed, Louis. You look terrible."

He did, but a big beaming smile suddenly lit up his ugly mug.

"Fraleigh, I . . ." He trailed off.

Dr. Obnoxious cut in, "I don't think the patient is quite

up to visitors yet, Captain. He's been unconscious for twelve hours."

"He's been unconscious for years, Doc." Louis grinned.

"Paul and the Block?" Suddenly, I felt myself drifting back into sleep. Fighting it until I heard Louis's answer, I tried to sit up and screamed as the pain hit my shoulder.

"I told you that you were seriously injured." The doctor's bedside manner would have delighted the KGB.

Louis put his big black hand over mine and squeezed. "You know how tough those two are. They're going to be O.K."

I didn't like that nonanswer at all, but I couldn't keep my head off the pillow. I hoped I wouldn't dream about all the tubes they had connected to my nose, arms, and God knows what else.

The next day was one of semiconsciousness. I was in and out all day. The dreams were hard to separate from reality. At one point, I woke to find around ten young doctors in white coats staring at me. Dr. Obnoxious was talking about me. I wanted to say something outrageous but was too exhausted. I drifted back to sleep.

That evening Louis showed up. I don't know how long he had been sitting there, but as soon as my eyes opened, he asked, "How are you?"

"Fine. Want to go a couple of rounds?"

"I knew you were going to pull through, Fraleigh. Only the good die young."

"How are they, Louis?"

"They're O.K. You were the one nobody was taking any bets on. We pieced together what happened as best we could. You were set up. The Moral Reaffirmation people haven't been near that office for a week. It was definitely a hit. The two guys you took out jimmied the lock. We found a hot car in the rear that they had used. But it was brazen—broad daylight." He shook his head.

"Why?" I asked.

"We don't know," he continued. "But I'll tell you one thing, Fraleigh, you wouldn't be here if it wasn't for that reserve cop, a guy by the name of Harry Sharpe. He was one of the bunch unloading a truck when you pulled up. He made the car as official and saw you get out. When he heard the first shot, he was already on the way over. He saw you fly through the window and shoot both of them. By the way, that was some clutch shooting, Fraleigh. Before he could get there, you had crawled back through the broken window. He found you passed out on top of the Block and English. You bled all over them. Lucky he used his belt and got a tourniquet on you right away. Another minute the way you were bleeding and it would have been all over."

"I didn't radio for help?"

"No, he grabbed your keys and got right through to Central. Why?" he asked, looking puzzled.

"Who were they?"

"We don't know," he said. "They weren't local. We sent their prints to Washington and Sacramento, but it'll be a while before we get anything back."

"What does Stone have to say about all this?"

Louis hesitated before answering. "We haven't talked to him yet. First he was out of town, now his lawyer is setting up an interview."

I wanted to do a lot more talking about that and get him to answer my questions about Paul's and the Block's conditions, but exhaustion hit me again.

He saw it and got up. "You take it easy, hear?" he said, squeezing my good shoulder.

I wanted to tell him no, I wasn't going to take it easy because I was going out dancing, but it wasn't that funny, and I had no energy. The door closed after him, and I felt a real depression slipping into sleep with me.

Things were very bad after that. People kept waking me

up. Every few hours someone would either take my temperature, force me to swallow pills, give me a sponge bath, or force me to have soup or to do something else that I really didn't want to do.

All I wanted to do was sleep. Ah, perchance to dream. That was a problem. The dreams were bad and continuous. The man with the shotgun was a star. He appeared and always had a leading role. He had a hairy mole on the left side of his face. The dreams varied, but usually I stared, hypnotized by the mole, as he shot the Block and English. I had my magnum in my hand, but just couldn't raise my arm. He knew it and laughed. He would shoot into the Block's body, and the noise and flash would leave me yelling, "No! No!"

By the third day, I was afraid to drop off, and at the same time I was so tired that it was unbearable. A couple of times the pain in my shoulder woke me screaming. I suspected, in my more lucid moments, that it occurred when they screwed up my dope. I knew they were dosing me heavily. The first few minutes after a shot made me feel warm and pleasant, but inevitably, the feeling of well-being ended in dreams that woke me and left me terrified and depressed.

One dream ended with a police funeral. Hundreds of uniformed officers were lined up. There were flags and pallbearers. Sometimes I could see into the coffin. It was me. I wanted to get out but couldn't. Foley and Louis were among the pallbearers. I pleaded with them that they were making a mistake, to let me out. But they showed no signs of hearing. Louis had tears streaming down his face. Foley was smiling happily. He said, "I warned him about the operational orders." I tried to tell Louis that he was lying, but he never heard.

Once, the Block was delivering my eulogy.

"I'm crying for him," he said, "but he never cried for me—just for the girl . . . and English."

In the coffin, I yelled, "No! Look! I'm crying for you too." But no one heard me.

At other times, Paul was in the coffin. I was sitting in the first row in front of the open grave. He would sit up and look at me with a hurt expression in his eyes. I wanted to stop the funeral, but no one else saw him sitting up. Sandra Fortune was sitting next to me, bare-breasted. She said calmly, "He never passed therapy at Stanford."

"It wasn't his fault. It was the war, don't any of you understand?" I cried, but no one heard me.

Louis, in his captain's uniform, looked at me as he let go of the casket. "They expected you to take care of them, Fraleigh."

The most disturbing dream of all was about Bini's funeral. Awake, I couldn't remember the details as clearly as in the other dreams. But I did remember that there was no dialogue. Just a coffin that contained Bini. It probably bothered me more because he hadn't been in the ambush. Somehow, that made dreaming about his funeral worse.

Half conscious, propped up against my pillow, I daydreamed about years ago when I had been assigned to Bini for some on-the-job training as a rookie investigator. It came back to me how patient he had been over my bumbling enthusiasm. Like a dope, I had seen his drinking problem but not his skills as a dick. Instead of teaching me a lesson, he had taught me his trade.

One of the early cases involved a barroom stabbing in a Filipino joint. Not surprisingly, we were batting zero as far as getting anyone to admit he saw anything. Each afternoon for a week we hit the place. Much to my disgust, Bini was more interested in drinking than in doing any questioning. Stubbornly I drank only Coke and insisted on paying for all my drinks. Bini was all too willing to allow generous quantities of rum to be poured into his glass and to stuff the same unbroken five-spot into his wallet when leaving.

Referring to me constantly as Champ, he would get a nice glow on, then waddle to the door precisely at 1700 hours so that we would not be late signing out of the squad room. Each day my walk out of the bar got a bit more rigid. He wasn't doing a damn thing except watching afternoon base-ball on TV and getting a free load on.

What finally pushed me over the edge was a coincidence. I drove past the place about ten o'clock one night. Glancing through the open front door, I spotted Bini's fat rear end perched on the same stool he claimed each afternoon. I knew the same five-spot was decorating the bar.

The next day I was determined to have it out with Bini. I wasn't a prude, but what he was doing was just too much.

"Morning, Champ. How are you today?"

"O.K., I guess." He was just too likable to get sore at. Nevertheless, I started to take him on.

"Bini, about that Filipino bar stabbing, the guy died on us, so now it's a homicide."

"Splendid piece of deduction, Champ." His eyes were twinkling.

I felt my face getting a little red. Rookie dick or not, I asked, "Don't you think we should be doing more on it?"

"I certainly do, lad. How would you like to accompany me this afternoon to arrest the perpetrator?"

"Do you know who he is?"

"She, not he," Bini said.

"You're pulling my leg."

"Not at all, Champ. While you've been looking down your nose at my methods, I made it possible for people who hang out in the bar to talk to me."

Now my face was really red. It was a variation on the Mutt-and-Jeff interrogation: nice guy–bad guy. He had used me as the heavy. Each afternoon Bini had used me to scare the piss out of the patrons, then returned at night to gain their confidence and listen to their stories.

"Do you really have it wrapped up, Bini?"

"Yeah. No big problem. The victim was popular, the gal is a real witch. No one liked her."

"Then why the hell didn't they tell us?"

"You never gave them a chance, Champ. You strutted around like Jack Webb. They couldn't wait for me to come in at night. There it is." He pointed to a pile of typed and signed statements.

"You did it all without even telling me."

"Now don't get touchy, Champ. You actually helped by playing it straight. Come on, I'll buy you a rum and Coke, and we'll arrest a murderess."

Actually, I was the one who bought. Bini stuffed the same five-dollar bill into his pocket after the expressionless bartender had nicked me for the four rum and Cokes we consumed. But it was worth it. During the next two years, I learned more about criminal investigation than I thought existed, and I remembered the hurt and loss when Bini told me he was adopting a new rookie to break in because he had nothing left to teach me.

My mind was spinning in and out of dreams. The uniformed cop had to touch my arm a couple of times. "Fraleigh? I know you're not supposed to see anyone, but this kid outside says he's got to talk to you. He claims it's about the shooting."

"Kid? What time is it?"

"It's 0130 hours. Look, I can tell the kid to beat it. To come back in the daytime."

"He says it's about the ambush? What's his name?"

"Eric. He won't tell me his last name. What do you say? Should I tell him to walk?"

I was hazy, but not so hazy that I didn't remember Eric Stone and his father's call, which had sent us off to get shot. "Bring him in. But sit in the corner and keep an eye on him while I talk to him."

Young Stone looked haggard, but there was no sign that he had been snorting coke recently. He looked over his shoulder at the uniformed man. Reassured that he was out of earshot, Eric said softly, "I was sorry to hear that you were hurt. It was really my fault."

"Your fault? I don't get it."

"I should have warned you about my father."

I fought off a spasm of dizziness, trying to keep my mind focused on what he was saying.

"Look, I can see you're in bad shape. Maybe I can come back when you're able to understand me better."

"No. Go on," I whispered.

"My father's dangerous. If I told you some of the things he's done to me you wouldn't believe me. He's capable of corrupting anyone. And God forbid, I'm afraid he's succeeded with Judy and Lisa."

"But they're dead." I felt that I was losing the thread of conversation. Was this another dream?

"Keep in mind that you can't believe anything my father says. And Sandra Fortune . . ."

I heard the cop telling him, "That's all, kid. The poor guy just passed out on us."

I awoke early. Sunshine was flooding the room. I rang the buzzer. A cop stuck his head in the door. "What's up? Do you want the nurse?"

"No, but tell me something. Did I have a visitor last night?"

"I don't know. I just came on duty an hour ago."

A female nurse built like the Block and almost as heavy ignored my feeble protest and dragged me out of bed. Somehow she maneuvered me once down the corridor and back.

"There, didn't that feel good?" she prattled.

My head was spinning and legs trembling. As much as I hated her, I silently yielded to her sponging me off. Tears of frustration over my helplessness were on my face.

"There, there. A big, strong man like you shouldn't cry," she said. She must have gone to the same school as Dr. Obnoxious.

That afternoon a chubby short character in a flashy open-necked sport shirt stuck his head in. "Ah, we're awake today," he said cheerfully. "We seem to be recovering nicely, I daresay," he said, beaming at me.

We? I had a private room. The only one in it was me. I wondered if he was a nut who had wandered down from the psychiatric ward. I slipped my hand toward the call button. If he was violent, I was in trouble. I was as weak as a baby.

"Any dreams?" he inquired eagerly. "Don't be concerned, I've done a lot of work in shooting cases. Or perhaps," he laughed, "I should say police officer shooting cases."

He saw my hand reaching for the call button.

"Bedpan? Here, let me do it. I'd just as soon we not be interrupted for a few minutes."

With that, he grabbed a bedpan and lifted me up, placing the coldly unpleasant metal contraption under me.

"Who are you?" I asked, not totally sure this wasn't another nightmare.

"Dr. Morin, the staff psychiatrist. Didn't Nurse Griswold tell you I'd be in today? It's standard in these cases, you know. No wonder you looked so hostile."

He had wandered down from the psychiatric ward after all.

"You've been through a traumatic experience, and although your body has survived, more or less," he chuckled, "the postshooting mental phenomena intrigue us just as much as your physical health. How's the potty? All done yet?" He lifted me up, peering into the pan. "No? That's all right, we needn't be anxious just because of me," he said matter-of-factly, tucking my balls back into the range of the bedpan.

"I'm tired. I want to sleep," I said in a pathetic gesture of self-defense.

"Totally understandable, old boy, under the circumstances, but first tell me about these dreams of yours. We don't want to bottle them up, do we?"

I closed my eyes with determination, letting my head nod. He sat there patiently for a minute. I peeked through my eyelashes. He was writing rapidly in a notebook. Getting up, he carelessly bumped the bed, sending a shaft of pain through my shoulder. I stifled most of my moan, but he was on his way out, oblivious of me. In fact, the dumb bastard left me on the damn bedpan. I disturbed my shoulder getting it out from under me. I threw it on the floor and went to sleep, determined to escape as soon as I could walk.

The next day was even worse. They kept waking me during the night for needles, pills, pulse-taking, and other annoyances. Even when they left me alone, the noise from the nearby nurses' station was only a few decibels less than the Super Bowl game. I felt sorry for people who never got quite strong enough to get away before their health was completely destroyed.

Right after some crummy mush that was supposed to be breakfast, the heavyweight nurse arrived to waltz me up and down the hall. It made me sick and nauseous, but I was game. I wanted out and knew I had to be able to walk to pull it off.

After she was gone, the cops started arriving. Only a form of martial law had kept them away until now. At first, I was glad to see them. They told me not to worry, they had traded me for one of the new female sergeants, who not only was stacked, but also knew how to keep her team's case load up to par.

That afternoon Raoul Chavez and Bini showed up. It was silly, but after dreaming so vividly about his funeral, I was reassured to see Bini.

I looked at him more closely. What was it? His face looked a little more flushed than usual but . . .

"Hi, Champ," he said.

"Bini! You son of a bitch, that's my new sports jacket you're wearing."

"Yeah, well, you know how it is, Fraleigh. No one figured you was going to make it, and we do take about the same size, you know."

Two more dicks came in after Raoul and Bini left, telling me that they had drawn lots for my prime three-week vacation pick around Labor Day, since I would be on disability leave if I survived in the first place. The fatigue caught me, and I dozed right in the middle of a sentence, realizing as I slid into slumber that none of them had mentioned the Block or Paul.

When Nurse Battle-Ax arrived the next morning for our stroll, I told her that I wanted to visit my two partners.

"I'm afraid that won't be possible."

"Why not?"

"You're in no condition. That's why not."

"You don't know what you're talking about. I'm checking out this afternoon."

She almost dropped me. "It will be a long time before you are recovered enough to check out."

"This afternoon," I said stubbornly.

I woke up to see Dr. Obnoxious and the shrink with their heads together.

Obnoxious spoke. "Sergeant, you don't seem to realize what your body has been through."

"You don't seem to realize what this joint puts a body through. You ought to camp here some night and see how much sleep the patients get. I want out. At least at home I can get some sleep and start getting better."

"I'm afraid that would be very unwise. You lost a lot of blood, have a major incision in your left arm, and a multitude of superficial punctures and lacerations, as well as a fractured shoulder blade that needs complete immobilization. The healing process for your injuries, in addition to the postshock trauma, are energy draining. Furthermore, you will still be under heavy sedation for another week because of pain from your shoulder blade fracture. All of this means that you should be under constant monitoring."

"O.K. I'll give it three more days, provided that you let me visit my two buddies."

"Sergeant Fraleigh"—the shrink took over—"we're not your enemies. It is natural after an incident like the one you were involved in to go through certain guilt stages, with the resulting tendency toward depression, delusion, and third-party aggression. In extreme cases, paranoia may develop. Therefore, we practice patient segregation. It's best for you and for them."

"You ought to practice in the Soviet Union. You'd do fine. But tomorrow I'm checking out of your little zoo. You can get another guinea pig."

Obnoxious said, "We can't keep you from checking out, of course, but we will require a complete written release absolving us of responsibility for your health."

Later that evening, Louis came in. "I've got one thing to say to you, Fraleigh. You pay attention to the doctors and stay away from the Block and English, and you stay put in the hospital until I tell you otherwise."

"That's two things! And you can go to hell," I told his retreating back.

Twelve

THE NEXT AFTERNOON A SOMBER CROWD WITNESSED ME
signing out of the hospital. I would have been impressed if I
hadn't been so doped up. Dr. Obnoxious was there. He
sternly warned me, "This medication is extremely powerful." He was holding a little plastic container. "You take
one before going to bed at night and one during the night if
the pain wakes you. Under no condition take more than four
during any one twenty-four-hour period."

Raoul Chavez had agreed to drive me home. "You sure
this is a good idea, Fraleigh?" he asked.

By this time, I wasn't sure of anything. I was ready for
sleep again, but a worried-looking nurse was handing me
my schedule.

"Today is Sunday. You come back here to the outpatient
clinic on Wednesday afternoon. Now remember, it's very
important. Your bandages have to be changed and an X ray
taken to make sure your shoulder is knitting properly. Then
Thursday morning you have an appointment with Dr. Morin. His office is on the third floor."

"Yeah, O.K., I understand," I said, taking the papers while fighting my leaden eyelids.

"Don't use any machinery, Fraleigh," said Physician Obnoxious, watching me intently.

"Don't take any wooden appendixes, Doc." It was feeble, but the moment we were in the car I was asleep.

My bed was a luxury that I would never again take for granted. I sank into it ready to sleep for a month. The pain caught me in the middle of the night. It ran from my left shoulder right into my brain, and I found myself openly whimpering. It took about twenty minutes for the pill to take hold. I walked up and down the living room, into my small hallway, around the kitchen, and back into the bedroom, not stopping for an instant in a desperate attempt to divert my mind from the pain. Nothing worked, but the pain seemed a little more intense when I was still. Finally, I sank back into bed, exhausted by the experience.

So passed the night. Time became a blur. My daytime routine didn't differ from the night. Occasionally, I wondered if I had eaten. Once I couldn't believe the electric alarm clock—it said 4:10. Out of habit, I called the phone company. A voice confirmed that it was 4:10, but a moment after hanging up, I couldn't remember whether they had said P.M. or A.M. Not that it made any difference anyway.

I was sitting watching television, or actually the television set, because the set was off, the screen dark and silent. The light in the living room created soft shadows. It was pleasant and dreamy. The door opened. It was Sandra Fortune.

"Oh, my God," she said. Her hand flew to her mouth as she looked around.

It was all quite confusing. I wondered if it was real. One way or the other it was certainly better than the kind of dreams I had been having. I wanted to know how she got to my apartment, but somehow the question got twisted.

"Who are you, Sandra? No, wait. I mean, how, how . . . ?"

Her eyes had misted as I struggled with the question. Her voice caught a little. "I'm so sorry to see you like this. Somehow I feel responsible. I called yesterday to see if there was any news on the murders. I never knew about you being hurt until Captain Robinson told me. He's very concerned about you. I thought about you last night. I called you this morning. Don't you remember?"

"This morning?" Dimly I remembered. I had answered the phone. I couldn't take my eyes off her. I wanted to talk, but my brain and tongue were tied in knots.

She looked away from my fixed stare for a second. "You sounded so . . . so disoriented, so in need of help that I got the address from the phone book and came here. How could they leave you like this?" She actually sobbed.

I rose from the chair. I was a detective. I wanted to let her know I didn't accept all this bullshit, all this coincidence. My phone wasn't even listed, although suddenly I wasn't sure that was true. The drugs befuddled me, destroyed my confidence. Still, I was going to let her know I wasn't a fool.

Instead, as she was helping me to my feet, I put my arm around her and kissed her full on the mouth. I held her tightly. Her full breasts were pushed against my chest and I felt a surprised gasp move through her body. "I wanted to do that from the moment I saw you in the kitchen."

"But . . ." she said. Her eyes were wide. White teeth and pink tongue showed through her slightly open mouth. The same look she had shown for a moment when we first met. When she realized how quickly she had aroused me.

I covered her mouth with mine. I knew this was crazy. But it was like the drugs had unleashed a new me. A reckless one. I had violated a cop's first directive: Don't get emotionally involved with anyone connected to a case. Yet I didn't care. She was returning my embrace to the point where the pressure began to hurt my shoulder. Then the drugs in their fickleness swung me to a mood of guilt.

"Your husband, your stepdaughter, I mean. I don't want to take advantage."

"Shut up, you idiot," she told me, reaching through my robe. My cock had no scruples at all. It was hard as a steel rod. Unbelievable. For a week, the shock and medication had made me forget it was even there. She moved me to the bed.

I lay there, watching as she quickly took her clothes off. First she threw off her blouse and unhooked her bra, appreciating my fascinated glance. Without hesitation, she discarded her slacks and light pink panties. She was beautiful and knew it. Gently, she took my robe off, then my shorts. Her eyes had clouded momentarily when she saw all the bandages, but without hesitation she got on top of me and began rocking up and down.

That was her foreplay. In a minute she was screwing with a vengeance, bouncing up and down on me. Between the drugs and the pain she was causing my shoulder, it took a lot longer than otherwise. She was frantic, her eyes wilder and wilder. Her breasts, full from nursing, swung furiously up and down as she tried to drive me through the mattress.

Finally I released. She gave a sharp cry, halfway between moan and scream. She was lathered with sweat. Cuddling into my good side, she said, "I'm terrible. I knew I was hurting you, but couldn't stop. Are you all right?"

"Sure," I lied. It felt good to have her there. The warm softness of her seeped into me like sunshine. But my shoulder was throbbing. We lay there, slowly letting our breathing subside to normal.

"My husband hadn't touched me in a year. The day you came was one of his rare visits to the children. He didn't live with us. Nor does Judy very often. Unfortunately, she's always been hostile toward me."

I was holding her very close. My good arm was around her shoulder. Her head was on my bare chest. She had spoken so softly that I had to strain to hear. "Don't. You don't have . . . You don't need to explain . . ." I was still having trouble with words.

"I know. But I didn't want you to think that I'm some kind of heartless ghoul. I am badly shaken by what happened, but it's not as if . . ." I stretched to put a finger to her lips, silencing her.

A delicious drowsiness was sweeping over me, and I could see that she, too, was beginning to doze. My drowsiness was being pushed out by the steadily rising crescendo of pain in my shoulder. Sandra was in a light sleep, and I didn't want to disturb her, but after about five minutes, I couldn't stand it any longer.

I eased out from her embrace and walked unsteadily into the bathroom for a pill. The water glass slipped from my fingers, shattering noisily on the tile floor. I stared numbly at the pieces, surprised that it broke so easily.

"Don't move. You'll cut your feet."

Incredibly, I had forgotten her. She was nude and gorgeous standing in the bathroom doorway. She took my hand and led me gently back to the bed.

"Christ, are you out of it. What kind of pills are you taking?"

"Percodan. But I need one bad now." I had shoved my knuckles into my mouth to stop the whimpering, which I couldn't seem to control.

"Be careful of your feet," I told her as she left me.

She looked over her shoulder at me on the way to the kitchen. I could see moisture in her eyes. The two of us were going to get waterlogged if this didn't stop soon.

Taking the broom from the closet, she carefully swept the glass from the bathroom floor as I watched from the bed, worrying about her feet. My teeth were almost drawing blood from my right knuckles. She returned with a glass of water and the pill container, reading the instructions. She rattled it. It sounded almost empty.

"How many of these damned things have you taken?"

"Just give me one now. Don't start diagnosing me, for God's sake."

She thought for a moment, then handed me the pill and water. After swallowing it, I lay back, watching her dial the wall phone in the kitchen. There was one right next to the bed, and I felt a pang that she didn't want me to hear her conversation.

As she talked, I realized with relief that it wasn't another man. She was talking to someone at the hospital. She was giving them hell. I heard something about "irresponsibility" and "malpractice," and once she actually called someone a "son of a bitch." I hoped it was Dr. Obnoxious. She was tough, but what a lovely ass, I thought, watching her, still nude, barking into the phone. She hung up.

"You're a mess, Fraleigh," she told me angrily from the side of the bed, with her big breasts jutting out over me. "Look at you—you haven't shaved, you haven't bathed, and you probably haven't eaten since you got home. You're a damn junkie."

I thought of a snide crack about how she hadn't felt so repulsed a few minutes ago, but swallowed it. This was a tough lady and she was steaming.

"I'm going to clean you up, feed you, and take you to the hospital."

"Please, don't put me back in the hospital." I realized with disgust that I was crying—begging. The lousy pills were driving me crazy.

"You're coming home with me." She had lifted me up, once more jolting my shoulder, which had just begun to feel a little better with the pill taking hold. But then she tenderly held my head to her warm breasts and things were very fine indeed.

In a few minutes, she had me standing weakly against the shower wall. A wonderful stream of warm water was bouncing off me. She had cleverly rigged one of those plastic covers they put on clothes coming from the cleaners over my bandaged shoulder. From somewhere she produced a shower cap for herself and moved in with me. She gently washed me from head to toe.

"O.K., now your head," she commanded. "It looks like it hasn't been washed since you left high school." She bent my head down so that she could work the shampoo into a lather. I realized I had her by two or three inches. Up until then, it seemed that she towered over me by about a foot. I nibbled at her breast a little as she was working my hair. She hit me a stiff hook in the ribs.

"The next one will be into your bad side, buster."

I had an uneasy feeling she meant it and I wasn't about to gamble.

Out of the shower she carefully dried me after watching me fail at it with my good arm. She puttered in the kitchen after ordering me to get dressed. When she came in to see how I was doing, I tried hard to keep my frustration from showing. I couldn't even get a pair of drawers on, let alone socks or shoes.

"Sit down," she said.

I sat. Then she slipped my feet into the shorts.

"O.K. Now stand up."

I did. She raised the shorts up around my waist.

"Sit down."

Then she patiently put a pair of socks on my feet, slipping a pair of loafers on with a shoehorn. I was so helpless that I was fuming.

"I think we'll skip your undershirt today, sport."

She moved to the closet, pulled out a sport shirt and

slacks, and ordered me to raise my legs. She couldn't get the slacks on over the shoes. I felt better. She wasn't so smart. If she had asked me, I would have told her to put the slacks on before the shoes.

"Don't be so smug, you jerk, or I'll let you do this yourself," she said, calmly taking off the shoes, slipping the slacks onto my legs, then having me stand while she fastened the waist button and zipped the fly. She paused for a moment, looked straight into my eyes while I stood, then lightly kissed me on the lips. Emotion ran through me like a warm flood. I just stood there, thinking it must be the pills. I leaned against her, and she slipped her arms around me, holding me firmly but tenderly.

"Tough guy, huh?" she said softly.

Then she put the shirt on me, deliberately buttoning it without looking at me. I was dressed. She took my hand and led me to the kitchen. Some soup I didn't know I had was simmering on the stove. I sat on a stool.

The kitchen was narrow, and the towel she was wearing slipped a bit as she stood on her toes facing away from me trying to reach soup bowls. I goosed her.

"You bastard!"

She managed to get the dishes and turned, glaring at me.

"You've got a dirty mouth, babe," I told her.

She poured soup into the bowl. It was delicious. I had been starving without realizing it. She sat opposite me, looking like the cat who swallowed the canary, as I wolfed down the soup.

"This is good. What kind is it?"

"It's chicken soup, you ass."

"Chicken soup? Then it's really true, Sandra, what they say?"

"You better quit while you're ahead, Fraleigh," she warned.

She drove her miniature Toyota station wagon toward the

hospital with the verve of a New York cabdriver. The car hadn't surprised me—Californians regard it as unpatriotic to drive an American-made car. But the smell was different. It smelled of children and the beach. It was delicious. I remembered what the hospital smelled like.

I was hunched in the seat. We stopped for a light. She turned and looked at me. "For God's sake," she said, "it's not going to be that bad."

She didn't know. I felt the chicken soup and stale croutons floating ominously. My shoulder was temporarily in a state of truce, but I had no illusions about what was coming.

We pulled into the hospital complex. It was around four o'clock on a lovely August afternoon. The brilliance of the sunlight had me squinting somewhat as she led me through a door marked Outpatients. I sagged into an empty seat while Sandra went up to a white-outfitted witch guarding a window with a sign warning you to have your Blue Cross card ready. The broad in the window tried to give her a number and orders to wait until it was called, but she was overmatched. Within a minute, Sandra had her flushed and reluctantly telephoning someone on the hospital staff.

I had made a poor choice of a seat. There was a man of about seventy sitting next to me with a consumptive cough that was obviously tubercular. I knew that in my weakened state I shouldn't be exposed to a communicable disease, but I was afraid that if I got up to move, I'd collapse and get rushed into one of their torture chambers cleverly camouflaged as a private room.

Sandra won. She was back.

"They're going to take you into that room. I'll be right here."

I was in a cold sweat. It cost me a lot, but I got out, "You won't let them keep me here, will you?"

"You're coming out of here with me," she said, lightly touching her hand to my cheek.

I felt better. Not much, but better. I walked through the door marked Treatment Room. A kid in a white coat put down a file. I read my name on it with dread. He eyed me briefly, sort of the way you glance at the live lobsters in the tank of a seafood restaurant on the way in to dinner. Then he was washing his hands. Why, I don't know, because he had a nurse immediately help him put on gloves. In the meantime, they stripped me to my shorts and had me sitting on the table.

"I want you to know what I'm going to do," he told me.

I didn't want to know. In fact, I didn't even want to know why they were all so goddamned young.

He continued. "You have one hundred eighty-two lacerations of different magnitude, sixteen incisions, and four punctures. In addition, you have a broken shoulder. I'm going to change the dressing on all of them. It will hurt as I pull the adhesive off and possibly as I treat the open wounds. However, it is essential to ensure that no infection is occurring."

"Look, I'm not going to medical school, so just do whatever you have to do so I can play in my polo match tonight."

Two hours later he left. I lay on the table, a beaten man. We had paused once, about halfway through, to let me vomit the chicken soup into a sink, which had a couple of things lying in it that must have been extracted from a previous customer.

I don't think he made it hurt any more than it did normally. In fact he was too conscientious. Each time he ripped a piece of adhesive off, I prayed he would just burn it with whatever kind of acid he was using. All too often, he decided I needed a little pruning first. The first few times, he told me, "This may hurt a bit." After I blacked out on one of his carvings, he did his butchery silently.

He gave me an injection before leaving. "Don't drive," he warned and disappeared to carve up someone else.

Drive? I didn't think I could walk. Only the fear of being admitted to the hospital got me off the table. Even so, it took about fifteen minutes before my head stopped swimming to the point that I could walk out of the room.

My face, reflected in the mirror behind Sandra in the lobby, was chalk white. She paled a little herself as she looked at me leaving the treatment room.

"Now we'll go see the Block and English."

"No way," she said. "You're coming home with me before someone mistakes you for a cadaver."

Thirteen

IT WAS UNCONDITIONAL SURRENDER, BUT IT WASN'T SO bad, I thought. She covered me with a blanket and put on a tape of Debussy's "La Mer" as she steered expertly onto the freeway, aiming toward the ocean. The injection was slowly easing the pain and memory of the last two hours of cutting and snipping. I didn't sleep, but wasn't really awake, either. It was kind of pleasant.

The car windows were open and Sandra's soft brown hair was blowing in the wind stream. The last golden light of a summer evening played about her smooth flesh, and I felt overwhelmed with pleasure. She was taking me home with her. The memory of her afternoon nudity coupled with the intensity of her personality filled me with happy anticipation. And the little red warning light blinking deep in the back of my brain with the message that when you think something is too good to be true, you're usually right was simply covered by drugs, weakness, and, yes, desire for Sandra. Besides, being with her would give me a chance to find out more about Don and Judy Fortune. Who knows? It might even lead to clues about how and why we got bushwhacked.

A mile or so outside of Santa Cruz, the clear sea air came into the car, promising intangible wonders of release from the massed population of the valley and its morass of corroding problems. Yet I knew deep down that the promise, like the sea itself, was also a measure of quicksilver—deceptive, dangerous, full of illusions.

I breathed deeply of the dark, salty, balmy air before following Sandra into the house. She carried a small bag that she had packed for me before leaving my place. I stood awkwardly in the front hall waiting for her to reappear. We hadn't used this entrance before. She came back and introduced me to a gray-haired woman in her sixties, who had been baby-sitting for the children.

The woman got paid and left. Uninvited, I followed Sandra as she checked on the children. First she visited the baby. Babies all look alike to me; it was the mother who held my attention. Love flowed as she lifted the infant to her cheek and swayed with it briefly before returning it to the crib. Then we went to another room where the other two rosy-cheeked kids were asleep in separate beds. Gently she touched each of them.

"I always have a compulsion to check them as soon as I get in, even when I have to pee as bad as I do now," she said, rushing off.

Once again, I stood alone, waiting for her to come back. When she did, she led me into the kitchen and placed me on the same stool I had occupied when we met. Going to the refrigerator, she paused, eyeing me speculatively, then took two bottles of Henry Weinhard's beer from the shelf. She opened them cleanly and poured for each of us. My stomach felt terrible and I had a real fear that the cold beer might cause cramps. I matched her silent toast, however, downing a respectable mouthful. I would have done a lot worse things rather than have marred her pleasure in serving me a beer following the afternoon's hospital ordeal.

"Let's make a deal, my hero," she said. "Don't eat or drink something because you want to please me. And don't try to tell me that you wouldn't mind staying up for a while and talking, because I can see that you're about to fall down and you're much too heavy for me to carry."

She poured my beer into the sink and, taking my hand, led me into the comfortable-size bedroom. Turning the cover down on the king-size bed, she said simply, "You go ahead, I've got to read for an hour or two to unwind."

I managed a couple of buttons on my sport shirt before she rushed back in from the living room. "I'm sorry. Here, let me help, and stop playing John Wayne, will you? Ask me for help when you need it."

She pushed me into a sitting position on the bed, quickly taking off my shoes and socks. Working together we got the slacks off easily, and I lay back in my shorts, prepared for instant unconsciousness. But she would not allow me to sleep without some covering on my chest, with its multiple wounds. Averting her eyes from the mass of bandages, she slipped my pajama shirt on. Then she slipped my shorts off. I noticed she wasn't averting her eyes, but curiously appraising my privates as she pulled on the pajama buttoms. Looking up, she saw I had caught her at it and turned red.

"Shut up, Fraleigh. Go to sleep."

But she kissed me lightly on the lips before turning out the light.

It was around two weeks since I had come to this house with the Block and English. Now I was lying where Don Fortune had. Sandra and I had done a lot of nontalking. Both of us knew that he was dead. He had died because I followed Foley's stupid orders and now I had taken his place in bed. Strangely enough, it seemed perfectly natural to me, but maybe that was only because of the shock of the ambush and the drugs.

What about her? She had come and picked me up at my lowest ebb. Somehow I could understand that. Something had passed between us that day in the kitchen. I knew now that the realization that her husband was gone had registered deeply with me when English had broken the news in the courthouse. I had suppressed it consciously, but I had known I would be returning to this woman.

My own agonized whimpering awoke me. For a moment I didn't know where I was. Then Sandra touched me. She was next to me, in a plain blue nightgown. Her eyes were sympathetic.

"I wish I could do something. I'll get you a pill," she said.

The pain of this injury was like nothing I had known before. The medication seemed to diminish it only halfway and then only temporarily. To stop chewing my knuckles, I wrapped my leather wallet in a handkerchief and bit into it to stifle my moans. She sat watching me. I got up and walked through the house, back and forth, until I was asleep on my feet. But every time I got back into bed, the pain drove me up again within a few minutes.

"Go back to sleep. I'll be O.K."

Shaking her head no, she got up and returned a minute later with a double brandy. We both knew I had been warned about mixing alcohol with the drugs. I drank the brandy in two gulps, waiting for the warmth to hit my stomach. It took about ten minutes before I stretched out.

I was soaking wet from sweat. She wiped my face with a hand towel, then moved next to me. Her closeness, the brandy, and the pill got me a fitful hour and a half of sleep before the process started all over again. I couldn't wait for dawn, but when it came, things were no better. Both of us were tense and red-eyed. She hadn't bargained for this. Taking care of the house and three kids under the circumstances was more than enough. By preventing her from sleeping and adding to her worries, I would quickly push her to the breaking point. Maybe I would have to go back to the hospital for her sake. It had finally penetrated that I really couldn't hack it on my own. And I knew neither of us could take another night like this.

At 7:15 A.M. Sandra provided coffee and croissants. Almost casually she warned me that she hadn't told the children anything about their father and Judy. "Until . . . You know what I mean. The kids won't make anything of their absence for a while. I just haven't been able to bring myself to talk to them about it." Toddler Don appeared. He irritably fought off Sandra's hug, kisses, and nose-rubbing.

"What's wrong with you males anyway? You don't want to show affection and enjoy all that good hugging," she said.

"Try me."

"Big talk. I didn't hear any of that last night."

"You were exhausted," I kidded.

"I have only one thing to say to you, Fraleigh."

"Yeah? What's that?"

But she remained silent, just looking at me.

When both kids sat down for breakfast, she brought up the subject of my presence.

"Do you remember Mr. Fraleigh, the policeman who was here a few weeks ago?"

I realized I had been slightly uneasy and guessed that Sandra was also.

"I like him, he's nice," said that darling, bright child, Lily.

"Tawley," shouted little Don, "you big shit cop."

I gaped at him.

"Don, wash your mouth. That was a bad thing to say,"

his mother scolded. Once again I noticed that she was twice as beautiful when she blushed.

"I don't know where they pick up these things," she said.

But I think we both had a pretty good idea and I found myself laughing at her embarrassment. She picked it up pretty quickly and moved to bring some more coffee from the kitchen.

"You're really not very nice, Fraleigh," she told me over her shoulder.

So I had made an impression on Don, the bus driver–investor, after all. From the mouths of babes, as they say.

She returned composed, carrying more coffee and second helpings of cereal for the children. I sat enjoying the scene, for the moment able to ignore the pain that had hounded me for the past week. She went back into the house while I got acquainted with the two youngsters. They were both so cheerful that it was contagious.

"We go to the beach. Do you like the beach?" Lily asked with her little-old-lady precision.

"Yes, I used to be a lifeguard."

"You too old, Tawley," contributed her brother. "And too skinny," he added.

"Mr. Fraleigh is not skinny. He's just sick this week. You don't remember him from last week, that's all," the little girl lectured.

"Yes I do," he shouted. "He's big—"

"You better not say that," Lily cut in, her expression and tone so much like her mother's that I couldn't help laughing.

We made plans for beach excursions and building elaborate sand castles until they disappeared, leaving me to study a couple of noisy jays bullying the smaller birds away from a redwood feeder that would soon be empty.

Sandra reappeared in a white blouse and dark blue slacks. She paused for a moment, savoring my appreciative look.

She was a striking woman, an attention getter in any setting. I hated to let her out alone.

"Why don't you try to lie down and get some rest. I'm taking the kids to do a little shopping, should be back in an hour. You'll be O.K., won't you?"

"Sure."

"Fraleigh? Please don't take any more pills while I'm gone. O.K.? It won't be that long."

"Oh, for God's sake, cut it out. I'm not one of your children."

She took my hand. "I don't think you realize the state you were in. Those pills are dynamite. I won't leave unless you promise."

"O.K., O.K.," I said, somewhat ashamed of myself. She was right and had gone to considerable pains to undo the trouble I had gotten into with the pills. How was she to know that now that I had her, it was no longer a problem? I stood up and, putting my good hand to her cheek, kissed her lightly.

"I'm sorry. I do appreciate you getting me straightened out, but that's all behind me now. I can hold off until you get back if the pain comes on again."

"Remember, you just had one before breakfast. You shouldn't have another until at least eleven o'clock," she warned.

I went inside the house and back to bed, listening as she pulled the car out of the garage. It was silly, but I was really sorry she was leaving.

The same excruciating pain attacking my shoulder woke me about an hour after they left. I started toward the bathroom for a pill, then remembered my promise. The electric alarm clock read 10:10. It's ridiculous, I thought. What's fifty minutes with pain like this? But I had promised. The minutes crept by so slowly that twice I checked the clock to be sure it hadn't stopped. I roamed the house nonstop, trying to think of things to distract myself from the pain. As usual, nothing worked.

Sandra returned with the kids around 10:45. She looked at me. I didn't say anything.

"It's bad again, isn't it? I can't stand to see you suffer like this." She drew a glass of water and took the pill container from her bag, spilling out a single yellow pill.

"Don't be mad at me for taking the pills with me. I would never have forgiven myself if you had some sort of accident while I was gone."

I just put my arm around her and hugged her to me.

"You're trembling. Poor baby. It can't last much longer. The doctor told me the intense pain would only last a few more days. It will still be achy, but nothing like this," she said.

A few days more. How could I last? Not only the pain, but I couldn't stand what I was doing to her. As a cop, I always thought watching people screaming in agony was the worst part of our job. For a person like Sandra, watching someone she loved in great pain would be even worse. Stunned, I realized what I had thought. Someone she loved. She did love me. I had been suppressing that and, less successfully, the fact that I loved her. The truth had broken through only in a moment of agony.

"What is it?" She had drawn slightly away from me and was staring into my face.

"I suddenly realized how much I love you, but you knew all along, didn't you?"

"What does it matter?" she answered. "As long as I can hold you like this and have you here, that's all I care about."

I lay down again, listening to her and the children unload the packages in the kitchen.

"Where does this go, Mom?" Lily asked.

"In the cabinet next to the sink, darling."

She sounded happy. I loved the sound of her voice. It was

full and throaty, and it changed. Speaking to Lily she conveyed a warmth and, somehow, an intimacy with the child. A moment later, answering toddler Don's excited scream, "Where this go, Mom? Where this go?" her voice held just as much affection but also an amused and loving patience.

"That's shaving cream for Fraleigh. It goes in Mommy's bathroom."

Lying there, I rebuked myself for letting such mundane chatter cause me so much happiness. But the fact that she had shopped for shaving cream for me and now directed that it belonged in her bathroom, touched me deeply. It must be the damn pills, I thought, but I knew it wasn't.

My dozing was unpleasant. An ugly thought kept intruding. It had to do with my unlisted number. She had said that she looked up my address in the telephone book. But if it wasn't in the book, then she was lying. I had given her the number. I remembered that, but maybe I had given the address to her during the phone conversation that I didn't remember. No. She hadn't said that. I didn't want her to be lying. I didn't want to question what we had going. Finally, before pain pushed me into sleep, I remembered that I had given her my card and written my home phone number on it. But *not* my address. And my address was not in the phone book where she claimed she had found it.

She roused me for lunch. There was a cocktail glass full of bay shrimp, covered with a spicy red sauce, and some sourdough bread. In addition, she expertly uncorked a bottle of Mirassou Mountain Chablis. "I'll expect you to do this," she said, "when that bum shoulder of yours is better."

After lunch, she decided that I should sunbathe. I managed to get out of my pajama top without excessive effort or pain, but getting the damned bottoms off forced me to bend in a way that sent dizzying pain through my shoulder. She had been watching from the doorway.

"Why are you so stubborn?" She had tears in her eyes.

"I thought you were going to ask for help when you needed it?"

I didn't answer. She came to the bed and pulled my bottoms off easily. Then she slipped my bathing trunks over my feet and said, "Stand up, dopey, unless you'd like to do some more calisthenics to see if you can make yourself faint?"

As she pulled the trunks into place, I got hard.

"Now you see what you've done. How can I go out with a bulge like this? That's why I don't ask for your help, you're too damned sexy," I told her.

She responded by tongue kissing me in the ear before I could wiggle away from her.

The sun soaked into my shoulder. The lunch and wine combined to lull me into a pleasant doze stretched out on the patio chaise longue. After an hour, Sandra reappeared in a bikini, which immediately led to the same embarrassing space problems in my trunks.

"Mrs. Smith takes the children and baby for a walk to the beach in about fifteen minutes. Then you're going to earn all the good treatment you've been getting around here, buddy."

"I have no idea what you mean. I thought we'd all go to the beach together."

"That's what you think, big boy. You've got some service to perform to compensate for your keep."

We were alone. Without embarrassment, both of us savoring the moment, holding each other's naked form in the huge bed. I held her lightly with my good arm. We were lying sideways, face-to-face. The fit was perfect. She snuggled into me, her right arm lightly circling my bandaged shoulder. My left arm was strapped, immobilized against my chest, but her hand reached beyond the tape, and its firm pressure pulling me into her made me feel wanted. We stayed that way for a few minutes, until I had to shift my weight to keep my right arm from going numb with loss of circulation.

I lay flat on my back, while she, on her stomach, raised herself slightly and kissed me on the mouth, I lightly fondled her breast with my right hand. It was slow and almost painfully delicious. We had both been aroused quickly but held back, enjoying the closeness. Now she started to swing on top of me as she had the first time, but I stopped her. Holding myself easily on my right arm, I moved on top of her. She gave a sharp cry when I entered her, and began to move rhythmically with me, placing her hands on my buttocks, pulling me hungrily into her. But I hadn't realized how weak I was, and her pressure pulling me forward upset my fragile, one-armed balance. She, moaning, eyes closed, was unaware. Suddenly my arm failed and I crashed down heavily on her, my head banging hard into her skull. She screamed. I was dizzy from the force of contact and exertion. Sandra was in shock, sobbing hysterically. To make things as bad as they could get, my shoulder, jarred by the fall, sent agonizing pains right through me, and I blacked out for a second.

She jumped from the bed and ran into the bathroom. I never felt lower in my life. I didn't want to be there when she came back but wasn't even man enough to manage to get up and walk by myself.

She came out of the bathroom in her robe. All desire was gone, and an awkwardness was between us. We avoided each other's eyes. I couldn't think of anything to say and she was silent. She turned and was halfway out of the room, then came back and squeezed my hand. But I noticed the tears, which she had controlled in the bathroom, had started again. She left hurriedly.

I don't know how long I stayed there, dozing on and off, before she came back. She was in a light blue blouse and jeans. I could hear the children in the background. I was in a depressed funk and didn't really care whether I lived or died.

"Get up." She took my hand and pulled me into a sitting position, but there was no tenderness between us now. "You can't stay in bed all day and expect to sleep tonight."

I stared at the angry red swelling over her left eye where my head had made contact.

"It's not the end of the world, you know," she said. "Come on, let's move it. I want to straighten up in here. You can sit outside. There's still some sun left."

Sensing that I wanted to do it myself, she left, and I managed to slip on a shirt and, with considerably more difficulty, a pair of jeans. I was in sweating pain. Socks were impossible, so I padded out to the patio barefoot. The kids were inside watching television, so I had the sun all to myself. For the first time I wondered if there was something permanently wrong with me, wondered if I would ever heal, ever be normal, strong again. The sun didn't induce the same feeling of well-being, and after an hour or so, evening fog appeared, making it too cold to sit outside. I went in. I didn't want to talk to anyone or be with anyone. I realized I was a stranger, alone in someone else's house. I didn't know what to do with myself. I sat in the shadowy den from which I had called Foley. My thoughts weren't cheerful. The mood of depression deepened.

After about an hour, Sandra came in. She was subdued. Without a word she poured two martinis from a pitcher. I left mine untouched as she sipped hers. She was back into eye contact now, but I wasn't much for it.

"Drink it," she ordered.

I looked at her. "Go ahead," she coaxed.

I didn't want the drink and left it standing. I couldn't help thinking of the last time I had martinis with the Block and English. Suddenly my eyes filled as I thought of them. I looked away from her.

"Fraleigh, I never told you that I'm a clinical psychologist. I have a small office in Santa Cruz. I see patients by appointment for diagnostic and therapeutic sessions. I'm going to say a few things to you now that may hurt, but you need to hear them. First of all, I made martinis deliberately. Louis Robinson told me the story of your binge."

A psychologist. It figured. I remembered her use of language. Without thinking, I picked up the martini and took a sip. It was ice cold and potent. It sent a shiver right through me.

She smiled slightly at the impact. "What you have to realize is that the doctor's right, you should see the psychiatrist after an experience like the one you had. You're trying to bury everything, even to the extent of not drinking martinis again."

I resisted telling her that I didn't drink martinis period, with the exception of that one night. Facts always get in the way of beautiful shrink theories.

"Your self-image has been shattered as much as your shoulder," she continued. "First of all, you blame yourself for the fact that the Block and English were hurt, for . . ." Here she faltered. "And for everything that happened before with the girls and Don," she finally got out, leaving me the only one with terrible buried guilt. "The pain, your dependence on me, losing your great physical strength, which is as much a part of macho you as your hair, and what just happened in bed—all of these things and more—have fragmented your mental psyche. It's important to talk to a psychiatrist and begin the mental healing process."

With something of a shock, I realized I had sipped away half the martini while she had been stripping my psyche or whatever.

"Even the fact that the three of you aren't immune from injury or death was something you had never acknowledged before, and now you have to cope with that at the same time you're in great pain and exhausted from your injuries.''

"If these martinis and pills ever hit the market as a combination, they'll be best sellers," I observed.

"Now, you needn't take it so hard," she told me, placing herself on my lap and putting her arms around my neck. "Broken shoulders lead to impotence only forty percent of the time."

I had created enough moods talking to witnesses and suspects to know exactly what she was doing so skillfully. She had conned me right out of my depression.

"We can make the best of it. I'll carry on like Lady Brett. You remember *The Sun Also Rises*. Ava Gardner was great in the part," she said.

"I don't think I could ever pull off the Tyrone Power bit with my nose, though," I joined in.

"So you'll let me schedule you for a session with the psychiatrist when we go to the hospital on Monday?" she wheedled.

"Hell, no."

She pulled back from me and I almost let her fall on the floor. "Damn you, Fraleigh, you're so stubborn. Why won't you see him?"

"Because he's as screwy as the rest of them. What profession has the highest suicide rate? The highest rate of drug addiction? Do you think I'm going to put myself in their hands? Besides, I need all my neuroses to survive. It's a tough world out there and I'm in a tough business. Suppose they convinced me that I was crazy to be doing what I do. Where would I be then? Even your kids know I'm too old to be a lifeguard."

"I wouldn't let you out there on the beach with your gorgeous body and all those women," she said. "But how about me, a psychologist? Do you think we're all crazy, too?"

"Of course. How else can you explain yourself? Driving all the way over to the valley to rescue a punch-drunk, over-the-hill flatfoot, then adopting him. No one in their right mind would do something like that."

"No one who wasn't in love," she said, and the last of the depression was gone, except from the tiny corner of my mind that never stopped thinking like a cop.

Fourteen

NIGHTTIME NOW HELD TERROR FOR ME. MEDICATION, weakness, and fatigue combined to push me into a bed that I dreaded. My head drooped as she stroked my hair.

Watching quietly with her big green eyes, she said, "Don't fight it."

But fear of last night's horror, of dreams, pain, and inability to get back to sleep made me reluctant to hit the pillow. "You're one bossy bitch, you know."

She didn't rise to the bait. Finally I gave in and went into the bedroom. A couple of minutes later, as I wriggled under the covers, praying for a good night, she came in. Unnecessarily, she straightened the covers, looking into my eyes for a long minute.

"Sleep. I'll be here with you," she said, brushing my lips with a kiss. "The doctor explained it to me." Her voice was tiny without its usual vibrance. "It's not just the bone fractures you're feeling. The tremendous force—the blunt trauma that you took full on your shoulder—tore ligaments and other muscle tissue with nerve endings, which are sending messages of pain to your brain."

The sun coming through a stained-glass window woke me to confusion. It was 8:00 A.M. and Sandra was nowhere to be seen. With a shock, I realized I had actually slept six straight hours for the first time since the ambush. My face in the shaving mirror looked different. Puzzling over it, I saw Sandra come to stand behind me.

"Thank God," she said. "I couldn't stand to see that look of constant tension from the pain on your face much longer. Can you see how different you look?"

"Um," I grunted. "What's for breakfast? I'm starving."

She beamed at me and vanished into the kitchen, as I had guessed she would. She had made me nervous putting me under the microscope. I wasn't used to beautiful, sexy women standing close to me as I wielded a razor over my rough beard.

There were pleasant surprises in the sunny kitchen breakfast nook. Delicious-smelling hot coffee, toasted bagels, cream cheese, lox, and Sandra. She watched me like a mother hen. After a while, I began to clown.

"What's wrong?" she asked in response to my look of distaste.

"Is this Nova Scotia salmon?" I asked.

"Don't you like it?" She looked at me uncertainly.

"I'm used to Nova Scotia," I said.

"I got this on the wharf; it's the best they had."

I grunted. "Humph, we always get water bagels."

"We? Fraleigh . . ." Her eyes were blazing. "I should have left you . . . we? And who might the other party be that you are accustomed to having breakfast with?"

"Oh, no one you'd know," I answered.

"Feeling much better, aren't you?" she said with exaggerated phony sweetness. "Well, you're much nicer when you're drugged and out of your head with pain and . . . the things you said."

"What?" I asked too quickly.

"Oh, I don't think it would be ethical, you know; after all, you were under medication, but oh, so sexy."

"Sexy?"

"Yes, and who was to know all those things you felt about little old me." She rolled her eyes outrageously. "My goodness, a big macho man like you talking all that mush. And the things you wanted to do, really, Fraleigh."

"You get even too quick."

She came over and sat on my lap. It amazed me how she could be stacked the way she was and be so light. "And another thing, Fraleigh, all the time you were talking this non-stop erotic stuff in your sleep, your thing was hard." She reached down between my legs. "Goodness, is it like that all the time?" she teased.

"Yes, you lucky devil," I told her, finally realizing Mrs. Smith must have taken the three children for an early-morning visit to the beach. We moved into bed in mutual haste, and on this, our third try, it was the way it should have been, except that it was too fast for both of us. "We need to practice," I said.

She touched a finger to my lips, ordering silence. We stayed holding each other in contentment for a good half hour. Then she moved quickly, her mother's ears hearing what I hadn't: the voices of the children returning. She was dressed and out to greet them before I even began my one-armed struggle with clothes.

That afternoon I took the two children to the beach while the baby slept. Sandra pushed us on our way, solemnly telling the children, "Don't let Fraleigh get caught in the undertow. You know he's old and feeble."

"No, Mom," little Don screamed, "he's a big . . . ." We were all holding our breaths, but the little urchin was laughing at us and ended his shout with "lifeguard."

We trooped the short blocks to the beach, juggling pails, shovels, beach blanket, suntan lotion, and what seemed to be eighteen different variations of sand molds. It took three times as long to get to the beach as it should have because the impatient little boy had to hold each form up to me, announcing, "Fish, Tawley, see? Star. This one frog." Naturally, there was a great deal of dropping of forms, shovels, etc., during this exhibition. And for me, free from all but a dull shoulder ache, life was sharp and precious. Each little sound from the children, the deep clear blue of the sky, warmth of the sand, ocean smell, and roar of the waves were things I wanted to keep. Yesterday's pain made today's routines into treasures.

Slightly more than a hundred yards from the beach entrance, a nondescript, blue, two-year-old Chevy was parked, facing down onto the beach. The man behind the wheel was shielded by an open newspaper, but he hadn't turned a page since I spotted him. I memorized the license plate, chiding myself for being ridiculous.

It was fun watching the kids play on the beach. I got bawled out a couple of times for making unappreciated improvements in the various sand-construction projects under way. After a while, I got the hang of it, though. I wasn't supposed to actually participate in the building, but some unconscious mechanism registered in the kids' minds when my study of the female bodies tanning, jogging, jumping, and somersaulting got so intense that I wasn't paying enough attention to them. At one point, just as I watched in fascination, convinced that a loosely fitting bikini top would fly off in the violent exercise its shapely owner was subjecting it to, Lily and Don loudly demanded, "Look, Tawley. Look." And look I did. But looking with one eye on female pulchritude and one on their achievements was not acceptable, I soon found out. The kids somehow knew when to be the most distracting. Sandra would have been proud of them. Nevertheless, I did manage to observe that there had been some remarkable changes in the shape of female youth and the amount of shape you were allowed to look at since my lifeguard days. It was disgusting, of course.

Don and Lily finally gave up asking me why I didn't take my shirt off. The two of them had been disdainful of my excuse that I didn't want to get sunburned. They quickly pointed out that I didn't wear a shirt in the backyard.

"I bet he doesn't want people to see his bandages," Lily said.

"Tawley doesn't want people to see his bandages," chortled Don at the top of his considerable voice. A number of people paused to stare.

"It's not that. Just be quiet, will you?" I asked. Of course, it was a mistake. I realized somewhat uneasily that these kids seemed to have their mother's intelligence. My denial only increased their pursuit. Finally, I stooped to the truth. "You're right, I don't want people to see my bandages, so please stop yelling about them," I pleaded.

"Why don't you want people to see them?" they asked together.

"Because. Is that tunnel finished? It looks like it might cave in if you don't build some supports."

"Do people think you're bad if you have bandages?"

"No, Lily, it's just that it's none of their business."

"Mom said it's because you're a very shy private man, even though you pretend not to be."

"Daddy said you big shit," giggled Don, as his sister slapped his wrist.

"That's naughty," she said.

He socked her in the eye and she countered with a nifty straight right to the nose before I lurched between them.

"Hey, hey, you shouldn't do that," I complained, as both of them attracted everyone's attention by bawling at the top of their lungs. Don's nose was bleeding and Lily had the beginning of a mouse under her eye. Jeez, I thought, packing them up to go home, it's lucky they weren't armed with shovels.

The blue Chevy, with its newspaper reader, was gone, but as I looked up the side street, I saw a car back around the corner before I could determine if it was the same one. Suddenly, I wanted badly to sprint the short block and see for myself if it was the Chevy. Looking at the kids, loaded down with beach material and their anger, I shrugged and continued walking. But at the next cross street, looking to the parallel street, I was shook to see what appeared to be the same car edge up to the stop sign. It was too far to be certain, but I could have sworn that the driver, seeing me look in his direction, gunned the vehicle through the intersection. On the other hand, I told myself, it could have been a teenage rubber-burner.

Sandra greeted us at the door, her welcome smile vanishing as she took in little Don's bloody nose and Lily's swelling eye. "It wasn't my fault," I said in response to her accusing look. Then, as she started to bustle them off, cooing comforts, I said the wrong thing: "They have their mother's temper. They batted each other before I could do anything."

I thought she was going to attack and actually stepped back defensively, turning my injured shoulder away from her as she charged up, hands on hips and eyes shooting flames. "You gross incompetent, don't you talk about my temper. If you hadn't been lost in your state of cop-anomie all these years, you might know something about children and be capable of functioning as well as a twelve-year-old baby-sitter." With that, she spun around, whisking the children into the bathroom for comfort and first aid.

Cop-anomie. I remembered the word "anomie" vaguely from one of my college courses, and Paul had said it recently, but I couldn't put it together the way she had used it. I started toward the bookcase for the dictionary but stopped, not wanting to have her come back and see me looking up the word. I hadn't even been watching broads when the main event took place. I had been talking to the kids, and the same thing would have happened if she had been watching them, probably. Twelve-year-old baby-sitter, ha!

She led them both into the room. Sheepishly they apologized according to the script for fighting. Then, "Tawley," the little one implored, "will you take us tomorrow, even though we were bad today?"

"Sure," I said with a big stupid grin. They disappeared, but their mother stood there, her smile warming the area for at least half a mile around.

"You uncouth ruffian, do you think you could make us a civilized dry martini before dinner?"

"There's nothing I can't do, sister."

"Phawr!" she replied with gestures.

The martinis were pretty good, if I do say so myself. The four of us then sat around having a light supper. Sandra was marvelous. She made each of the kids feel unique and somehow found a way to occasionally let her eyes fall on me in a very special way. Noisy and happy, the two youngsters trotted off to their two hours of authorized daily television. Sandra had some very firm ideas on that, as well as other things.

"Fraleigh, did you ever do anything else? I know you mentioned lifeguard, but I mean any other real job?"

"No, the first time I saw 'Gunsmoke' and 'Hill Street Blues,' I knew my calling."

"I don't like to be made fun of. The only reason I tolerate it is because I know it's your way of avoiding personal questions that you don't like to think about."

Fortunately, the phone rang and she spent a few minutes politely yessing someone on a subject that I couldn't identify. She hung up and resumed.

"I mean, really, you're a bright guy with real ability, leadership ability. I know, I've done a lot of psychological counseling in some of the big corporations. You are a lot sharper than many of the top executives I've met."

"Anything on television?" I asked politely.

We stared stubbornly at each other for a couple of minutes, then she got up and cleared the dishes into the sink, where Mrs. Smith would take care of them.

"Sleep well," she said affectionately.

And I did. I was awake before her, at 7:30 A.M. Looking at her sleeping serenely next to me, I thought, Something's wrong, I can't be this lucky. Her eyes opened and we looked at each other in silence for a while.

"Good morning." I brushed her lips lightly.

She stretched, her nightgown wrinkling to expose a luscious breast. "You were looking at me while I slept."

"Nothing illegal about that."

She snuggled into me. "Wouldn't it be great if things never changed?"

I had the same wish. But her question touched a nerve. It was almost a hint that she knew of things lurking under the surface. For now I was too exhausted to question anything that might threaten our happiness. My body and spirit needed this woman too badly to let my mind's nagging warnings of danger surface for very long. I just held her, enjoying the warm, soft fullness of her body. So I didn't answer. Eventually, we moved, she faster and more efficient. Coffee and croissants were on the table before I wandered out.

"Do you think you could take the children to the beach today? It's going to be beautiful and Mrs. Smith gets Sunday off."

"Uh, this morning?" She had caught me by surprise. I hadn't really decided what ought to be done about the occupant of the blue Chevy and what meaning it might have for all of us.

Misreading my hesitation, she said, "I'll warn them. No nonsense. They'll behave."

"No, it's not that at all." I was uncomfortable. She was studying me closely and I didn't want to frighten her.

"The kids will be so disappointed and will think it's because of yesterday," she said.

"I'll be happy to take them. I just wondered how they'd feel about it," I improvised.

"You're sweet, Fraleigh. Don't you know the two of them adore you as much as I do?"

They all had more faith in me than I did, I thought, as we repeated yesterday's journey to the beach. My eyes roamed nervously for the Chevy or anything else out of the ordinary. Nothing. The Sunday-morning scene was laden with tranquillity. So why couldn't I relax?

The blue Chevy whizzed by on the street behind us just as we stepped onto the sand. The glimpse of the driver was too fleeting to be useful. I didn't like being out on the beach, exposed. A half-ass marksman could have snuffed the three of us from any of the bluffs overlooking the beach before someone noticed he was double-parked blocking traffic.

Hysterical. What had the hospital shrink said? Even paranoia was possible. Yet, over strenuous objections, I moved the kids right in front of an incredibly large family of active children with two inert parents. Unless someone wanted to be a mass murderer, he wouldn't dare take a shot at us. It was an unanticipated blessing. Little Don got cranky after one of the tribe stepped on his sand masterpiece and demanded to go home before we had been there an hour. Lily made no objection.

"But we just got here," I protested with a deviousness foreign to my generous nature. That got both of them to put up a howl that they wanted to go home. I scanned the street and bluffs above us.

"Very well," I gave in, "but remember, when Mommy asks why we came back so soon, you tell her it was because you wanted to leave."

It was an unnecessary ploy. Sandra was about to go shopping and was as glad to take the kids along as they were to be taken. "The baby has just had his bottle and should sleep until we get back. If not, there's a bottle in the fridge, but he may need a change. Do you think you can handle that?" she asked.

"Of course, but maybe you had better just run me through it."

"But there's no need if you know all about it, Fraleigh," she said.

After another moment of childish gloating, she explained the diaper process to me, which I could certainly have handled anyway.

As soon as she left, I called the squad. At 1100 hours on a Sunday morning, there was a fifty-fifty chance no one would be there to pick up the phone. But on the third ring, it got picked up, and a hoarse, whiskery voice grunted, "Bini, Homicide."

"How goes it, Bini? This is Fraleigh. What's happening?"

"Well, Champ, only the Zombie is with me, and I got three barroom homicides from last night, a dope killing, a felony robbery murder in a jewel snatch, the rumor that someone tried to off three homicide dicks a few weeks ago, but nothing I don't have under control right now. Of course, you know I can't devote as much time to police work as I used to, carrying on the way I am with that socialite dame from Atherton."

"That means you're sitting on your fat ass reading the Sunday *Mercury-News*."

"Only the comics; the rest of the paper ain't intellectual enough for me."

I grinned, picturing him alone in the squad room. The Zombie didn't count.

"Hey, Bini, I'd like you to do me a favor, check a license plate for me, O.K.?"

"Sure, I remember when you used to be a cop, too, Fraleigh. How's the nookie over there in Santa Cruz?"

"The registration is two A-Adam, G-George, G-George four-twenty," I responded professionally.

"Hold on, my dear Watson, while I employ the marvels of modern technology in your behalf. I guess you don't want to talk about nookie, eh? I hear she's something else, a ten and a half."

I resisted the temptation to comment on his crudeness, knowing that it would only further delay our law-enforcement work.

"Fraleigh? All right, I get a registered owner as George Bosco, resides 1123 Pacific Street, Oakland. There will be no charge until I catch you in Gordon's."

Gordon's was the headquarters' pub. "Bini, I hate to overexert you on a Sunday, but would you also run a criminal history check on the lad?"

I heard Bini tapping away on the same terminal that he had queried the DMV, Department of Motor Vehicle file. Now he was searching CJIS, also in Sacramento.

"Damn. Hey, Fraleigh, bad luck. The system just went down. You know how it is on Sunday. Lots of down time for maintenance and updating, but he did have a couple of aka's and some arrests in the Bay Area. I could see that before it went down. His DOB is six-twenty-forty-eight."

"You probably broke the terminal, Bini. You know those things can't withstand your breath on a Sunday morning."

"Hey, Fraleigh, I got a message for you, want to hear it?"

"No, and seriously, Bini, do the check for me when the system comes back up, O.K.? How do you figure, an hour or so?"

"Yeah, probably. Want me to check NCIC, too?"

"Please, and give me a call when you get the info and throw a copy of the Sacramento print-out in my mailbox, will you? I'm at 555-3175."

"Can I do anything else for you, like maybe your laundry or shopping for your condo, or something?"

"Hell, no. I couldn't afford all that booze you'd buy," I told him, hanging up.

Fifteen

IT WAS A NOISY, MESSY LUNCH. THE BABY HAD JOINED US and managed to miss the towel on my shoulder as I burped him. Sandra, Lily, and little Don thought it was hilarious. Smelling the sour gook running down the front of my sport shirt, I didn't see anything at all funny about it. My reaction sent the three of them into helpless gales of laughter. Or I should say, the four of them, because even the baby joined in, cooing and smiling. Naturally, that sent some more spittle onto my shirt, and we would have been into a vicious cycle if Sandra hadn't taken pity and relieved me of the baby.

When I returned wearing another shirt, she asked, "Would you mind holding down the fort for a few hours this afternoon? I have three clients scheduled for sessions between two and five."

"Can I do the dishes and laundry also?"

"Don't be a rat. It would really help out. It's too late to line up a sitter now," she wheedled, stroking my chin in a disgracefully blatant female way.

"I'm delighted to support you in the pursuit of a career, my dear."

She laughed. "God, you are a lousy actor. You're actually pleased that I counted on you, and you don't fool anyone with your male chauvinist act."

"You're right, naturally," I commented. "The realization that you believe that I've conquered my state of cop-anomie and actually may be as competent as a twelve-year-old babysitter is tremendously uplifting to me."

"Oh, my poor baby," she cooed, pulling my head into her breasts and rubbing up against me. "Fraleigh's feelings were hurt by mean old me." This little performance sent Lily and Don back into their giggles.

"I don't get it. You mean these people like their heads shrunk on Sunday afternoons?" I inquired, breaking loose.

"Some people have normal working hours during the week, and it's more convenient for them to participate in therapeutic sessions on weekends."

"You mean they work at lousy jobs that drive them nuts all week so that they have enough money to pay you to work them over on the weekends. Why don't they quit their crummy jobs, make less money, and get sane so they won't need their heads shrunk? Then they'd be ahead financially."

"Why? For much the same reasons you change the subject when I ask you about being something other than a cop."

I started to say, "That's different," but realized that she was ready to pounce on that kind of answer. Instead, I asked, "Can I put on the roast or anything so that it will be ready when you get home?"

That got my face rubbed some more and a laughing reply, "Just have the martinis ready, you one-armed bandit."

She was right. I did enjoy sitting in the sun watching the kids play in the backyard while the baby slept. I worried that he slept too much, but Sandra accused me of being a Jewish mama when I asked about it. The sun was delightful and I could actually feel my shoulder and body healing. The kids had moved from the sandbox to the swings to the sliding pond before getting bored. "Tawley, I want play Breakout," little Don demanded.

"Fraleigh doesn't know how to work the computer, silly," Lily said.

The little boy said, "Daddy said it was easy. Not easy, Tawley?"

"Well, let me take a look at it," I told him, silently cursing the child's hyperactive imagination.

Two minutes later, I was looking intently at the computer data projected on the television screen.

"That's not game," Don yelled at his usual volume.

"It's Daddy's appointments," Lily said.

Fiddling with the apparatus, I managed to get one of the games into place on the screen, but my mind was racing as the children laughed and yelled excitedly over the play. Why in the world did Don Fortune's journal list a number of appointments with Adolph Stone, notations about Lisa Stone, and an entry on Fred Casey?

Somehow, I controlled my impatience for the half hour or so that it took the kids to get tired of the games. When they returned to the sandbox, I got the journal back onto the screen. I don't know why I wasn't surprised to find that four appointments were listed with Adolph Stone along with his telephone number. There was no way of telling if the appointments had been kept, but they were spread out over the three-week period prior to our interview on that memorable Thursday night. Also intriguing was that Judy's name was listed next to the entry on Lisa Stone, along with a question mark. Casey was listed with the letters "MRG" and several other initials that didn't seem to stand for anything.

I found the right button to press for print-outs of the entire journal. Then I worked my way through the rest of the business entries. They didn't mean any more to me than when

Don Fortune tried to explain them. I had been poring over the machine for more than an hour. Sandra was due home soon. I realized that I didn't want her to know I had been scrutinizing the records.

I pressed the switch to turn the machine off, but hit the wrong button. Instead of fading out, the screen now showed the names of six teenage girls, ranging in age from thirteen to sixteen. For good measure, I ordered up a print-out of that as well. It was past time for Sandra to return. I quickly put the print-outs in the side pocket of my empty suitcase, stored in the bedroom closet. No sooner had I stuck two cocktail glasses in the freezer to chill than Sandra bustled through the door, giving me a kiss and an affectionate squeeze before rushing off to the john.

It was a quarter to six. I realized with a start that Bini hadn't called back. I could have sworn that I put the pad with the registration on the night table next to the phone. After prowling for a minute, I found it on the writing desk near the window. Taking it back to the phone, I started to call the squad, then hung up. It was probably too late to get him and I didn't feel like talking to anyone else. I reminded myself to stop at the squad after the hospital visit tomorrow.

I had, after all, gotten proficient at making martinis. And a little too good at drinking them. Sandra was glad to be back home after her sessions. No wonder. God knows what kind of nonsense she listened to from these rich California kooks.

"Is something bothering you?" she asked.

"No. Why?"

"Come on, lover. I've already told you, you're the world's worst actor. Did the kids misbehave?"

"No. They were great. I'm O.K., honest," I said, trying not to guess whether or not she knew of all the computer entries.

Leaving her drink, she came over and fit herself snugly on

my lap. "It shouldn't be that bad at the hospital tomorrow," she said, misreading my mood. "And I'll be with you."

"You know you don't really have to drive all the way over. I could take one of the cars. I'll be all right."

"My big strong man, always so brave," she said, touching her hand to my rough beard. "But I want to be with you.

"Ouch!" she uttered, surprised at my fierce, one-armed hug, but she returned it with gusto, holding me very tight.

Neither one of us had much to say the next morning. She drove expertly, but illegally fast over the mountain to the hospital. I was tired, on edge after a poor night's sleep, disturbed by dreams I couldn't and didn't want to remember. After an hour wait, I faced yet another doctor in the treatment room. Unhappily, I wondered if they had some kind of an experiment going in which as many of the staff as possible would get a crack at me. Whether I was more distracted or the treatment less painful, I don't know, but finally, we were going to visit the Block and English without me being groggy from pain.

She stopped me as we approached their rooms. A uniformed cop was sitting between the adjacent rooms perusing a magazine. "Brace yourself, Fraleigh," Sandra said. "Both of them have been hurt as badly as you and their physical appearance will be altered."

Despite her words, I couldn't keep the shock off my face when I saw the Block. He was actually skinny. I gaped at him. "You don't look so good yourself, Fraleigh," he said.

"My God. How much weight have you lost? Hey, goddammit!" I winced. Sandra had slammed me in the side, my bad side. I was almost doubled over with pain.

"You gotta hit him in the head, lady," the Block advised her. "He's too thick to get the message otherwise."

"How are you feeling, Block?" I asked, keeping one eye on her.

"Lousy. You were lucky to get outa here. I wished I had

a broad, er, I mean someone to take care of me; I'd get away from these creeps. They don't give me enough to eat and I haven't even had a beer since I got here.''

"I'll bring you a six-pack."

"You will not, you oaf. It would be the worst thing for his health."

To my amazement, the Block demurely agreed. "Yeah, you're probably right, lady. And to tell you the truth, I don't feel that much like having one right now."

I didn't know what to say. "Are they telling you anything about the case, Fraleigh?" he asked.

"No. I don't get it. When cops get shot, they're supposed to pull out all stops. I don't get it. Do they tell you anything?"

"Nothing. And Paul . . . ain't no use telling him anything," the Block said.

"What do you mean?"

"Ain't you been to see him yet?"

"No, we're going in there next," I said with a pain shooting downward through my stomach.

"I'm happy to have met you," Sandra said, getting up and shaking the Block's hand. "We'll be back to see you in a few days. Fraleigh thinks he's stronger than he really is and we'd best be going."

"Yeah, he looks terrible," the Block told her, like I wasn't there. "I heard he almost croaked. Take care of him. He don't always have good sense, you know."

"Yes, I know," she told him.

It was unbelievable. Like one of my dreams. These people were discussing me as if I were deaf and dumb. Numbly, I started for Paul's room. When we got outside, Sandra grabbed my hand, pulling me up short. "Maybe that's enough for today?"

"What? We're right here." I pulled away and went into Paul's room. It was dark, gloomy. For a moment, I looked at the empty bed, not seeing him sitting motionless in a chair, staring at the wall.

"Paul, how are you?" I asked.

There was no sign that he had heard. "Paul, Paul, can't you hear me?" I shouted. The cop came in quickly. He and Sandra crowded me away from English. He hadn't even reacted when I touched his shoulder. We walked toward the door. I couldn't handle it. He had been sitting in the dark, just looking at the wall.

"Wait." She wiped my face with her handkerchief. Dimly, her fragrance came to me from the cloth.

"I need to stop at the squad room. It's only about five minutes, and I'll be right in and out. Just need to pick up something."

"Do you really think you should? This has been emotionally draining for you and you really haven't been well."

"I'll take a cab."

"Oh, for God's sake, grow up, will you? I'm just trying to protect you, you know."

We rode in cool silence to headquarters. "I'll wait here if you don't mind," she said.

"O.K. I'll be less than five minutes."

The squad room was subdued. I expected to be mauled and bombarded with cops' black humor. I checked my mailbox for the print-out from Bini on the name check. The box was empty, and all I got from the dicks were stares. It was an odd feeling. One of the cops popped into the captain's office. Louis came out immediately.

"How'd you get here?" he asked, shaking my hand.

"Sandra drove me. It was hospital day. We just came over."

"She outside?"

"Yeah, what's with you people, anyway? Remember me? I used to work here."

Louis whispered something in the dick's ear and led me into his office.

"How you feeling? You don't look so good."

"I'm kind of tired," I admitted. And suddenly I felt completely without energy. "What's going on around here? The place seems like a morgue."

"Hello, Sandra," Louis said, as the dick he had sent for her showed her into the office.

"Hello, Captain," she said in a small voice, her face very tense and white.

"Louis, as an old buddy, would you mind telling me what the hell is going on around here?" I demanded.

He actually came over and put his arms around me. "You think you're indestructible, Fraleigh, but you've been through a lot." For a crazy moment, I wondered if he had been drinking.

"I asked Sandra to come up because I have some very bad news for you and I wanted her to be here when I told you. Bini was killed yesterday. I'm sorry. I know you were closer to him than anyone else."

"But I talked to him yesterday," I heard myself say.

"What time?" Louis asked.

"In the morning. I asked him to check out a license plate. He never called me back."

"He never made it back from lunch. You know he liked to eat at Gordon's. Well, he left there and started across the street. A pickup truck hit him. It was really moving. He was dead before he hit the ground."

"Drunk driver?" I asked reflexively. What did it matter? Bini gone. It was unbelievable.

"We don't know," Louis answered. "It was a hit and run. The truck was stolen. We found it a few blocks away."

I couldn't help it. Leaning forward, I just put my head in my hands. I was completely empty.

"Come on, Fraleigh, we'll help you out to the car."

Louis had reached one of his huge arms around my waist and lifted me to my feet. "Can you get him home O.K.?" he asked Sandra.

She nodded yes. We made our way slowly downstairs and out of the building. I was aware that a lot of people were watching, but my head sagged, and Louis just about carried me to the car. He squeezed my shoulder. "Take care," he told Sandra as she started the car.

The drive back over the mountain was a blur. She put on a tape of "Greensleeves," and the music washed over my exhaustion. A cold, dismal, foggy night would have suited my mood. Perversely, it was a magical, soft, warm summer evening. Sandra had a short conversation with Mrs. Smith and was waiting for me as I emerged from the john. I wanted to sleep and headed in a stupor toward the bed.

She moved quickly, intercepting me before I could flop down into the softness.

"Come," she said, taking my hand. I had no will to resist and reluctantly walked with her to the car. She drove for a couple of miles, then pulled into a beach parking lot. The last thing I wanted was an evening walk. Yet that was just what we were doing. With determination, she led us to the sand. The noise of a gentle surf filtered through the golden light cast by a reddish-orange sun, slowly sinking into the ocean horizon.

Once again, I marveled at this gal's professional skill. She had arranged healthy outdoor exercise. Now her conversation floated over me in a pleasantly soothing melody. My concentration was in and out.

"Stressors can lead to cognitive rigidity, perceptual narrowing, impaired efficiency, and behavioral difficulties manifested in alcoholism, psychosis, psychosomatic disorders, and even organic disease. You have been under sustained stress of violence, threat of physical injury and death. Now you've suffered the additional loss of a significant other person, coming on the heels of a behavioral pattern reminiscent of Kafka's trial syndrome.''

That brought my attention on full. "How's that again?" I asked.

"There is a pattern in Western life associated with guilt and trial fantasies. If you remember, in *The Trial* by Kafka, the psychological process of the trial was itself an enormous stress inducer, exacerbating inherent guilt residues, building classic conditions for psychopathological consequences.''

"Look, my partners and I had a close call. We got hurt. It happens. Then hearing about Bini right on top of all this; it's been heavy, but all this garbage about trials and inherent guilt, I don't know.''

"There's a lot of research on combat neurosis. Cops and soldiers involved in lethal or near-lethal interactions evidence the most symptomatology,'' she answered, ignoring my comments.

"Yeah, I wouldn't be surprised if some of them fell right into a nasty pit of cop-anomie,'' I sneered.

"Fraleigh, listen to me. You killed two men in a violent encounter. The machismo reflex is a common enough reaction in your line of work, but it unfortunately is a stressor in itself and not a stress reducer, as you seem to maintain.''

I hadn't been paying attention to where we were going as we walked on the beach. I realized that we had reached Aldo's boat launch and outdoor restaurant. Sandra secured a table and we sat watching the boats return through the inlet to their moorings in the yacht harbor. The last rays of the sun glinted off the bottle of Paul Krug's Chenin Blanc, which she had selected to go with the shrimp and Dungeness crab salad we were nibbling on. I don't know how much she charged as a shrink, but she had done wonders for me. The wine was delicious and I was eating the seafood as if I were starving.

"The only thing I regret is that I didn't kill those two animals sooner, before they hurt us."

"That's the machismo and guilt combined," she continued. "You have fantasized a trial for yourself, not just on those events, but even going back to the night you followed Foley's orders. Consciously, you acknowledge that Foley left you no choice, but in your supermachismo subconscious, you feel guilt, the nagging feeling that somehow you should have rescued the young damsels in distress."

"Go on," I said, spearing a juicy hunk of crab and dipping it into the spicy red cocktail sauce.

"Then too, you really don't forgive yourself for bringing the Block and English to the Moral Reaffirmation office. You accept cognitively the fact that no one could have predicted the ambush, but again in the fantasy trials of your subconscious, you're the accused in the witness block."

"O.K., this is fascinating. Tell me how my subconscious figures I got Bini knocked off."

"You're so sarcastic, but what you said to Louis Robinson as soon as you heard of Bini's death is symptomatic. You immediately told Louis that you had spoken to Bini on the morning of his death. Right now, your subconscious is probably inducing guilt by somehow theorizing that your phone call had something to do with his death.

"What's wrong, Fraleigh? Don't take any of this so seriously," she cautioned nervously. "Part of it is designed to get you out of yourself. You have been through a lot recently and were slipping into a depression. I don't want you to let any of this bother you; it's just healthier to get it out."

I poured the rest of the wine into our glasses. The sun had finally set, but the evening was unusually warm for the beach.

"Something I just said about Bini disturbed you, didn't it? Tell me."

"Well . . ." I hesitated. "You know I did ask Bini to check out a license plate for me."

"A license plate. How could that possibly have anything to do with that poor man's death?" she exclaimed, putting her hand over mine.

"There was no print-out in my box. Bini would never have missed that."

"Now I'm really concerned about you, Fraleigh. It's not abnormal when the subconscious plays all those games we described, but when the conscious joins in, that's paranoia or psychosis."

"Look, stop all that goddamned jargon. I'm not crazy. In fact, I'm the best investigator this city has ever had, and I'm telling you, I smell something. It's too much of a coincidence, the more I think of it."

She had pulled her hand back and was making a half-hearted effort at a supportive smile, but there was a shade of fear deep in her eyes.

"Can't you even listen to what I'm trying to say?" People looked. My voice had gotten loud.

"Why don't we walk some more on the beach?" she asked.

"No. I want to explain this to you. It may affect you and the children. The license plate I gave Bini was from here, the beach. It was someone watching us when I took the children to the beach."

Wide-eyed, she waited for me to continue. I tried to choose my words carefully, knowing she didn't believe what I was saying.

"Who was it?"

"I don't know. That's what I'm telling you. The system was down. Bini was supposed to call back and stick a copy of the print-out in my mailbox. He never did."

"So what's the hypothesis? What do you think happened? Someone in the police department stole the print-out? Bini was murdered because he talked to you? You know I love you, darling, but I'm really concerned. The human mind is a fragile thing. It's possible after what you've been through that you only imagined the whole thing. You have been under medication.''

I wanted to slug her.

''Don't look at me that way, please.''

I sighed. ''Let's forget it. I don't have enough to hypothesize, as you put it. But don't forget, it ain't exactly normal to try to blow away three homicide dicks in an ambush, and we can't explain that, either.''

''Tell me again about the car,'' she said. What I said had registered after all.

''It was a blue Chevy, about two or three years old, with a dent in the left fender. I couldn't get a good look at the guy behind the wheel, but if you should see anyone hanging around, let me know. I don't want to scare you, but it could be important. I'll come out of my psychopathological fog long enough to check it out.''

We held hands on the mile-long walk back along the beach. I felt myself drawing strength from this woman. She had pulled me from the bottom of the heap at least three times in the last few weeks. I had never allowed myself to become dependent on anyone before. It had just happened with her. There was no going back, I knew, but the shadow of her husband's involvement in the case was with me constantly since the computer had spilled its guts. Only when she spoke, with her shining openness and sincerity, did the doubts leave me. At those times, it was simply impossible for me to believe anything bad about her. But when I was alone, the years of police experience worked their cynical impact, and my imagination grew the evil wings of a free-flying predator.

Back in the living room, with Mrs. Smith relieved of duty and dispatched home, we sat opposite each other. Sandra had her serious, thoughtful look going full steam. I hoped she was off the shrink kick. I was very tired and couldn't take any more of that jazz.

"Can we talk seriously for a while?"

"Sure," I agreed.

"How do you feel physically?"

"Tired."

"I know that, silly. You look as if you're about to fall asleep. What I want to know is how soon do you think you could go back to work? Can you go back?"

She never ran out of surprises. I hadn't faced the question; now tired, I tried to cope with it.

"Give an honest answer," she pressed me.

"I don't know. I haven't thought about it."

"Go ahead, think about it. What's involved? Are you strong enough physically? Do you need some more time mentally? You can probably qualify for a disability retirement if you wish. That opens a lot of new doors. Maybe you should get some counseling?"

She hadn't done anything annoying, so why was I annoyed?

"You're annoyed, aren't you?"

"No, dammit. Why are you always diagnosing me, telling me I'm this or that?"

"Someone has to," she said. "You're likely to flounder without direction."

I was no longer annoyed. I was burning. "Do you really think I could walk away? Just shrug off the fact that someone tried to kill us without going after them?"

"Ah, now we're getting someplace. Vengeance is mine, sayeth you."

"Look, Sandra, you win. I'm beat. I can't take any more shrinking tonight. Give me a break."

"I wasn't trying to put you through the wringer. There's a method to my madness. I figure you owe me big, lover. I took you from the ghetto, clasped you to my bosom, and haven't asked you for a dime in return.''

This was the damnedest woman. I just looked at her, with no idea what to expect next.

"I didn't think you would be able mentally or physically to go back to work for a while, but I needed to have you say it before I made my suggestion.''

"What suggestion?" I asked.

"We've both been through a lot. Now that I'm through breast-feeding, I'd like you to take me on a vacation, fully paid, for six days. Your paying will satisfy your macho drives and make you much more sexy. I want to spend four days in San Francisco, one in Mendocino, and one in Carmel.''

"I can see that you haven't given this any thought. Don't tell me! Mrs. Smith is already lined up, the car gassed, and the bags packed.''

"Yes, yes, and no. I'll pack in the morning. I can see you're useless tonight, but I won't accept any excuses for the rest of the week. You stand forewarned.'' And she was off to bed before I could say anything.

Why not? I thought. It would give me a chance to get away from the blue Chevy and try to straighten my head out. She had been on target with her questions. I was drifting and that could be bad—or lethal—with the kind of enemies we had.

She was right. It wasn't just that I was weak physically. I had been avoiding the whole question of whether or not my nerve was gone. Even now, I didn't like to think about it, but someday soon I had to come to grips with it. I was pretty sure I was going to be O.K., but it was another question to think about functioning again as part of a team. Right now, I didn't have the confidence to order anyone around, even her kids. I was capable of routine, spotting a tail maybe, but running any kind of an investigation was so beyond me that I wondered if I would ever do it again. Taking a vacation certainly wouldn't be time wasted.

Sixteen

WE WERE SITTING IN THE LOBBY LOUNGE OF THE ST. Francis Hotel. Sandra was dressed in a black slinky thing that made her look like a sophisticated society dame until you got to her face. Then she appeared about eighteen, with a rosy glow that completely destroyed my attempts at laid-back California coolness. Her happiness was overwhelming and contagious. People stared at us. Even she conceded that it wasn't my subconscious imagining it.

I could never adjust to her. Sometimes she was the almost frighteningly competent clinical psychologist, sometimes the mother and hausfrau, at other times the sex bomb and, like now, the wide-eyed little girl in the big city.

"I'm starving. Get me something delicious to eat, Fraleigh, please," she begged, never once pausing in her visual inspection of the crowd in the opulent setting.

"I've got something delicious for you, but I'm not sure I want to give it to you in the lobby in front of all these people."

"My God, you are absolutely the most low-class, vulgar man I've ever been with," she said.

Just to show her up, I ordered some Brie and crackers to go with our Beefeater martinis. I was careful not to look at the check until we finished enjoying our food and drinks. Sandra, drooling over the cheese, insisted on futilely questioning the waiter on its origins. I had told her to save her breath; waiters and waitresses weren't programmed to give the kind of gourmet lecture she was seeking.

"Stop laughing at me, you jaded cynic. Suppose he did know where to buy it, wouldn't it be marvelous to take some home with us?"

"It wouldn't taste the same."

"You're horrid. I don't know why I bother with you, and if you eye that gal at the bar once more, I'll maim you for life."

"Strictly professional, babe. That's one of the highest-priced call girls in the city."

"Oh, stop lying. I concede she's beautiful, with a gorgeous figure, and scores a full two notches above me. You don't have to apologize for looking."

She was right. The girl was absolutely stunning.

"It's the other way around, babe. You've got her by a couple of points, and she really is a hooker."

"You're just teasing me, aren't you? You don't know her at all."

"True, I don't. But I've been watching her and the John she's stringing for fifteen minutes, and I've got her M.O."

"Really? Tell me. Come on, Fraleigh, tell me how you know."

"Well, the John was the first tip-off. Look at him. How old would you make him to be?"

"Fifty-five or so?"

"I'd say that's about right. Now he was sitting at the bar by himself for about twenty minutes, looking at his watch and looking around, really pissed. Either his wife is late back from shopping or someone else was supposed to meet him at the bar. When she came up, they were very tentative; then he said a couple of things rather pointedly, she shrugged, just taking it, letting him come back to the deal. How old do you think she is?''

''Twenty-two?''

''About that, I'd say. So it's hardly a spontaneous love scene of boy meets girl at bar. Besides, after just a peek around, she headed right for him when she came in. Then she had to call her pimp to confirm whatever change in plans he was pushing.''

''Change, what change? I thought these things were all arranged in advance.''

''Most are, but as you know, a little hondling is inevitable. Then again, it might not have been the price.''

''Then what?''

''An all-night stand instead of a quickie. Maybe a ride someplace else, a little S and M, who knows?''

''God, it's hard to believe a beautiful young girl could be involved like that. And look at him. He's so distinguished-looking. He could be a corporate president, but he's certainly old enough to be her father, if not her grandfather. Are you going to arrest them?''

I looked at her. She was serious. ''Babe, hookers were around centuries before anyone decided they needed police forces, so no, I don't think I really ought to interrupt our vacation to strike a blow against prostitution.''

''Too bad,'' she said wistfully. ''It would have been such fun confronting them and getting a confession.''

''A confession? You're dreaming. You might get threatened with a suit for false arrest, but neither one of those two is a rookie. You'd have to make the case all by your lonesome.''

''He's probably some kind of executive. Don't you think he would be embarrassed enough to cooperate?''

"Are you kidding? Some of these corporations deal in birds by the dozen."

"Is that what they're called, 'birds'?"

"Yeah, among other things."

"Why does she have a pimp? Don't they mistreat them and keep all the money?"

"Usually, but some of the girls are pathetic. They get broken in at thirteen, fourteen, or sometimes older, and never really know anything different. It's nuts, but they actually brag sometimes that their pimp has the most girls in his stable and drives a Mercedes. But this class girl probably has a slightly better-class pimp. They have to have some muscle somewhere. There are always rumors that some sharp girls don't cut anyone in, work free-lance, but I've never met them. They simply need a man to protect them from other pimps, whores, and even the Johns."

"How do you know so much about this?"

"I'm a cop, remember? And I had to work a year in Vice once."

"Was it exciting?"

"No, it stank."

The graying executive gave me a cool look, passing with the bird on his arm. She stared straight ahead.

"What do they actually do? I mean, when they get to the room?"

"Come on. I'll show you," I said, dropping a small fortune in cash on top of the check and leading her out to the elevators.

It was our second day in San Francisco. It should have been our third, but we had stopped for a picnic lunch at Half Moon Bay, and I couldn't get Sandra away from the binoculars and the whales that were putting on a late-summer carnival. Each time one would sound, sending plumes of water high in the air, she would give a little-girl squeal. Her enthusiasm and closeness pleased me more than the whales. I was content to watch the afternoon fade away, even though I knew what the rush-hour traffic would be like in Union Square around the St. Francis.

Now, early in the morning, she was admiring the suite with its magnificent panoramic view of the city and bay. "Fraleigh, how much is this room costing? I didn't want you to go bankrupt, you know."

"Glad you like it."

"Seriously, a whole suite, it's decadent, even for a couple of nights. How much?"

"To tell you the truth, I don't know. I made the reservations through a friend. This was his idea, including the welcoming flowers and wine from the management."

"Graft," she said in a stage whisper. "I knew it all along. You're on the take. That's why you wouldn't arrest that hooker last night."

"You got it babe," I leered.

"The first time I saw that crummy condo of yours, I knew it was a front. Not even you could be that poor or cheap."

"Very funny. But I don't have suckers to squeeze at seventy-five dollars a throw for a head shrink, and the only leverage I know about involves opening a can of apple-sauce."

"But your mysterious resources, Fraleigh, to be able to arrange for quarters like these. What valuable services did you perform for your friend?"

"Well, if you must know, you nosy little wench, I beat the piss out of him."

"Ah! That's extortion. I saw it on 'Hill Street Blues.' Television doesn't lie. Can't you go to prison for that? I'll have to testify against you, of course. I'll be stunning. My black dress, I think. It will be just right for the television interview. Then maybe they'll want me on some of the talk shows. Eventually I'll have my own national column on psychology. But I should also have my own show. Wouldn't I be just great on television?''

I tried to think of a wise answer but couldn't. She really was great, in person, on television, whatever.

''But first, I must worm a confession out of you, using my wiles.'' She had put her hand in a very sensitive spot and was slowly stroking as she kissed me persistently on the lips.

''I'll cop out to anything. What do you want to know?''

''Well, just why did you hit this poor man? What's his name?''

''Bret Peters.'' I hurried my confession. In another minute, neither one of us was going to remember what we had been talking about. ''And he was trying to annihilate me, but he was outclassed.''

''Of course you outclassed him, darling,'' she purred. ''Did you kick him in the groin and fight dirty?''

''No. They wouldn't let me,'' I got out, between laughing at her and wiggling away from her caresses. ''We boxed each other in the California Police Olympics. Bret was San Francisco P.D. then; now he runs security at the hotel. I didn't think he would overdo it like this, although I did tell him you were special.''

She stopped her performance. ''Did you really say that?'' she asked, her green eyes deep and serious. ''You say the nicest things sometimes.'' She left the drapes open, and we made love looking out at the crystal-clear blue sky of San Francisco, holding each other long after passion had subsided.

Seventeen

THE ST. FRANCIS HAD ONE OF THOSE FANCY, INTIMIDATING beauty salons. No doubt a couple of hours of letting them work you over cost as much as the best room in the house, but the next day Sandra, in her little-girl way, told me that the trip would not be complete unless she was perfectly decadent and got the full three-hour treatment. Being a sport, I graciously agreed to her going, even though it was totally unnecessary. She couldn't have looked better.

I dropped her into the hands of a sweet young thing, whose curly dark chest hair was displayed by the peculiar shirt he was wearing. It was a kind of chartreuse or something, and they had saved dough on manufacturing it, because there were no buttons. Tied with a sash, it wasn't supposed to close over all that carefully spiraled hair and heavy gold chain on his chest, and it didn't. The hair on his head was as meticulously coiled, and it set off the discreet little gold ball decorating his pierced left ear.

He greeted Sandra as if they were old friends, although she had never been in the joint before. Hustling her away with just the slightest stroking of her arm, he purred, "This way, dear, we'll fix you up just loverly." Edging her gently toward an open female-style barber's chair, he batted his delicate eyelashes at me and bared his marvelously white teeth in just the friendliest smile. Hoping to secure good treatment for Sandra, I gave him a solemn wink, which set him off giggling. Sandra's reproachful eyes caught mine in the reflection from the mirrored wall, but in a moment, she was giggling along with him. I left them, grateful for her assurance that the cost of his tender ministrations wasn't coming out of my pocket.

Walking into the lobby, I had the strangest feeling. I didn't know what to do with myself. Three hours to kill. We had been together almost constantly for the past two weeks. I wandered absently to the newsstand and came close to squandering a quarter on a newspaper that I didn't want to read. Instead I headed for the coffee shop for coffee that I didn't want to drink and a danish that I didn't want to eat. A lovely brunette in a Pan Am stewardess uniform flashed a friendly Latin smile at me while she paid the cashier.

"Are you Kevin Adams?" she asked.

"No." I smiled. We both knew I wasn't Kevin Adams. When I didn't pick up on it, she shrugged, blew me a kiss with her hand, and swayed back toward the lobby, turning once to make sure I was paying proper attention to her retreating figure. I was. It deserved proper attention.

I dawdled over a second cup of coffee supplied by a waiter with enough facial blemishes to ruin your appetite. Just to keep my hand in, I surveiled a small Caucasian whose gray hair and veined hands indicated mid-fifties to me. I watched his expensive sport shirt, slacks, and one-hundred-fifty-dollar shoes glide with deliberation from the washed-out female cashier to the two counter girls, then to a dumb-looking busboy wearing a stained, brown uniform. After a couple of words, each of them handed the little dandy some green stuff. Before stashing the cash from a transaction, he'd casually glance around. He had started talking to a young brown-skinned kid who was lackadaisically sweeping the floor, when he finally spotted me watching him. Without the slightest pause, he sauntered through the door, heading for the street. The only trace of his presence that remained was the puzzled expression on the porter's face.

I was absently trying to decide whether he had been picking up numbers, sports bets, or payments for supplies of grass or coke—everybody's favorite candy in everybody's favorite city—when Adolph Stone slid into the seat opposite me.

"Sergeant Fraleigh, I thought I recognized you," he greeted me.

With surprise, I realized I hadn't lunged across the table to squeeze out his explanation for the Moral Reaffirmation ambush call.

"I'm in the city for a business meeting. I couldn't believe my eyes when I saw you. I heard you were almost killed, but you look so well," he lied.

I looked lousy and knew it, but he looked like the millionaire that he was. He wore a tasteful blue pinstripe suit with a silk tie. His tie probably cost more than I paid for my new sports jacket.

"I hope your two partners are doing well. I was horrified to learn that my call had put you men in danger and led to your being injured."

"Yeah," I threw in, still trying to come to grips with his suddenly appearing.

"I know that our interview wasn't all that friendly, with Eric and his antics, but"—he chuckled—"you and your colleagues handled it well."

I eyed him in silence. He was different. The charm was flowing and he was exhibiting an embarrassed guilt for having set us up. So why wasn't I convinced that it was real?

"Thank God, the three of you survived without permanent injuries . . ." Here he paused to see if I might be going to contradict him.

"We're going to be O.K.," I filled in.

"I never would have forgiven myself if . . . Well, you know what I mean. I suppose I feel especially bad because of the unpleasantness of our first meeting. I hope you understand that I was highly upset because of Lisa. I can assure you that I'm normally quite civilized." He smiled.

"Er, Mr. Stone—"

"I can guess what you're going to ask, Sergeant, and I don't blame you," he interrupted. "My phone call to your office sent you into an ambush. You certainly have every right to be curious and . . ." he hesitated, "even angry, perhaps suspicious of me, but I assure you, my only thought was to provide you with information that would help you to find Lisa," he said, oozing sincerity.

"I understand, sir," I oozed back. "How did you happen to learn the location?"

"Doris called me from Rio Del Mar. She was concerned about Lisa as a result of your interview with her. She can be quite effective when she wants to be," he said.

I sure wasn't going to argue with that. In fact, I wasn't even going to guess what he meant by it, but he solved that small mystery for me.

"She made some calls and found the location of the Moral Reaffirmation office. I thought you should know about it, so I called your number, but you were at lunch, I believe."

"Mr. Stone, do you remember if she mentioned who gave her that information? It could be important."

"No," he answered too quickly. "I only wish I did. I certainly don't mean to be uncooperative with the police, although it occurs to me that it may appear that way to you fellows. It was simply that I went to pieces after"—he choked a little and his eyes teared slightly—"after identifying Lisa's body."

I looked away from him for a moment. The acne-troubled waiter poured a cup of coffee for Stone, who stared down into the cup. Suddenly I was exhausted. I knew this was a crucial interview, and I was blowing it. I was overwhelmed by it all. I just couldn't pull myself together enough to establish a pattern of questions. My mind was blank. I couldn't think of what to ask next.

He looked up. "I can see you're fatigued, Fraleigh. I'm sorry that I intruded and brought all of these unpleasantries back to you while you're trying to recuperate." He started to get up.

"No. That's perfectly all right. You haven't even finished your coffee. Why don't you stay for a while? We can talk about other things," I stalled, not wanting him to leave.

He eased back into his seat while I searched my mind, trying to come up with something I had in common with this very polished rich man. I had narrowed it down to our acne-faced waiter when Stone saved me the trouble.

"Do you know much about my business?" he asked.

I shook my head, no.

"Here in California, I got my start in the semiconductor industry. Fortunately, I was able to move in at the beginning. I started two highly successful companies that were among the first to exploit the development of silicon chips. Our early healthy capitalization made it possible to spread seed money, which helped new entrepreneurs. My venture capital activities produced profits beyond my expectations. It also led to business and political connections that were invaluable. That kind of networking provided information that led to highly successful real estate investments, including offshore oil enterprises and some mineral and precious metal exploration in western states. As you know, those fields of commerce have proved extremely profitable." He paused for my acknowledgment.

I nodded shrewdly, rejecting a momentary silly impulse to tell him that my knowledge of commerce was limited to a once-a-year investment in trying to pick the winner of the Preakness. A fine-looking, expensively dressed woman in her mid-thirties passed our booth. She had the kind of poise developed by a good prep school and college and money, money, money. Her eyes passed right over ole stumble-bum me, but lingered with open interest on Adolph Stone's perfectly barbered and manicured good looks. He blinked in acknowledgment, but it was old hat to him. His whole bearing made it clear that he took for granted people acknowledging his presence.

He continued complaining, as if we were both men of the world together. "It's simply amazing how few competent people there are around. I've built a business requiring management expertise, which is becoming as rare and precious as the minerals we search for."

Remembering his humble mansion, I avoided tears, but made what I hoped were appropriate sounds of sympathy.

"The incredible part of it is the financial remuneration for people who actually are quite mediocre. For example, I'm paying the man who manages my businesses in Southern California one hundred and fifty thousand dollars a year, not that he's worth it, but what else can I do?"

"A hundred and fifty grand a year is a lot of dough," I mumbled.

Stone continued. I was getting interested and he knew it. "And his management is strictly routine. I provide the creativity and imagination. His value is that he's consistent. He stays away from gambling, cocaine, and keeps his head about women. Yet for what I'm developing now, he would be useless."

"What would that be, Mr. Stone?" I asked.

"I've begun an international shipping business. Come to think of it, Fraleigh"—he paused speculatively—"I'm looking for someone just like you to steer it. There might even be positions for your two colleagues."

Jesus Christ, I thought, he wants to hire us as smugglers.

"It's not smuggling or anything remotely illegal," he said. "Of course, there is some risk, but it is financial, not physical, except some slight possibility of nastiness in Marseilles, but nothing of the magnitude you face every day."

"Mr. Stone, I don't know the first thing about business. I've been a cop so long that it's hard to think about doing anything else."

"That is what intrigues me. The position is, of course, different from law enforcement, but it requires a tough, no-nonsense mind like yours. And then too, such businesses require security systems with checks and balances to prevent theft and fraud, which almost require a police mind to put in place."

Stone had surprised me by appearing. Now he had dumbfounded me with this offer. It had seemed spontaneous, but nothing this man did was spontaneous. Yet he was so smooth that he had given a preposterous suggestion a ring of truth. I was speechless.

"Don't misunderstand me," he said, "I feel some sympathy and responsibility for you and your colleagues being hurt, but I am a hard-nosed businessman. I make the offer only because I am convinced that you would be a definite asset to me. And I didn't mean to imply that the salary range is similar to my man in Southern California. Business start-up costs are significant, and it usually takes three years to get into the black. However, one hundred and fifty thousand for the three of you is not unreasonable. It could be divided as you see fit. If you perform during the first year as efficiently as I think you would, we can work out a contract calling for a percentage of the profits. I favor the arrangement in my enterprises. It encourages productivity and loyalty.''

"That's quite a generous offer, Mr. Stone."

"I'm not in business to be sentimental or generous. If my judgment of your ability is incorrect, I assure you that I'll know it rather quickly and will look for someone else. But I don't think I'm wrong, and unless I miss my guess, you are sitting there right now, confident that you can do the job I described.''

Stone was good all right. I had been daydreaming, thinking about travel to Europe, executive perks, no more hassles with Foley . . . I caught myself.

"Naturally, it would be unreasonable to expect you to make a decision this morning. Why don't you think it over for a few days and give me a call. You have my home number. Just leave a message if I'm not there. That is, if you are interested.''

"I don't know, Mr. Stone," I hedged. "You see, this case we're on . . . someone tried to kill us. In this business, you don't walk away from something like that until it's finished.''

"Did I misunderstand?" Stone asked. "I thought the two men responsible for the attack were dead.''

I locked into Stone's slate-gray eyes. Once you got past the veneer of civilization, it was like looking into a black tunnel plugged at the other end. "The two men who attacked us are dead. But not those responsible. The contest isn't over yet.''

My words didn't alter the darkness I was peering into. I tried again. "Then too, something tells me that my case connected to the Washington Housing Project isn't over, either.''

Deep, deep in the pitch-darkness beyond his eyes a bright pinhead of intense white light flared and died.

"I see. I didn't comprehend how complex your police

code of behavior is, but who knows, perhaps sometime in the future we will have another opportunity to discuss this." He looked at his watch and rose. I went along with him, stopping at the cashier's counter to pay the three-fifty for the coffee. Stone made no offer to pay the check, but patted me on the back and said, "Take care of yourself, Fraleigh. I hope your health improves quickly."

His right hand traveled across my shoulder, dropped lightly against my hip, and then extended for a handshake. Simultaneously, his left hand gave me a friendly pat on the other hip. If I hadn't done the same thing myself a few times, I wouldn't have believed it. Suave millionaire Adolph Stone had given me a quick, efficient brush frisk.

I kept him in sight, crossing the lobby headed for the O'Farrell Street exit. I was close enough behind him to be able to observe a well-dressed chauffeur emerge from a gray Rolls-Royce and open the door for Adolph Stone, who moved into the backseat with practiced ease.

Checking the time, I saw there was still an hour before Sandra was due back from the beauty parlor. Using one of the lobby phone booths, I called Raoul Chavez at the squad.

"Raoul, Fraleigh here. What's doing?"

"Not much. How are you?" He had lowered his voice, which was an indication that something was odd. You would have thought the three of us were suspects instead of victims in the case.

"Raoul, I need to know if there is anything new with Adolph Stone. Has he come in to make a statement?"

"No, and the odds around here are that he won't. Guess what law firm he hired?"

"Tweedledum's brother's firm?" I hazarded.

"You got it, amigo."

Tweedledum was an unaffectionate department nickname for Capt. Walter McCarthy, widely regarded by the troops to be city hall's man in the P.D. We went through one figurehead police chief after another, but few people had any doubts about McCarthy's staying power or influence over department policy.

"Has anything else developed in the case?" I asked.

"Not that I know of."

"How are the Block and English doing?"

"Pretty good, Fraleigh." I waited, but nothing else was forthcoming.

"You're a regular gossip, Raoul. Do one thing for me, will you? Give me Doris Learner's telephone number from the file, O.K.?"

I heard him rustling through the file. "It's 555–4212, the area code is 408, and forget where you got it, right?"

"Sure thing, Raoul." I hung up, wondering when and why we had become officially unpopular.

Fishing out some more change, I called Doris Learner's number. It was busy. Sitting there in the booth, I tried to remember the last time I had dialed a woman's number and it hadn't been busy. Sandra would be out looking for me in fifteen or twenty minutes, I guessed, and dialed the number again. A fat, gray-haired lady, carrying a Cost Plus shopping bag and a camera, passed by the other occupied booths and camped outside mine. I threw some coins in the slots and dialed again. Busy. I held. My would-be successor glared. A guy in drag, with the shoulders and legs of a longshoreman and the mascara and lipstick of a cover girl, walked by. The lady with the shopping bag turned to watch him. There would be some great stories to tell when she got back to Kansas City.

I hung up. Once again I dropped change into the phone and dialed the number. Unbelievably, it rang and was picked up on the third ring. My friend the tourist was scowling now.

"Hello."

"Doris Learner?"

"Yes."

"This is Sergeant Fraleigh. Do you remember me? My partners and I spoke to you about Lisa Stone."

"What? Oh, yes, of course. You . . . I read in the paper that the three of you were wounded. Is that right?" she asked.

"Yes. I wonder if I could talk to you for a minute—"

"For one reason," she cut in. "If you hadn't been hurt, I wouldn't bother talking to any of you, the way you let those two youngsters get butchered. I can't believe it."

The tourist was gone. I felt very tired. What was it again that I was going to ask Doris Learner? "Yes," I said, "I know how you feel, but we're still trying. That's what I wanted to talk to you about."

"How is Paul?"

The small, dapper man I had watched in the coffee shop passed by. His pace quickened when he spied me in the booth.

"Paul's doing just fine," I told her.

"Sergeant, do you think I could visit him? I mean, in the hospital . . . you know . . ." She trailed off.

I thought about righteously informing her of the department's rule prohibiting investigators from getting personally involved with females on cases. "Sure. It would do Paul good. I'll tell you what. As soon as the hospital starts letting him have visitors, I'll call and let you know."

"You mean he can't have visitors? I thought you said he was fine," she said.

"Well, what I meant was . . ." I groped. I wasn't doing much better than I had with Stone. "It's Valley Hospital, Doris. They run it like a prison. You know, only immediate family is admitted when someone is in critical condition. And they put everyone in 'critical condition,' " I added.

"Immediate family? Is, er, is he married?"

"Paul married? No." I was soaking wet in the booth. I

wanted to ask her questions. Instead, she had me on the ropes, trying to come up with answers for her own questions.

I took a deep breath. "Doris, what I wanted to ask you is, do you know anything about an outfit called the Moral Reaffirmation Guild?"

"Moral Reaffirmation Guild? No, I'm afraid I'm not religious."

"Well, it's not exactly a religion. It's more like a cult that lures kids into its activities."

"Oh, yes, a couple of weeks ago Lisa mentioned that she was trying to persuade her friend Judy not to get involved with them. I got a phone call just then, so I never did learn anything about the group or even where it is located."

"Are you sure?" I pressed. "We've heard rumors that they have been active in your area, and Lisa may have been somehow—"

"Look, Sergeant, or whatever you are, you guys haven't been exactly impressive up until now, but trying to tell me I know something about a group of kooks that I never heard of is too much."

"I'm sorry, Doris, really. I mean, honestly, we feel lousy about this case in every way and don't have much to go on. That's why it may seem like I'm pressing you, but believe me, I don't mean to."

"I suppose so," she answered.

"Just one more question," I pleaded.

"O.K., go ahead," she sighed.

"Adolph Stone. Did you hear from him lately?"

"Listen, Fraleigh, if you wanted to really piss me off today, you succeeded. No. I haven't heard from Adolph Stone and don't want to hear from him. But the first alimony payment he misses, he'll hear from my lawyer. Now—"

"You mean he hasn't even called you after what happened to Lisa?"

"Fraleigh, I thought the heavyset guy was the slow one among the three of you. Now I can see I was wrong. No. I read about Lisa in the paper. My former husband didn't even have the decency to call me. Now, if you don't mind—"

"Thank you, Doris," I said, too late to beat the click.

I sat in the hotel lobby, waiting for Sandra to appear, beautified. Interesting-looking people were flowing back and forth on the way to doing interesting things, but I wasn't observing. My mind was full of Adolph Stone. Years of police work had convinced me that I had a special skill for figuring people out. Stone was my comeuppance. I had to admit that I couldn't get a handle on what made him tick. It was annoying. I tried to let myself off the hook by theorizing that the injuries received during the ambush had taken a lot out of me. The trouble was that even before the ambush, Stone was a mystery.

His daughter is missing, but he doesn't call the police. He gets the lieutenant governor to write a letter to the mayor asking the police to hop to it on behalf of Adolph Stone. Then on the phone with me, he's just as puzzling. He can't remember whether or not the callers asked for ransom. And we never find out why, but he sure doesn't like the Moral Reaffirmation Guild. Then at his house, he really gets ticked off when his son mentions the Washington Housing Project. On the other hand, it seems to me that he was very much on the level a few minutes ago when he was offering us a job. How does that fit with him calling Louis after identifying his daughter's body and demanding our scalps? Sure, now he feels a little guilty about sending us to the MRG shoot-out the next day, but when he tells me that wasn't a factor in the job offer, that he's really a hard-nosed businessman, I believe him.

Another thing, I stay at the St. Francis exactly once in my

life and happen to run into Stone. What are the odds on that happening? Who knows? Maybe Stone's in and out of here every day. Anything else is crazy. Not even the department knows where I am. Finally, the lie about Doris Learner being the source of information for the call that sent us to the MRG shoot-out. How could he expect that to get by? Unless he figured that I'd never check on it. That maybe we'd take his business offer, or that maybe the department wouldn't let us work on the case again, or . . . ? And the parting frisk. Did he think I was going to shoot him? If so, he must feel better. My gun is locked up in headquarters.

And his son Eric's visit to the hospital. I didn't really believe that I had fantasized the whole thing, but all I could remember was something he said about his father being dangerous and devious. Something about the old man trying to ensnare him and Judy and Lisa. I could swear that he had also mentioned Sandra.

I realized I could go on forever speculating about Stone. One thing that didn't need speculation was the manner in which he had marched across the lobby and waited for the door of his Rolls to be opened for him. Adolph Stone was a man very confident of his own importance.

"You should smile more often. It lights up your whole face." Sandra had arrived, waiting to be inspected and admired. My smile had been unforced admiration. My reservations had been unfounded. The beauty salon had made
her more beautiful. I studied her.

"Don't get any carnal ideas this afternoon, Fraleigh," she warned. "You're not messing up this hairdo. We'll be tourists. I want to see the Rodin exhibit at the Palace of the Legion of Honor, come back to change, have cocktails at the Top of the Mark, and dinner at Jack's. Got it?"

"Yes, ma'am."

It was yet another Sandra. With the formal hairdo, all

was dressed in a casual but expensive tan summer suit, and her poise and assurance equaled that of the woman in the coffee shop who had admired Stone.

"Don't frown, lover. It's a beautiful day. The museum will improve your mind, and I promise I'll get it all out of my system today."

Eighteen

THE NIGHT BEFORE IT HAD BEEN DRINKS AT PERRY'S AND dinner at Sam's Grill, where we both salivated over delicate petrale sole, cooked to perfection. It had been complemented by a four-year-old Mirassou Chardonnay, selected by Sandra after a slight argument with the waiter. She won all arguments, as I had already noticed, but she had never been wrong on wine before. I would have sided with her if she had ordered grapefruit juice. She was absolutely radiant.

Now, as we left the St. Francis for our night out, she postured, "I must feed my macho man rare meat to keep him in the mood. The fish last night was superb, but we must guard against your impotence. Anyway, during our brisk walk, we will work off most of Jack's scrumptious excessive calories."

I had discovered that she regarded it as sacrilege to drive anywhere in San Francisco. As a result, the car was where I had parked it in the garage two days ago. And indeed, we had walked many a mile up and down San Francisco hills. I loved it, although by the end of a day of trying to keep up with her, I was tired, a reminder that I still wasn't out of the woods with my injuries.

On the top of the Mark Hopkins Hotel, the hubbub of cocktail-lounge noise paused for a respectful couple of minutes as the sun sank.

We had enjoyed two glasses of the house Chablis, savoring the moment, each other, the sunset, and more. "The schmaltz is thick enough to slice, you gorgeous, sexy broad. I'm almost ready to introduce you to the police positions."

"Is that something to do with sex?" she asked.

"You jest. But the police positions are precisely that—sexual positions evolving out of police training programs."

She gazed adoringly at me. "You know something, Fraleigh? You're full of crap."

"Very well, have it your way," I replied.

"I never even heard of the police positions. You just made that up to tease me."

"Humph!"

"You sound like a toothless old man when you 'humph' like that."

"We should leave to get to Jack's before the crowd gets there. You know there's no place to wait once it gets mobbed."

"You're insufferable. All right, I'll indulge you. How many police positions are there?"

"Seventy."

"Seventy?"

"Yeah."

"Why seventy?" she asked.

"Why not?"

"You're impossible. When you give those deadpan answers like that, I can't read you. You're such a terrible actor, I can't tell if you're acting or not."

"That's your problem, sister," I said out of the side of my mouth.

"All right," she said, laughing. "That's back to your normal untalent. But why police positions?"

"It's elementary, my dear. There are certain physical requirements for police academies set by the state of California. About ten years ago, there were two recruits in one academy, I forget which department it was. One was a female. She had been a college phys. ed. instructor. He had been a chorus boy. One thing led to another, and they were living with each other before the class was half over. They hit on a unique way to practice their physical exercises."

"This can't be true. You're making it up as you go along."

"Both of them were unusually dexterous people because of their previous occupations. And each had an exceptional knowledge of the human body. Every night they fooled around with calisthenics, and pretty soon, they were also fooling around with each other. After a while, they noticed that they were getting sensations they had never experienced before and their appetites and stamina noticeably increased."

"God, you are a rogue, Fraleigh."

"Suddenly word of it got around, and it was sensational almost throughout the state. The two of them put together a booklet describing the training and the positions."

"Then why haven't I ever heard of it?"

"Well, the police brass got wind of it and naturally suppressed it. They threatened the two rookies with 'conduct unbecoming an officer' if they ever dared to publish."

"And you, my hero? What's your role in all this?"

"Only that I was one of four cops in the state who got a copy of the original book." I smiled.

"Just like that, huh? Because you were so sexy?"

"No. Well, actually, that may have had something to do

with it. I did meet the female phys. ed. gal once, and she certainly was interested, but you see, I had just stopped boxing and they were using me to set up statewide physical-defense courses for cops. Four of us in the program at Sacramento were sent copies in the mail by some dumb bureaucrat who didn't realize the material had been banned."

"That's the biggest crock I've ever heard."

I shrugged nonchalantly.

"Will you demonstrate the positions, Fraleigh?"

"What? I thought you didn't believe a word of this?"

"I don't. But how can I lose? What fun!"

Summer weather in San Francisco can be tricky, sending tourists home freezing, shaking their heads in wonder. But the night was mild as we strolled toward the restaurant. Turning into Sacramento Street, I unhooked my arm from her shoulders, not really conscious of what had alerted me. Three men in dark clothing had moved from the building's edge. I noticed that the street was deserted and that both of the two slighter males were wearing tennis shoes. My body had already positioned itself, so when the youngster in front broke into a fluid running motion, sweeping Sandra's handbag from her, spinning her roughly to the ground, I hit him with a full right, flush in the side of the head, before he had taken another step. He bounced into a car parked at the curb and fell heavily, the handbag skittering toward me.

Out of the corner of my eye, I saw the other pair of tennis shoes in full retreat, standard M.O. for a purse snatch, I thought, turning to see how Sandra was. The third member of the group, older and considerably heavier, hadn't fled as per script. Instead, he was charging at me, throwing a formidable right at my head. He was strong but untrained, and it should have been easy. The defense against his punch was simply to move forward slightly, tuck my jaw down while using my left hand to deflect the blow away from my head, then move into a counter-punching position for a right hook to the body. So I moved forward, tucking my chin downward, and only as I felt the brass knuckles grazing the side of my head did I remember that my knees were wobbly and my left arm was strapped helplessly to my chest. He hadn't landed the punch solidly, but the force of his rush sent me crashing into the wall and down. Recovering his balance, he drew his foot back to kick me in the face. Sitting helplessly against the wall, out of it, I watched his foot coming with incredible force. At the last minute, I managed to turn my head sharply. He screamed in agony, probably breaking his toe on the wall. Unfortunately, he quickly recovered and kicked twice as hard with his other foot into my ribs, where he couldn't miss. I felt the familiar pit of blackness coming over me, but as he went for my head again, he suddenly stiffened and yelled in pain. Sandra, bless her, had come up behind him, reached down, grabbed his testicles, and pulled up. I hoped she wouldn't finish the maneuver.

She did. The hold is taught so that the subject goes up on his toes, off-balance as pressure is exerted upward on his balls while the aggressor throws a shoulder into his buttocks, taking him off his feet. I don't know where she learned it, but that's exactly what she did, and two-hundred-plus pounds came crashing down, completely pinning me.

She continued yelling and kicking ineffectually at him while he reached in his pocket for what I was pretty sure would be a sharp, nasty knife. It was. As he got it out, I heard Sandra's voice wail high in horror as she saw the blade. I reached my head forward, fighting off the terrible lethargy urging me to just let it go. With a last-second surge of adrenaline, I bit into his exposed left ear. With a roar, he was off me and racing down the street. I spit and stared fascinated at the tip of his ear lying on the sidewalk. There was blood all over me—his, from the ear—and a good deal of mine from where the brass knuckles had taken a chunk out of my head. It didn't stop Sandra from getting right down with me, hugging and comforting.

She yelled at the ambulance driver that I was a policeman. The arriving squad car cop gave us a siren escort to the emergency room instead of doing his job and nailing the very unusual and deadly purse snatcher. I tried to tell them as they were loading me into the ambulance, to get him, but the words weren't coming so good, and Sandra kept shushing me.

They puttered over me in the emergency room. I was in and out of knowing what was going on. A couple of times, I caught myself thinking how sick and tired of doctors and hospitals I was. They really had an army of people fluttering around me. I didn't feel very good, but the fuss was puzzling. I had suffered some lost flesh because of the brass knuckles, but it certainly wasn't the first time I had needed a few stitches on my mug. And getting knocked down, a couple of kicks to the ribs, wasn't exactly terminal cancer. I was glad to see that they at least had a middle-aged doctor in the joint. He had strung up some X rays they had taken and, pointing to them, was having an intense conversation with Sandra. It was too far to see or hear what was going on, so I went to sleep.

It was only a couple of minutes, but when I woke, they were loading me into an ambulance with Sandra sitting next to me. For a stunned moment, I thought they must be taking us back to the scene.

"Where are we going?"

"Don't talk, darling," she said. "Everything's going to be all right."

I gave up on the conversation. We rode and rode. Finally, they pulled into Valley Hospital. It had taken over an hour.

"Sandra, please tell me why we're here," I whispered.

"You're going to have to stay in the hospital for a while,

and I wanted you to be here, closer to me, and you can be with the Block and English,'' she said.

"I only had a little fistfight; I don't get it.''

"Do you know what a spleen is?'' she asked.

I nodded. We had handled a couple of cases where victims had shuffled off with ruptured spleens. I pondered that a little uneasily. The cases that came to mind had both been barroom brawls, not very different from the recent rolling in the street. The other thing that came back nastily was the memory of the coroner saying there was no cure for a ruptured spleen. "Once you have it, you've had it,'' the ghoul had laughed.

"I can see that you know how serious it is, Fraleigh. When are you going to accept your own mortality and think about getting out of this lousy business? The good guys die the same as the bad,'' she sobbed into my chest.

There was no use pointing out to her that I hadn't exactly sought out the encounter. Oddly enough, my mind wasn't focusing on the incident, my new injuries, or police work. The only thing I could think of was that Sandra would have to pack a bag to bring me pajamas and other necessities. And I saw it vividly, my small gray bag sitting on the floor of her closet, and hidden in the side pocket, the print-outs, along with my doubts and questions that I had never had the nerve to discuss with her.

Nineteen

I WOKE IN THE MORNING, HUNG OVER. THEY, ONCE AGAIN, had really doped me up. If I ever got back to the police department alive, I'd sic the narcs on the joint. Unbelievably, the Block was standing at the foot of the bed in a white jacket, the same style worn by Dr. Obnoxious, who was standing next to him. They could have been making their morning rounds together.

"Heh, heh, you got mugged, Fraleigh," the Block snickered. I couldn't believe him, skinny and in a doctor's jacket. Maybe it was the dope and I was dreaming. "You're getting too old. I heard the broad saved your bacon."

"There were three of them, you asshole, and I only had one arm."

"I'm afraid I must warn you once more, Sergeant," Obnoxious cut in, "your health is in a fragile state, and these encounters are courting disaster."

"Are all you people crazy around here? I was just walking down the street when they jumped me. I didn't schedule the goddamned bout."

"Nevertheless, you are extremely ill and your condition is grave."

"Well, I'm not in one yet, so don't get all broken up over me. I wouldn't want it to interfere with your bedside manner. Do I have a ruptured spleen or not?"

He paused, speaking carefully. "No. We see some bruises in the X rays, and it will be a few days before we can determine the extent of trauma. Of more immediate concern is internal hemorrhaging. We have been unable to identify the origin and have scheduled a series of tests, including a blood dye test. It will be somewhat painful."

"Look, I'm not going to medical school. I don't want to know what you do. Just do it."

"Yes, I know, so that you can get back to your polo matches," he said without expression, turning and leaving the room.

I shook my head. Despite the dope, I was sure it had been another doctor I had used that line on in the outpatient treatment room. The sons of bitches even put wisecracks in your folder.

"What's all that crap about polo? You ain't been on a horse in your life."

"Block, what the hell are you doing in that white jacket?"

"I lost so much weight, my bathrobe and stuff don't fit no more," he answered a little self-consciously. "But that was all right, Fraleigh. You don't take no shit from those doctors. 'Course, they're going to make you pay for it. I had some of those tests, and they hurt like hell."

God! They put a white coat on him and he was beginning to sound like them. He turned on my television set and plopped down in a lounge chair, all the time describing the series of tests he had been through.

"Dammit, Block, I don't want to hear any of that stuff."

"You know, working days, I never knew they had all

these good programs on TV," he said. "This one is 'Life-Flow.' See that snatch—she's been screwing with this guy's brother, and the kicker is that the clown is her husband. Get it? His own brother?"

How the hell was I going to get out this time, I wondered. Nurse Battle-Ax came through the door. "Well, you just couldn't stay away from us, I see," she laughed. "I'm sorry, you can't have any food this morning. Tests, you know. Your stomach must be empty, or the blood analysis—"

"I don't want to know about tests and blood analysis. Just leave me alone."

"Now there's no need to shout. I thought policemen were supposed to be brave enough not to let a little pain upset them?"

"Only some of us," the Block chipped in.

"Don't you have a television set in your room?" I asked him.

"Yeah, but I figured you could use a little company since your little lady ditched you."

I looked around for something to throw at him.

"What are you doing?" I yelled at Battle-Ax, who had swept back the blanket and was pulling me roughly forward.

"Doctor's orders. You must walk, keep the blood circulating."

"Are you crazy? My blood's got trauma; it's scarce and exhausted. I don't want to walk."

"Nurses have to follow orders, just like policemen," she gushed. "See, it didn't hurt that much to start moving, did it?"

The damn fool had pushed me forward off-balance a couple of steps, and the room swam dizzily around. I would have taken a header right into the sharp corner of the metal bed table if the Block hadn't reached out, grabbing a handful of my hospital gown.

"Dizzy, huh?" he asked, never once taking his eyes off the soap opera.

Undaunted, Battle-Ax literally dragged me up and down the hall a couple of times, ignoring my protests.

An hour later they began the tests. The Block had returned to his cage for lunch. A thin jerk, looking to be no more than eighteen, waltzed in wearing the standard white coat. "Blood," he smiled. He took a rubber strip from his jacket pocket. I noticed there were some bloodstains across the front of his jacket. This place works so hard to instill confidence in the patients, I thought, while he caressed my veins, swollen by the rubber strip he wound tightly around my arm. I didn't see how he could miss the vein, but of course, he did—twice. By the time he had finally jammed the needle in and got the blood flowing, I was ready to slug him.

Sometime during the agony of the prodding, pricking, poking, X-raying of the next two days, I became convinced that I was getting better. I took Dr. Obnoxious on about it the third morning. "I feel better. What have all the tests shown?"

"Fortunately, the internal bleeding has stopped. The tests, however, have been inconclusive. We're thinking of repeating them."

"Bullshit. I'm not going through all that again. You mean you never even found out where the blood was coming from in all those damned tests I had to put up with?"

"That may be surprising to a layman, but it's not that unusual."

"I bet it's not around this joint. When can I plan on leaving?"

"I would advise another couple of days of observation. Your shoulder fortunately escaped further injury in the latest incident and is doing well. The older lacerations, by and large, have healed or are close to it. I'm going to take the stitches out of your face wounds this afternoon. That leaves the hairline fracture of two ribs, which should heal without problems, providing, of course—"

"Don't tell me," I interrupted. "Provided I don't get ambushed by assassins or attacked by muggers until you medics sign off on me. Well, I'll try my best not to."

"I'll be back shortly to remove the stitches," and with that, he was gone.

The next day, I said to the Block, "Let's put our heads together in English's room and figure out where we go on this investigation."

"He's catatonic. He ain't going to be able to hear you."

"Catatonic? Hey look, Block, just because your bathrobe's too big and they gave you a white outfit, don't mean you have to sound like the rest of these assholes around here."

He shrugged. "Do you think they're going to let us work on it again?"

"Why not? Someone has to." But I had the same misgiving. Most times, officers would not be allowed to work a case where a personal involvement existed, and what could be more personal than someone trying to snuff you?

We were in Paul's room. I greeted him. There was no sign that he had heard or was in any way aware of our presence, but I raised my eyebrows at the Block, who was all set to ignore him. Somehow it seemed important that we include Paul in the discussions. "Hello, Paul. How are you?" the Block asked, with a self-conscious grin.

I hadn't really expected an answer and there was none.

I pulled out a clipboard and pen stolen from Battle-Ax's desk at the nurses' station. "Let's try to get a handle on this. I'll start at the beginning, O.K.? We'll list everything in chronological order. Maybe some things will fit that we haven't been seeing up until now. Then we can figure a game plan.

"Let's see, we caught the squeal about—"

"It was five weeks ago yesterday," the Block cut in.

"God, five weeks, was it that long?" My mind drifted, the photos of Lisa Stone, Foley's bumbling introduction to what hadn't even appeared to be a case . . . and Sandra. In just a few weeks, I had experienced what had escaped me for my entire life. Where was she? There hadn't been a word since she had dropped me here two nights ago.

"Fraleigh, you ain't said nothing for ten minutes. You're almost as bad as Paul. I don't know. You changed. I mean, maybe it's the dope. You were stoned out of your head for at least a week, you know. Maybe it's that Fortune broad. I seen guys hooked before, but if someone had told me that you, hard-guy Fraleigh, would go gaga the way you get when she's in the room . . . then you getting downed by punks. I don't know, Fraleigh, maybe you're losing it."

I was dumbfounded. Cumulatively, in two years, he had never said as much. "Listen, Block, if you had been getting the shit knocked out of you as often as I have lately instead of watching soap operas on television, you might just know what I'm going through."

"Wait a minute. I got shot in the chest, you know."

"Don't brag about it. It could happen to anyone."

But he was right. Instead of lining up the case synopsis, I had been mooning like a love-sick teenager. But where the hell was she? Not even a phone call? I looked at my watch. It was three o'clock; Sandra should be at her clinic sessions.

"Let's break it for now. We'll meet again tomorrow morning to continue."

"Continue?" the Block protested. "Fraleigh, you got a screw loose. We didn't even start, so how can we continue?"

I would have demolished him with a scathing reply, except that I was already moving. In my room I dialed the number and held my breath. It was annoying. At thirty-six, I was acting like a teenager. Like I hadn't even acted *as* a teenager.

"Hello."

"Hello, Lily, how are you, honey?" I had been calling for news of her mother. Yet it surprised me how pleased I was to hear her voice.

"Mommy told us you got hurt again. Are you going to be O.K.?" the little old lady asked.

"Yes, sweetheart, I'm almost better. How's little Don?"

"Tawley, you got beat up!" My eardrums were suddenly shattered by his shout from an extension phone.

"There were three people, silly. It wasn't his fault. He was very brave," his marvelous sister said.

I resisted the childish impulse of asking her if she had gotten that account from Mommy. "How's your mother, honey?" I finally brought myself to ask.

"She's O.K., I guess," Lily answered. "But she cries a lot. I think she misses you, Fraleigh. Did you have a fight?"

"No, honey. It will be O.K. I promise you."

"Tawley, I want go to beach. When you take us?" Don screamed into the phone.

"As soon as I get well, Don."

"You promise? Tawley, you promise?"

"I promise, I'll see you soon," I said, hanging up.

The next morning we reconvened. The Block protested that he was missing "General Hospital." Ignoring him, I looked at my clipboard notes from yesterday. "Five weeks" was the only notation.

"Let's start," I said. Paul was sitting, clean-shaven by a nurse, looking out the window, oblivious to our presence. "We caught the squeal from Foley, 0815 hours, Thursday, August 20."

"0830 hours," came from the Block. Overlooking his nitpicking, I scribbled onto Battle-Ax's clipboard pad, which had spent the night secreted under my mattress.

"At roughly 1030 hours, we interviewed Adolph Stone, who told us about little Lisa being missing. He was a cooperative witness—

"How really cooperative was Stone that day?" I asked myself out loud.

"He never told us why he didn't call the cops or her friends when he thought she was missing. In fact, you never even bothered to ask him," the Block said.

"Stop drooling all over your white coat or they'll take it away from you. I had reasons not to ask him."

"Yeah?"

"Yeah. Then we drove over to Santa Cruz Pier for lunch, where you set an all-time record for gluttony."

"I could file a grievance for you saying that, you know."

"It would get thrown right out because five years ago the department took judicial notice that you were a glutton. Now the next thing that happened is that Paul rapped with the surf-guru and you extorted a beer from him."

"You had one, too."

"That was different. Sergeants are allowed, for good community relations."

"Heh, heh. You allowed to do things to the broad, too, for community relations?"

It was ironic. Here I was finally rid of English's constant chatter, and the Block got born again as a verbal ball buster. "Then we interviewed Doris Learner."

"Yeah, heh, heh. I wish you could have seen your face that day, Fraleigh."

"I wish your doctor friends had seen yours. Right now, they'd have you up in one of the padded-cell wards with the sex nuts."

"That's another grievance."

"What'd you do, join the union since you're in here? Anyway, we didn't get much out of her, aside from Paul's feeling her tit." I sneaked a glance at English. Nothing.

"She did make a crack about Stone, remember?"

"Very good, Block. I'm glad that you were able to notice what she said as well as staring at her other crack the way you did that day."

"Grievance three. You'll pay for this, Fraleigh."

It was accurate. We hadn't gotten anything specific out of Doris Learner, other than a definite impression that she didn't care for Adolph Stone, to the point of hating his guts. But she had hinted at some tie-in with Casey, etc., that presumably made cheapskate Stone get generous in the divorce settlement rather than see it publicized.

"Then we went over to Fortunes' shack, where you and Paul had a jolly time playing Space Wars instead of doing police work."

"Is that what you were doing with her in the kitchen, Fraleigh, police work?"

"It turns out Don Fortune was involved with Stone some way," I continued.

"Fortune? I don't remember him saying anything like that."

"He didn't. It was on the computer. I found it by accident last week. He had a journal logged in the computer, with notations of meetings with Stone. There was even one for Fred Casey. And some other stuff. I got a hard copy, but it's stashed in my bag at Sandra's house."

"So that's why she ditched you. You were playing cop instead of being hypnotized by her snatch. I think you made a bad deal, Fraleigh; she's a nifty broad."

I was beginning to envy English's catatonic state after ten minutes of the Block's witticisms. "Then our great leader called us off the case. The next day we got word from the sheriff's guys in the mountains that they recovered Lisa's body."

"Not really." I looked at him, not completely concentrating on what he was saying, reliving the anger and despair of losing those two girls. "They never said it was Lisa. All they had was Stone's ID and the story about how the kids had disappeared from the camp. We ain't never examined any of the forensic stuff.''

"That's true. It seems like we've all been medical guinea pigs ourselves since the case started. There sure hasn't been much investigation.''

"Except what you been investigating with the lady," he leered.

"O.K. It was the very next day that we got set up.''

"You're leaving out you trying to kill Foley and your little martini binge at Morty's.''

"No wonder there's so much crime in this country— there's no respect for authority or rank anymore," I said. "Then after lunch on Saturday, we hit the Moral Reaffirmation office and got hurt.''

"You forgot . . .'' I sucked in my breath, hoping he wasn't about to say, "You forgot whose idea it was to go over there," but he didn't. He said, "You forget that Louis put the Zombie on some name checks and he just sat on his ass, doing nothing, while we had lunch. Except maybe taking Stone's call setting us up.''

"Do you think Stone sets us up?''

"Who else? He was the one called, and we don't hear no different explanation, do we?''

"But, Block, all Stone did was call with the address while we were at lunch. He had no way of knowing that we were even working. Remember we were scheduled to be off?''

"Yeah, ain't that hot shit? You got to be real smart to get shot on your day off.''

"Stone wouldn't have known whether we would check out the place then, in two months, or maybe never. And the two hoods who hit us certainly didn't steal that car and stake that place out indefinitely.''

"Do you know that the car and office had been wiped

clean, no prints at all, except some of ours in the office?'' he asked.

"How do you know? I thought you said they hadn't told you anything about the case?"

"They haven't, but some of the guys visiting have talked about what's come up so far."

"What else did they tell you?"

"The pickup truck, it was wiped clean too."

"Pickup . . . what pickup?"

"You know, the one that did Bini."

"Bini! Goddammit, Block, can't you keep track of what we're talking about? We're talking about how we got set up, not about Bini's hit and run."

"Did you ever know joyriders to wipe a car clean or dump it two blocks from the scene, where they just happen to pick up another car?"

"You got all this stuff from the guys in the squad?"

"Yeah. If you hadn't decided on sea air and nookie for treatment, you would have gotten the same stuff."

"All right, all right. Let's see if we can get back to the chronology. Where were we before you jumped in? We were set up. The question is why and how?"

"Questions."

" 'Questions'!" I repeated. He could be exasperating.

" 'Why?' is one question and 'How?' is another, so it should be plural, 'questions.' "

I happened to be looking at Paul and thought a trace of a smile had appeared for a moment on his face. "Block, are you giving me an English lesson or is there some significance to what you said?"

"Who knows?" he answered.

It was like old times. Trying to keep your mind on an investigation with this team was a major challenge, even with one of them on the sidelines, deaf and dumb. "Why," I said aloud, "would someone want to hit us? We did make a case

against the Hell's Angels, one against the prostitution syndi-
cate, a couple against the prison gangs, and that one last
year involving the organized crime family, but none of them
really like to hit a cop if they think it can be traced to them.
Too much heat. But even if they wanted to snuff us, how the
hell would they have known to set up the hit there and
then?''

The Block didn't answer.

"Since then I've spotted a guy watching me take the Fortune kids to the beach. The next day is a Sunday, and I call
Bini for a license check on the vehicle and a name check on
the owner, never thinking that it's for real. The computers
go down a lot on Sundays for maintenance and data base re-
newals, so Bini only gets a partial for me. It was a local.
George Bosco, Oakland, with a number of aliases and, according to Bini, an extensive sheet. By then the computer's
down, so I ask Bini to give me a call when it comes back up
and to stick a hard copy in my mailbox.''

"Why didn't you get back to him on it?" the Block
asked.

"Because that afternoon I discovered the stuff in Fortune's computer, and by the time I got it all out, it was 1815
hours. I figured Bini left for home and since I was due here
at the hospital the next day, I could run over to the squad to
pick it up.''

"I heard it hit you pretty hard when you did go over
there.''

"Yeah, Bini and I went back a lot of years. Then just
three days later, I have the lousy luck to get caught in a purse
snatch in San Francisco.''

"Purse snatch, my ass!" the Block said.

"It was. They took Sandra right off her feet. The little
bastards were wearing tennis shoes. If I hadn't got set in advance, I never would have touched any of them.''

"Fraleigh, how long you been a cop? Twelve, thirteen

years? In all that time, did you ever hear of a purse snatcher staying to duke it out with a guy your size? They're gone as soon as they grab the poke."

"And the guy who came after me was no kid, and he wasn't wearing tennis shoes," I said. So many coincidences and a disturbing feeling that the volume of events of the last weeks had been too much. I had lost my cop skills, wasn't coping, simply drifting from one event to the next without being able to understand or do anything about what was happening.

"Let's figure how we go about investigating what we've got," I said, trying to regain my own confidence. "First we need to take a good look at the forensic evidence from the girl's homicide. After all, that's what started it. Then we need to work Stone. There are too many unanswered questions about him. He's too slippery to take on direct, but I can try young Eric while we get the case enhancement people to do extensive file checks on Stone senior, his business, his friends. And it would be nice to get Doris Learner to open up on him. I got a feeling she knows plenty."

"I'll take her on."

The Block and I gaped. English was smiling his pleasant dreamy smile, just as if he hadn't been looking holes in a wall for weeks.

"Do you feel strong enough, Paul?" I asked. The Block and I were trying not even to breathe, out of fear that he'd disappear again on us.

"Not right now," English said, "but in a few days. It's an interesting case. I'm going to bed now, do you mind?" he inquired with his typical politeness.

Just then the phone rang. I grabbed it. "Fraleigh here."

"Fraleigh." It was Louis, sounding harried and almost whispering. "Three of the brass are on their way over to see you guys. They've got you slated for disability retirements. I tried to stop them, but someone is really moving it. I think we can beat them, but they're counting on you to blow your top. They've got a recorder with them, and it will be open and shut if you explode. Stay cool. I'll be by around 2200 and we can talk. Take care, hear?''

"Thanks, Louis," I whispered before hanging up and breaking the news to English and the Block.

Twenty

TWEEDLEDUM AND TWEEDLEDEE CAME IN, ALL SMILES. Captain Bently, behind them, had the heavy shoulders of a career cop, which he was. The expression he now wore and the distance he kept between himself and the other two reflected that also. They were administrative captains, hatchet men. Tweedledee, Saunders, was tall and thin, a nondescript nonentity. Someone never known to make a decision in his life, as forgettable as the wallpaper in a police world of distinctive characters.

Tweedledum, Walter McCarthy, was all too distinctive, dressed in a dark-striped, expensive suit and a Pierre Cardin tie. No one in the department had illusions about his decision-making ability; they just hoped the decision didn't involve them. His father had been mayor for eight years and had run the city for ten before taking office. There were legendary stories about land-development deals, fortunes made and hidden. When he died, he left a modest treasure to his two sons and widow. One son was a partner in a downtown law firm that did a lot of political work. The firm had been recognized for its legal excellence by having three of its eight partners appointed superior court judges during the present governor's administration. "Heavy" was the word applied to them around town.

Our visitor, the other brother, Tweedledum, had chosen the simple life of a dedicated public servant, a police officer. Somehow he had never, in fifteen years, been on the street or made an arrest. Nevertheless, his talents for police work and knowledge of administration must have been considerable, because during the past ten years, he had been administrative assistant to three police chiefs. The incumbent chief was some months overdue for the normal tenure in office. As a result, there was five hundred dollars in a pool for the lucky dick who had drawn the appropriate week for the chief's departure out of the raffle hat. My pick was eighteen months hence, an impossibility in everyone's judgment. It served me right for investing ten bucks in an illegal gambling venture.

McCarthy sounded like our best friend, an admirer. "I just want to tell you men how proud we are of you. I'm happy to bring to you Chief . . . Brown's commendation for outstanding valor." We had all managed a straight face as he had struggled for a moment to come up with the current chief's name.

"Personally, I'd like to say that your courage and performance under great danger and stress surpass the finest traditions of the department. You all went well beyond the normal call of duty. Sometimes it may seem to the men that the administration is unaware or unappreciative of their work. That's not true. We're very busy, but . . ." He paused for more flowery phrases, while I contemplated giving him the Miranda warnings if he actually started telling us how he was so busy. Not that there was any fear of that happening. His wife probably wondered what he actually did for a living. But we knew he spent more time running between his brother's law office and city hall and Sacramento than he did in the police department.

"We appreciate your taking the time to come here with the Chief's praise, Captain. It means a lot to us when we do end up in the hospital to know that you share the pain," I said. I noticed some apprehension in Captain Bently's eyes and an almost imperceptible shaking of his head from side to side. I knew he played racketball twice a week with Louis Robinson, which was a good clue as to where the warning had come from. Now he was nervous, but what had I said wrong?

McCarthy chewed that one over for a minute, then continued, "Yes, I can assure you that we, who also serve, see our job as helping you do yours. I think the purpose of our visit today is proof that the administration does care about the welfare of the troops. I'm happy to inform you that the department, in consideration of the ordeal you men have been through and the severity of your injuries, has cut through the red tape and prepared applications for disability retirement for your signatures," he said, smiling. Then he frowned, for the first time noticing the pocket recorder that had all the time been on the tray table in front of me. A cop would have spotted it immediately. Bently had, but hadn't said a word.

"You don't mind my recording this, do you, Captain?" I asked.

His eyes had grown hard. With an effort, he got back to his good-natured approach. "Actually, there's no reason to record this. As I said, it's not an adversary situation; the department wants to do what's best for you men." He nodded pointedly at the recorder.

I said nothing, looking blandly at him. "Of course, I'm in no way suggesting that you have to turn it off or anything . . ." He paused significantly.

I gazed innocently back at him, attentively awaiting his words.

When he saw that I was not about to take the hint, he continued, but I noticed he seemed more thoughtful. "I'm authorized to inform you that your pension under this retirement will amount to three quarters of your present pay, with annual adjustments for cost-of-living increases. It can hardly make up for your suffering, of course, but nevertheless, it's generous when you consider each of you would have to complete close to another twenty years to qualify for the standard half-pay pension."

"It sure is generous, Captain. I don't remember anything like this ever happening before."

"Oh, come now, Fraleigh, unfortunately we've had some disability retirements every year for as long as I can remember."

"No. I meant someone being offered a retirement without even applying for it. Has that happened before, Captain?"

"Well, as I said, your injuries are so evident that there's no reason for the usual medical mumbo jumbo, and in consideration of your courage and the general impact on morale, we thought it more advisable, more humane, to save you the trouble of formally requesting retirement."

"I want you to know we are deeply touched by the department's reaction, Captain; in fact, I think we sensed that kind of commitment. It's one reason why the three of us have talked it over and decided not to ask for disability retirements. The doctors feel we are well on the way to recovery, and we're all career policemen. We want to continue working."

He was frowning, but I noticed Bently, sitting to the rear, had a twinkle in his eyes and his head was now nodding up and down in approval.

"That's commendable, Fraleigh, but sometimes loyalty and dedication aren't in your best interests. Your health has to come first, and it wouldn't be right for the department to exploit your emotions at the price of your long-term health."

"I guess that's what's confusing, Captain. We don't think our injuries are that serious, and as far as we know, the city hasn't even seen the medical records yet, has it?"

"Actual written records, no, but some of the verbal reports indicate problems that would be exacerbated if you continued on duty."

"For example?" I asked.

"I don't think we should continue at this point. I can see that you men are emotionally upset right now. We'll let you think it over for a few days. Naturally, the final decision on your capabilities to perform police duties has to be made by the city's physician."

"I'm not at all emotionally upset, Captain, and I don't wish to speak for the rest of the team, but you're wrong in this case. I mean about the final decision being made by the city doctor."

"Wrong? What do you mean, Sergeant?" he asked, leaning forward. Bently, in back, drew in his breath, his head now shaking from side to side, again fearing I was about to blow.

"In my case, at least, I'm a young man in good health. I would appeal in court any attempt to retire me forcibly."

"I agree with Sergeant Fraleigh, Captain," Paul chipped in.

"Me too," the Block grunted, making it unanimous.

Tweedledum was no slouch. We had surprised him, refused to be intimidated, and hadn't exploded the way he had hoped we would. Yet he got up smiling, shook our hands, and left with Tweedledee and Bently trailing. The last one out, Bently, turned and gave us a wink. We had done O.K.

"*Muy bueno, amigos,*" Louis said, grinning to the three of us gathered in my room for his late arrival, in violation of hospital visiting hours.

He still looked tired, terrible. No wonder, I thought, losing key investigators like us.

"I hear for once you didn't go *loco*. Tweedledum was in some temper when he got back, but he still doesn't know what hit him."

"He will, though, Louis. You and Bently better watch your ass," I warned.

"It's unbelievable, Fraleigh. You had to almost get knocked off, turn into a junkie, and get senile before you ever expressed any appreciation for my carrying you deviates. To think what heaven the last year or so would have been with even a modicum of concern for me by the three of you."

"Deviates" and "modicum." Louis was throwing his master's degree around again.

"Louis," I said, "we have always had concern for the psychopathological consequences of our actions on you. It was just that you were suspended in a state of cop-anomie, so let's stop the bullshit. Tell us how you've screwed up the case since we left you on your own."

His eyes lit up like old times as he started to come back at me. Instead, he said, "We don't have much. The two hit men, we finally got identified through the FBI. They were soldiers in the Cappozo family, Chicago, strictly button men, no status. The FBI doesn't know, or at least they say they don't, what the two were doing in California."

That didn't surprise me. It was an open secret to everyone but the news media that the FBI had pulled out on us as unreliable some five years ago. We got some dribs and drabs of intelligence, but it was strictly on a personal basis between one FeeBee and one dick. Most of us on the inside didn't blame them. Once the department got to be dominated by Tweedledum and the like, sensitive intelligence information dried up on all fronts. Nothing chilled the process like the thought that the information would end up being used for political purposes. For us, it meant keeping the files in our head and sharing only with a select few. There was a big price to pay when you operated like that. A lot of crooks, big and small, profited, slipping through the net, but this was different.

"Are you telling me you think those sons of bitches are holding out, even though they know we almost got blown away?" I asked.

"I can't swear to it, but they got their sources, too, you know. They must be wondering, the same as we are, why Stone has never been brought in for questioning and why you three are being greased for retirement. Would you give them info if it was the other way around?"

"You know he lied to me in San Francisco about the call. He told me that Doris Learner had supplied the MRG location to him. He just passed it on to us to be helpful. I called her and she didn't know anything about it."

They were all looking at me. Louis exploded. "Goddammit, Fraleigh! What do you mean, Stone told you in San Francisco? Are you conducting some kind of secret investigation?"

"Don't get your balls in an uproar, Louis. It ain't good for a guy your age who's also overweight. Stone happened to run into me in the St. Francis a few hours before the purse snatch that put me back in this joint. This is the first chance I had to tell anybody anything."

I paid no attention to their sullen looks. It wasn't my fault if they were going to act like prima donnas about who got what information on the case. "Still, Louis, it doesn't make sense that you can't bring him in. Trying to hit three cops isn't something that can be covered by any amount of political juice. It just can't be done."

"No, if people think that's what you're doing. Let me try this out on you. Two stickup men blast three cops and lose. They're small-time hoods from Chicago, good riddance, case closed. Cleaning up loose ends, like finding out how Adolph Stone located the Moral Reaffirmation office, and why two 'stickup men' thought it would be loaded with dough, gets low priority, especially since Stone seems to be flying all over the world.''

"That's bullshit. They weren't two-eleven men and he may travel some, but he can't hide, Louis. Whatever it is that he's up to, he's got to be around enough to stay on top of it.''

"Yeah, you're right. But you see, all I get is what his lawyer tells me every morning when I call. He's very polite, and very expensive, from what I hear.''

"What firm?'' I asked, knowing the answer from Raoul.

"You guessed it. Tweedledum's brother's gang.''

"Can't you send someone to grab Stone on the way out in the morning or on the way home at night?''

"That's a great suggestion, Fraleigh. I don't know how we've been managing since you've been laid up. 'Course, maybe you could elaborate on whom I might put on it. I lost you three, Bini, the Zombie, and the normal complement of sicks and vacations. The black and Chicano teenage gangs declared an undeclared war on each other with four fatalities since you guys left us, and we got a two-eleven team hitting gas stations and fast-food grocery stores. They have provided us with three DOAs and more media publicity than we can handle. So you see, a twenty-four-hour stakeout just because you got hurt ain't going to fly.''

Section 211 of the Penal Code is armed robbery. Something that all police departments give top priority to. Yet . . . "It used to be they hesitated to hit a cop because they didn't want the heat. What happens when they get to think differently?'' I wondered aloud.

Louis's color got a shade deeper. "Well, son, while you've been recuperating at the beach and whatnot, some of your colleagues, instead of going home after twelve hours of overtime and stuff, have been working with Bently and me, strictly on the QT.''

"Then why the hell didn't you say so, Louis?" I was more angry at myself than at him. "You could have saved some time."

"Not much because you won't like what I have to tell you," he responded. "We've got nothing more to go on as far as the homicide in the mountains. The crime scenes weren't handled that well. They don't have the kind of expertise we have on our tech crews. In fact, we still don't have forensic confirmation that the body parts recovered in the mountains belong to Lisa and Judy. It's weird. No heads or hands were found, so fingerprint and dental identification hasn't been possible. All they have is Adolph Stone's statement that a blouse found near the torso was Lisa's." He paused for a moment, looking at me. "Two days ago, Don Fortune's body, or what was left of it, washed up off Point Lobos. So far, no coroner's opinion on cause of death."

I felt all three of them eyeing me curiously, but I didn't give a damn. All I could think of was maybe that was why she hadn't called, maybe it wasn't the print-outs after all. But I knew better.

I dragged my mind back to what Louis was saying. "The other thing that's going to stun you, Fraleigh, is that there's no record in CJIS that Bini ever did a name or license check that Sunday morning."

"What? That can't be. He gave me the information, or part of it anyway, right then. And the system makes a record of all inquiries by the investigator code number for security reasons. You know that, Louis."

"Yeah, that's what makes it so weird. I checked under the registration you gave me. Not listed in the DMV. I checked under the name you gave me, no listing. I checked under Bini's code number. No inquiries listed for Sunday; a couple of routine queries were recorded on Saturday. Those he did for two uniformed rookies on a robbery pinch. After that . . . nothing.''

"I don't get it. I thought the system had all sorts of safeguards so that investigators and agencies couldn't erase their queries?''

"It does. We actually talked for a while about whether you were on a trip or something.''

Seeing my look, he held up his hands, continuing, "But we did approach it from the point of how it could be done, not whether or not it was.''

"Gee, thanks, Louis.''

"It's nothing,'' he said. "But what is heavy is how much trouble someone had to go through to phony the DMV file and the CJIS file. It could only be done at a fairly high level in the Sacramento Data Processing Office—in the executive branch.''

"Executive branch . . .'' I wondered. "The lieutenant governor would have some juice there, wouldn't he?''

"Probably,'' Louis replied. "About three years ago, I went through an FBI training session at Quantico. For a couple of weeks, I shared a room with an investigator in the California attorney general's office. The AG only controls the top three percent or so of appointments to his staff, the rest are civil service. Anyway, this guy, Tony Rodriguez, has been with the state about twelve years. He knows the system backward and forward. I called him and gave him our little scenario without getting specific. At first he gave a flat no. It couldn't be done. But a couple of days later, he called back and said it was possible but so involved that it was almost like science fiction. I can't give you all the gobbledygook, but when the system goes down for maintenance and updating, it would be possible, through about eighteen maneuvers, for someone who was an expert to purge the basic files and to carefully erase all of the cross-references, effectively destroying the memory of any transaction. But it certainly was a hell of a lot of trouble for some-one to go through.''

''And what about me?'' I asked. ''Did they think I was going to shrug it off or just forget what happened?''

''If that cat in San Francisco had gotten to use his blade on you . . .'' The Block left his sentence unfinished.

No one said anything for a moment. My mind wasn't crazy about dwelling on the implications of the Block's comment. ''Wait a minute, the NCIC is run by the FBI in Washington. They couldn't fool around with that data base.''

''Precisely, and when we checked on one George Bosco of Oakland, the terminal printed out the information exactly as you said Bini had given it to you, leaving only the ques-tion as to why our state files in Sacramento suddenly devel-oped faulty memories.''

''And this discussion you guys had about whether I was on a drug trip or not, did it take place before or after you got the brilliant idea to check Washington to see if there was a George Bosco?''

''I'm not sure I remember, Fraleigh.'' He smiled.

''We ought to plot out where we go now, Louis. You know the Block, English, and I are checking out of here, probably tomorrow. We need copies of all the case files and the cooperation of the Case Enhancement Unit.''

''Wait a minute,'' he said. ''Tweedledum has shelved you guys indefinitely by putting you on convalescent leave. You'll have no official status, and any requests for work or information are sure to raise all kinds of hell.''

''So?'' I asked.

''A couple of things,'' he said. ''I'll let Raoul Chavez be our secret liaison. You guys feed him everything you get and he'll brief me daily. Goldberg, the police reporter for the *Mercury*, has been bugging us every day on what's new on the hit attempt on you guys. We'll let Raoul brief him off the record, enough good background stuff to produce a story speculating on why not much of a follow-up investigation is being conducted. That should be embarrassing enough to make them a little careful if—and it's probably when—they tumble to you guys doing an investigation. If the administration thinks about zapping you, they'll have to worry about how it would look in the paper, you know, disciplining three heroes for working on their own assault after it became clear the department wasn't doing much.''

"O.K., but we have a lot of things to follow up. We could shake Stone a little . . .''

"No, I don't think you'd get much out of him and you'd tip our hand, probably bring down Tweedledum and lots of heat.''

"Yeah," I agreed. "But Bosco certainly is worth pursuing.''

"He is," Louis nodded, "but that's a no-no right now, Fraleigh. And I mean it. He's very physical from everything we know. I don't want you taking him on. None of you is in the best shape right now, for one thing, and just like questioning Stone, it could blow us right out of the water.''

"Well, what the hell can we work on?" I demanded.

"Now, now, patience, my dear Sergeant. Who will take on Sandra Fortune?''

"Sandra?" I knew I wasn't going to like this.

"She certainly has to know a lot more than she's told you, Fraleigh," English contributed quietly. "Where are those print-outs from your bag? What connection was there between her husband, Stone, Casey, MRG, and on and on. Someone has to ask her about it.''

I was so down that, for a moment, I considered letting English take her on. I groaned inwardly. It was my job and Paul was not at all completely recovered. Even when he was, he was unpredictable. "All right. I'll get to her in a couple of days," I offered.

"How about tomorrow?" countered Louis. "We may have a break. The San Francisco P.D. notified us that they think they have one of your purse snatchers in custody. They asked if you and Sandra would be available for an ID tomorrow morning."

"O.K. I'll pick her up and drive up to the city."

"It might be better if I call her with the request," Louis put in diplomatically.

"Yeah," I agreed. How the hell did he know everything?

Twenty-one

LOUIS HAD ARRANGED FOR ME TO PICK HER UP AT 0900
hours. My disappointment was that she was ready, striding
athletically toward me before I had even turned the motor
off. She wore her light tan summer suit, with sheer stock-
ings and heels that were going to put her a half inch above
me. She carried a little black hand purse and was so goddamned gorgeous that I forced myself to look away after
mumbling hello. I had envisioned waiting, the way you always wait for a woman, and found that I was really disappointed not to have seen little Don or Lily.

Being unofficial as we were meant that I was using my
own car. Five years ago it had been new, full of pep and
good looking. Now it was a drab, five-year-old Mercury
sports coupe and, like its owner, sluggish, showing the inevitable dents and signs of wear. After a quick scrutiny, she refrained from wrinkling her nose at it.

The morning fog was thick off the ocean and carried an
unpleasant chill with it. The chill in the car was deeper. We
had nothing to say. Driving too fast, I headed us north up

Highway 1 and turned onto the Route 17 ramp, heading east to the valley.

"You're going too fast," she said, when I almost lost it on one of the steep turns. She was right. They had finally unstrapped my left arm the day before, and it wasn't all that reliable on these tight turns. I slowed down. As usual, we burst into bright sunlight about halfway over the mountain. Fifteen minutes later, I maneuvered us onto the Junipero Serra Freeway, less affectionately known as Interstate 280 to the thousands of commuters who got stuck on it every day. We whizzed past Stanford University's linear accelerator without an acknowledgment, and I tried to ignore her perfume. The gracefully curving foothills, lovely when green from winter rains, were dried out by summer heat. Like my emotions, I thought, once again pushing down too hard on the accelerator, only to ease up as she pointedly glanced at the speedometer. It was a day I wanted to end before it had gotten under way.

Precisely at 1030 hours, I pulled into the police garage on Bryant Street, where we argued for two minutes with a functionary clad in garage overalls. Then waited ten more while he called and argued with Inspector Comerford, the dick who was handling our case. Finally, he grudgingly allowed us to park, checking to make sure I obeyed his order to leave the keys in the ignition.

Comerford looked like Wallace Beery in an old Keystone Kops movie. Talk about burnout—he hardly had the energy to shake our hands. Red-faced, with wisps of gray hair, he must have been pushing sixty. His desk looked like it had been collecting reports for at least half that long without anyone ever removing or filing them.

Now he fumbled to find our file, knocking a few onto the floor. Bending over, he displayed an ample belly. I saw Sandra glance away and look at her watch. We had only been there five minutes, but Comerford was that kind of a guy. I thought of a certain hospital that would snap him up to head their security outfit as soon as he retired.

"We got this black punk. He cops out for seven jobs in the area. We think he's good for ten times that many. Let's see, you're Fraleigh, that's right, a cop from the valley."

He was impressive all right.

"Here, I got some mug shots of him you can look at."

"Hold on, Inspector," I cut in, "if we look at just his shots, it won't stand up in court."

"You're as bad as the lawyers," he said. "I thought from one cop to another . . . oh, well, come on downstairs. I'll let you look at junior through the one-way glass."

"Do you have a regular lineup scheduled?" I asked, knowing all too well what the answer was.

"Hey, Fraleigh, this is a big city, not some hick town. Do you think we got time to play lawyer games with all these punk purse snatchers?"

"Look, as a favor to me, O.K.," I pleaded. "I almost checked out on this one. I want it to be clean in court."

"It will take a half hour or so to set up a lineup," he muttered.

Sandra and I went downstairs to the public cafeteria, where Comerford promised to retrieve us when the lineup was ready.

"What was that all about? I thought we were just going to look and say whether or not it was the same person," she said.

"In 1967 the Supreme Court ruled that lineups have to be conducted so that witnesses make an independent identification; and the defendant has the right to have counsel present. If we had looked only at his pictures or only at him, the court would not have allowed any identification we made to be entered into evidence because it was prejudicial to the defendant. Comerford knows that. He's just being sloppy."

"Somehow I never thought of you as being a civil libertarian."

"I'm not particularly in favor of putting the wrong people in jail, you know. The courts were right. You can imagine what would happen if a couple of average, law-abiding citizens were upstairs and Comerford said, 'We think he's good for sixty purse snatches.' The victims generally ain't too happy to begin with. They figure that the dick must know what he's doing. In a borderline ID, they just might well feel pressured to go along."

"I never thought of that and I can see why it bothers you, the perfectionist."

I didn't have anything to say to that. Fortunately, Comerford's bulky two hundred pounds on a five-foot-eight frame was lurching around the cafeteria, trying to locate us. I waved to him, resisting the impulse to sit still to see if he was up to finding us.

"God, yes, it's him. The third from the left end," Sandra said. I had gone first. Playing it by the book, I looked and moved away from the one-way glass without any sign to her. The boy, Roy Graham, was seventeen. Looking at his juvenile record, which I had pulled from under a pile on Comerford's desk, I confirmed what I already knew: Roy had been around. From thirteen on, larceny, drugs, malicious mischief, burglary—a fairly typical pattern. No violence.

"Comerford, did he waive his parents and lawyer?" I asked.

"Yeah, the little shit has been in and out of here so much he knows more than the lawyers, and some of the cops, too," he added, looking at me.

"This time you charged him with attempted one-eighty-seven. He can be tried as an adult."

"Bullshit, Fraleigh. Even in the pastureland where you work, you know this kid is going to the Youth Authority for a few weeks' vacation, then coming back with a faster pair of sneakers."

"I'm not arguing with you, Inspector. It's just that I'd like a favor, a professional courtesy. You can understand why I'd like to know a little more about why the kid suddenly goes in for muscle work," I said.

"Who knows with these animals. We probably just ain't never nailed him on it before. But if you want to talk to him, go ahead. I don't give a shit. Er, pardon my French, lady."

"What's a one-eighty-seven?" Sandra inquired.

"It's murder, lady. What did you think that clown was doing with the knife, trying to sell it as a souvenir to your boyfriend?"

She got a little pale.

Unbelievably, the brass knuckles and knife were lying carelessly on Comerford's desk with evidence tags around them. I picked them up and took them downstairs with us. Comerford brought the kid into one of the interview rooms. I stuck my magnum, which Louis had returned to me, along with the two pieces of evidence, in an empty weapon locker outside the room, carefully turning the locking mechanism and pocketing the tiny key.

Then Sandra and I went into the interview room. I hadn't thought she would, but since Comerford made no move to stop her, I was glad that she came along. Who knows, it might influence the lad to be more talkative.

"Hello, Roy, I'm Fraleigh, and this is Sandra Jacoby. We just identified you in that purse snatch last week."

"Yeah, man, I'm real sorry. Lady," he said, turning to Sandra, "you got every right to hate me. I had no business doing what I did, but my old lady had no food in the house, I was high on drugs." He looked pleadingly at her.

"I don't hate you," Sandra told him.

"Hold on, Roy. I don't know if they told you or not, but I'm a cop."

"You a cop! You motherfucker, you almost took my head off for a stinking purse snatch. That's police brutality, man."

"Roy, I'm going to repeat the Miranda warnings to you. I know you already got them, but that's the regulations, I got to say them again."

And I did, carefully, word by word. He impatiently declined having an attorney or parent present. Sandra eyed me curiously.

"Now, Roy, first of all, I'm sorry that I hit you so hard. It wasn't just because of a purse snatch, you know that. What I can't understand is the switch in your behavior."

"Hey, man, I already told everything to the other cops. I ain't copping out to no more jobs."

"I'm not asking you to, Roy. I just want you to know we're sorry."

He looked. "You sorry. What about?"

"About you being charged with attempted murder and maybe going into adult court."

"Hey, man. What kind of jive-ass shit is that? I grabbed a purse. Just because she's your bitch and you a cop don't mean you can shaft me."

"Have you seen the evidence in this case, Roy?"

"Evidence, man, what evidence? I never even got the motherfucking purse. There ain't no evidence."

"Roy, I'm going outside for a minute. I put the evidence in a little locker out there. I'm going to hold it up so you can see it through the window."

Sandra, no fool, came out with me. I unlocked the weapon locker and held up the brass knucks. Then, flicking the knife button with a flourish, sent the evil-looking blade shooting forward.

We went back into the room after locking the stuff up again. Roy was sweating. "Man, I never saw that shit before in my life. I don't know what kind of a number you're trying to do on me.''

"That's why I said I was sorry, Roy. I think your partner who belonged to those two little toys set you up.''

"I don't know what you're talking about.''

"Let me show you what your partner did to me with those after you took off.''

I had prepared for this. Before Roy's unwilling but fascinated eyes, I took off my shirt. He looked uneasily at the mass of bandages and tape still surrounding my chest.

"Hey, man, I didn't have nothing to do with that. I didn't have no partner. It's the other way round; you slugged me.''

"You know the law better than that, Roy. You're both principals, equally guilty. He's gone, but we got you, and the jury's gonna look at those bandages and wounds. They took pictures of them in the hospital to use at the trial. I just wanted you to know there's nothing personal in it for me. I know you didn't actually do it, but the law says you're going to take the fall. Let's go, honey,'' I said to Sandra, slowly buttoning my shirt.

"Man, you can't do this to me. I never hurt no one. I steal, but I don't hurt no one. You seen my record.''

I finished with my shirt and turned toward the door. "See you, Roy.''

"Shit, I don't even know what that dude was. He just came up to us about ten minutes before we jumped the purse.''

"Come on, Roy, even the softest jury won't swallow that crap.''

"I swear it. We never seen that motherfucker before. In fact, at first, we thought he was a cop, but he was too goofy, and he spread the bread real quick, before we could get spooked on the job.''

Seeing that he wasn't going any further, I started him again. "How much bread?''

"Twenty each, but he told us it was a big score, that the lady had lots of cash and jewelry in the bag that he had given her."

"He had given her? And you believed him?" I asked in my most skeptical voice.

"Yeah, man. I know it sounds funny now, but the dude knew how to rap. He said she had been his bitch and you was going to run her, you know, cut him out."

"Come on, Roy, you think we believe that jive?" I stalled, mentally massaging what he had given up. Instinctively, he mixed truth and lies like other people put cream and sugar in their coffee. The question was, which was which and how much more was he willing to give up? Sandra sat spellbound as I got up, wincing exaggeratedly.

"You know something, Roy, that story is so crazy that I almost got to believe it. That cat sure left you in a pile of shit. You going to do some hard time if they nail you in adult court on a one-eighty-seven."

"You supposed to be a cop," he screamed. "What do you mean he left me? You supposed to do justice, catch the motherfucker. Don't have me do his time."

"Hey, Roy, you're a big boy. You should have thought of that before you went messing with him. Ain't no way we're going to catch him now. He's split, probably in New York by now."

"That motherfucker didn't split. I heard he dealt some smack the very next day from the pad he got in Daly City. You want to, you can find him. Maybe you don't want to."

"What makes you say that, Roy?"

"Word is, he's a crazy, very physical."

"Now you know that don't make no difference; we like cats like that. Once they get that rep, it's the Swat team and machine guns. We blow them assholes away, and no one says a word because of their rep." Looking at his eyes, I was afraid I had made it too obvious.

"Man, I don't want any of that shit on my record. You know I don't hurt people. I stay away from crazies. Whyn't you give me a break, man."

"Come on, Roy, you know I can't give you a break. You've been charged. Only the judge can help you, and the kind of heat they're taking on reelection now, they ain't likely to, especially when they see this," I said, tapping my taped ribs meaningfully. The wheels were turning.

"Suppose you caught that dude, what then?"

"He's the one I want, Roy. You help me, I'll help you," I whispered, leaning dramatically forward, really hamming it up.

"You ain't goin' to take that motherfucker alive, are you?" he asked.

I didn't answer, but leaned back, letting my best homicidal glint come into my eyes.

"3244 Dwyer, Daly City," he said.

We went back up to Comerford's lair. "How about lunch?" I asked Sandra.

"No. I really want to get back. I didn't think it would take this long."

It wasn't that she "had" to get back. She "wanted" to. I glanced at my watch. It was 1345 hours. "I'm going to be tied up here for about two more hours before the paper work is done. If you want, you can take my car. I'll take the train back and have someone pick up the car."

Comerford was listening as if this were the most exciting conversation of his career. She asked suspiciously, "What paper work? You got the address out of him. What more do you need?"

"For one thing, this isn't a *Dirty Harry* movie. We can't go over and break into the place. First I need to swear to an affidavit, then a judge of that county must examine it and sign a warrant. That means we need to work through the Daly City cops. It all takes time. Then too, Roy promised to look through the mug gallery that our friend Inspector Comerford is arranging of likely muscle men to see if he can ID the character who wanted to carve his initials on my ribs.''

"All right, as long as we can start back by three-fifteen," she agreed reluctantly.

Reaching for his phone, I headed off Comerford's objection that he couldn't possibly do all the work by then. Dialing the internal four-digit extension number, I asked the gal who answered to connect me with Capt. Harold Lutz. Comerford's eyes narrowed. Lutz, as I well knew, had a reputation for brooking no interference in cases he took a personal interest in. I knew he would in mine. We had fought to a draw twenty years ago in a Golden Gloves bout right here in the city, maintaining loose communications through the years.

"Fraleigh, what the hell are you doing here?" he boomed into my ear.

"Some of your local thugs jumped me the last time I was foolish enough to visit this den of thieves. I came in today for a lineup. Now I would like to use your vast expertise to arrange a table for two at Scoma's on the wharf so that I don't have to fight the tourist horde.''

"Sorry, pal," he said. "I got a conference set up by the boss. I just can't get away.''

"I wasn't thinking of you, you lunkhead. I'm taking the other witness.''

"Knowing you, I bet it's a female and that she's something to look at.''

"You're right, she is," I said, watching her.

She flushed slightly, turning away from me to look out the exceedingly dirty windows.

"Who's working your case?" Harold asked.

"Inspector Comerford," I replied. Comerford was now watching me with unwavering intensity.

"Put him on.''

I handed the phone to Comerford, who promptly identified himself with a good deal more energy than he had displayed all morning. He nodded a few times, twice, yes-siring Harold.

Hanging up, he said, "The captain says for you to go right over to Scoma's, they'll have a table for you. The lunch is on him, so don't ask for a bill or you'll be arrested," he recited without the slightest trace of humor. "I'll have everything you need from this end ready by the time you get back."

"Thanks, Inspector. I really appreciate how helpful you've been. I'll mention it to the captain."

"No problem. Glad to help out." He shook my hand with a little more firmness than had been there in the morning.

At Scoma's, the crowd waiting for tables was three deep at the bar, but the maître d' whisked us right into the dining room. We had a table looking out on the wharf, with boats, new and old, moored a shrimp's throw away. Sandra's complexion and eyes merely set off the brilliant blue of the sky, windswept, crystal clear of clouds and pollution.

"I suppose you must be pleased at the way you handled that boy this morning. Are many police officers as skilled as you in breaking down defenses during an interview?"

My fillet of petrale sole suddenly didn't taste so good.

"No," I answered with perfect enunciation.

"You even showed him bandages from the ambush that had nothing to do with the event here. That was clever. It scared him."

"Yeah."

She had ordered a turbot, much too mushy for my taste. Picking at it, she said, "Was Comerford right about there being little likelihood that the boy will be tried as an adult on the assault charge?"

"Probably."

"Yet, you quite skillfully created a psychological climate

built on falsehoods to lead him to give you the information you desired.''

"Yeah."

She sipped at the Geyser Peak Chardonnay I had selected on Lutz. "Does that pose any ethical conflicts for you?"

"No."

"That's interesting," she continued, daintily forking a piece of fish into her lovely mouth. "How do you reconcile the image you project so strongly of moral righteousness with your techniques of lying and inducing fear in a young boy held in confinement? It was a terribly unequal contest, you know."

"Wait a minute. He had a lot more going for him than you realize. For one thing, he had absolutely no physical fear of me. He's got great experience. He showed some of it when he put the con on you before he realized I was a cop. Also, confinement to someone like you and me can be frightening. A kid like him isn't that disturbed by it. He eats better and lives cleaner when the Youth Authority's got him than when he's roaming the streets. And all I did, really, was help him do what he wanted to do in the first place, give up the strong-arm guy.''

"Really?" she asked, her beautiful green eyes momentarily catching the reflection of the green harbor water. "It didn't seem to me he was all that willing to tell you what you wanted to know."

"He wasn't. In fact, automatically he would have obstructed the police. Only when he saw some possible advantage for himself did he start looking for a way to work it out."

"I'm not sure I understand."

"Forget about the myth of honor among thieves. It may happen occasionally, but it's so rare as to be almost nonexistent. We're deluged with crooks willing to put their colleagues in the can by giving us information in return for some favor for themselves. This kid was able to give the other guy up almost instantly. In fact, he's more than a little ticked off to realize he himself got conned into something.''

"Then why didn't he?" she challenged. "You had to work on him for almost an hour to get him to talk."

"Only because it took me that long to realize his stick."

"His stick? And we're accused of jargon. What does that mean?"

"Oh, it's really their word and has shades of meaning. What I meant is his motivation or concern. Once I tumbled to that, the rest was easy."

"Easy? I'm a psychologist, but I'm lost. What made him suddenly cooperate?"

"He was afraid of the strong-arm guy, afraid that if he gave him up, the guy would come after him. There's no Miranda warnings, lawyers, or appeals on the street. The sentence is carried out quickly and without mercy. He was actually feeling me out as much as I was working him. Once he was reassured, he gave him up without hesitation."

"Reassured of what?" she asked.

"Reassured that I would kill the person he was informing on," I said, looking straight into her eyes.

She winced, as the truth of the morning hit her. We finished the meal in silence, leaving a half bottle of Chardonnay that deserved better.

Twenty-two

IT WAS 1530 HOURS BEFORE WE WERE BACK IN THE SAN Francisco cop shop. Comerford was as good as his word. He presented me with the affidavits, establishing, we hoped, probable cause to believe that one John Doe, suspected of attempted murder as per Section 187 of the California Penal Code, as well as armed robbery, Section 211 of the California Penal Code, was residing in the dwelling located at 3244 Dwyer Street, Daly City, in the county of San Mateo, state of California. I signed the affidavits. A messenger took them for immediate delivery to the cops waiting at the presiding judge's chambers at San Mateo Superior Court. It was nice to have Harold Lutz around to expedite things.

Meanwhile, I knew my pre-lunch phone call to Raoul Chavez had by now reached Louis, and someone from our shop would be watching the house, ready to accompany the Daly City police when they hit the place. I guessed that would be within the next hour and that our representative would be either the Block or English, or both.

Comerford tossed a mug shot and criminal history record sheet at me. "Junior diligently searched our files and selected this winner for your approval. Don't ask me what the odds are whether or not he happens to be telling the truth this cycle of the moon.''

The same point had been troubling me. I had vivid recollections of my attacker's fist wrapped in brass knuckles as it bounced off my skull, his pointed boot as it bounced off my ribs, and his left ear as I spit the tip of it onto the sidewalk, but I had never gotten a good enough look at his face to identify him. I knew Sandra was in the same boat. So I wasn't overly charged up about Roy Graham's picking someone for us, thinking we didn't have much choice but to take it on faith. Thirteen years of dealing with people like him hadn't left me with lots of leftover faith.

The picture showed an ugly, heavyset character with hard eyes. Name: Felix George, aka George Stevens, and my eyes froze on the third alias: George Bosco. I took the material from Comerford for our file, mechanically thanking him. We rode down the elevator while I tried to come to grips with the information supplied by our young purse snatcher. I had the familiar feeling that I just couldn't handle what was going on. This character had watched me with Sandra's children at the beach. Fifty miles away, Bini had died violently within two hours of checking his name through the state's computer system. Then two hundred miles north in Sacramento, someone had used a hell of a lot of clout and effort to erase any trace of the inquiries. Two days later, one George Bosco approaches two punks in San Francisco, entices them to snatch Sandra's purse, and tries to off me under cover of the larceny.

The magnitude of it was beyond me.

''What's wrong, Fraleigh?'' Sandra asked, looking at me sharply.

I started to tell her, but suddenly she, too, was suspect. How had this bum known my movements, both at her house and here in the city? Where were the print-outs? How much else did she know? I looked into her clear green eyes, filled with concern, and stayed cautious. "Nothing, my shoulder is bothering me. I guess I'm not as ready for duty as I thought I was," I told her, walking to the car.

"Yes. I was wondering about that. How could they put you back on full duty so soon? Didn't you just get out of the hospital this morning?"

"How did you know that?" I asked.

She flushed slightly and her mouth tightened in a way I had never seen before. "Louis mentioned it to me when he called. Aren't you supposed to give me the Miranda warnings if I'm under suspicion?" she asked.

"I'm sorry. Look, I really feel lousy. Would you mind driving?"

"Yes, I would," she said.

I shrugged, turning the key in the ignition. Come to think of it, I didn't feel that well. I had asked her to drive because I wanted to be free to look around. If I had been alone, I would have had my gun in my hand. They had missed me twice. Hoping for a third screw-up was pressing my luck.

Nervously, I almost clipped a pedestrian who, normally enough for San Francisco, had started to cross the street just as the light turned green for us. Then, on the other side of the intersection, a cab startled me by shooting sideways toward us. Wrenching the wheel, I slammed on the brakes, grabbing for my magnum.

A wide-eyed cabdriver finished cutting in front of me, wondering what things were coming to when a little normal cutting and speeding provoked such reactions.

Sandra's eyes were wide. "All right, for God's sake. I'll drive. I've never seen you like this. What is wrong with you?"

"Someone is determined to kill me," I said more dramatically than intended.

"Are you sure it isn't you?" she asked, taking the wheel.

The silence had grown between us to the point where it seemed a third passenger was in the car. She drove purposely, eyes straight ahead. Mine roved nervously. I had cranked the mirror on my side so that I could keep an eye on traffic behind us. Every once in a while, I glanced out her side, checking cars moving to pass us. I unsuccessfully tried not to look at her when doing it. Her flowing hair set off the clean-featured profile and her smell taunted me with memories of our lovemaking. The pain deepened in my stomach.

She pulled the car into the curb in front of her house, significantly avoiding the driveway. She didn't even turn the ignition off, getting out of the car without looking at me and heading for the house. It was quite an uninvitation, and I cowardly wanted to take it, to jump behind the wheel and flee.

Instead, I called, "Sandra, aren't you going to invite me in for a drink?" My voice sounded funny, choked behind the lump that had formed in my throat. Turning off the ignition, I followed her. She hadn't paused to answer my question, but the sound of my car door closing stopped her.

With a look of contempt that shot downward with unerring accuracy to the pain in my stomach, she said, "No, and you don't want a drink, either, do you?"

"There are things we should talk about," I replied, avoiding the question. "How about inviting me in for a few minutes? I'd like at least to say hello to the kids."

There was fury in the green eyes now. "You're not welcome here. You don't even know who you are, and I certainly don't, either."

"What's all that about?" I asked, keeping my distance. Her anger was almost a solid force between us.

"I think you know very well what it's all about. You can't have it two ways—come here as a warm, loving man, share my bed, take my children"—here she sobbed before catching hold of her voice again—"to the beach, working your way into their hearts—and all the time, you're really a cop, a spy in our home, you bastard.''

I couldn't get any words past the lump in my throat. The impulse to run, to get in the car and drive away, was almost overwhelming. Instead, I followed her into the house.

I stood in the foyer while she disappeared. I knew somehow that going to look for the children would have been a mistake, as much as I wanted to see them. I moved into the living room, sat down on the sofa, and looked out toward the backyard through the picture window. It was growing dark. The rush-hour traffic had lengthened the drive back to over two hours.

She returned and sat directly opposite me, avoiding the sofa for a straight-backed chair. I wanted to reason with her. To recover some of our feelings for each other. To convince her that it hadn't been cop-spy stuff or anything like that between us, and she had to know it. Instead, I heard myself saying, ''I need those print-outs, Sandra.''

''Produce a search warrant or get out, Fraleigh.''

But her voice was exhausted, without any emotion or conviction.

''This isn't a game; it's a homicide investigation. People are in danger of getting knocked off, including me. You can't just pretend not to be involved. Your husband put those entries in his journal, not me.''

''You at least gave that boy the Miranda warnings. Is it because I loved you that I'm not entitled to them?''

''You have the right to remain silent. Anything you say can and will be used against you in a court of law. You have the right to talk to a lawyer and have him present with you while you are being questioned. If you cannot afford to hire a lawyer, one will be appointed to represent you before any questioning, if you wish one.'' Her eyes widened as I finished the warnings, and she was sobbing by the time I shut up.

"Go get those print-outs, Sandra. I want them. And while you're doing it, think of some answers to questions like, What was Don's relationship to Stone? How come their hit man knew every move I made over here? And you, sweetheart, if I was a cop in bed, what were you? You're sitting on plenty of information in this case that somehow you never let out in all of your tender moments with me."

Something had shattered with those words. I felt sinking loneliness, the worst kind, the deep-in-the-gut realization that I had been lonely before her without knowing it, but now would never forget it.

I don't know how we got into each other's arms, but I was stroking her hair, shushing her sobs, wondering what would happen next between us. It didn't seem possible that either of us could undo the suspicions, the bitterness, could unsay the words that had cut so deeply.

Then the glass shattered. The sound of the shot seemed to reach me a split second later. Probably a 30-30 rifle, I thought, sweeping a screaming Sandra off her feet and under me as two more shots sounded. From the floor, I made noise back, with my magnum, at the muzzle flash I had caught from the backyard. The picture window had vanished with the first shot, so my return fire was unimpeded. Not that it mattered. I hadn't even time to line up a sight picture, and Sandra's screaming movement as I pinned her protectively didn't help my steadiness. But something was terribly wrong. Even the world's worst marksman shouldn't have missed with a rifle at the twenty-yard or so distance from which the shot had come.

I fired more deliberately at the next muzzle flash, thinking that I had better hold my three remaining rounds in case they charged the house. The first two shots from outside had smacked into the wall behind us with resounding thuds. I tried to figure out why the third one was different as my eyes searched the darkness outside. Suddenly, the roof caved in on my head and I slipped into dark unconsciousness, thinking, my God, Sandra sapped me from behind. But my last thoughts were that she couldn't have, she's under me, pinned down. Then, with a childish pleasure that my nerve wasn't gone, I passed out.

Twenty-three

IT WAS THE BUZZING THAT AWOKE ME. WHATEVER DREAMS I had been enjoying vanished, leaving me with a colossal headache. When I opened my eyes, they were applauding. About ten of them, in their white jacket uniforms, happily clapping their hands and smiling. Obnoxious seemed to be pack leader. When I saw what he thought passed for a smile, I closed my eyes again.

There was some tittering. My head felt as if it were exploding. I ran my fingers lightly over a massive turban of bandages and one of those neck braces sold by lawyers specializing in whiplash lawsuits.

One of the white coat tribe had nice brown eyes, I observed, as Obnoxious began his monologue. She smiled at me as his high-pitched voice continued, "The outpatient treatment was successful until the patient engaged in some rough-and-tumble physical combat, receiving new injuries." En masse, they turned to the exit. Dr. Brown-Eyes had nice legs, I noticed. She trailed the group. Turning, she noticed me noticing and gave me a very lewd wink. No wonder the medical care was so bad here—the staff had its mind on other things.

I woke up. The Block and English were sitting motionless, watching me.

"Well?" I demanded. "How's Sandra?"

"She wasn't injured," Paul answered. "You did your usual John Wayne bit, covering her so completely that when the chandelier got shot away, it crashed down on your head. She was shook but unhurt."

"What I don't understand is why, at this point, they were only trying to scare us. They certainly have been playing for keeps up until now."

"Scare you? You're something else, Fraleigh," the Block grated in his truck-horn voice. "I guess you still think the San Francisco bit was a purse snatch and Bini a hit and run?"

"Wait a minute. No one with a rifle could have missed at that range. We'd be dead if they hadn't been just throwing a scare."

Paul said, "We checked the scene quite thoroughly because the same question bothered us. Finally, we realized what it was. The glass doors in front, combined with the hanging mirror behind you, created just the slightest optical illusion for the rifleman where he was standing. When we reenacted the crime, it appeared that you and Sandra were six inches taller than you actually were."

I didn't want to listen to what he was saying next.

"The holes torn in the wall behind you by the thirty-thirty slugs were exactly six inches higher than where we measured your heads were after interviewing Sandra. The third round was aimed lower and hit the chandelier."

"Does she know this?"

"You know the law, Fraleigh. We can't withhold information indicating a person may be in danger."

"How did she react when you told her?"

"It's hard to say," Paul answered. "She seems to be in a state of shock. Not panicky, but . . ." He trailed off.

We were all silent for a few minutes. Paul had a manila envelope under his arm.

"What's in the envelope, Paul, ballistics evidence?"

"No. We weren't sure how you'd be, so I brought this stuff along, just in case."

"Well, do I have to guess, or what?" I asked impatiently when he made no move to share the material.

"You really look like hell, Fraleigh. Maybe you ought to cool it for a few days, or even a few weeks. Maybe take a vacation."

A vacation. I almost got knocked off the last time I took a vacation. Paul just looked at me, unintimidated by my glare. It probably wasn't much of a glare at that. I didn't have much left. There had never been a case like this. I bounced from one injury to another and then got subjected to the tender ministrations of Obnoxious, Battle-Ax, and the staff of this asylum.

"Look, if I can survive these sadists around here for a couple of days, I'll recover. But if we don't break this case soon, I'm not sure that any of us is going to live that much longer. We've been lucky so far. It can't last forever."

"Yes, I guess," he said, handing me the package.

It was too light to be weapons or ballistics evidence. I balanced it in my hands before opening the flap.

"We hit Bosco's pad in Daly City last night. This is from there."

"And him?"

"No sign," Paul shrugged.

Looking at the first few photographs tumbling out as I turned the envelope upside down, I was disappointed. It was porn material. Pictures of young girls and boys with older men. It reminded me of my days on the Vice Squad. There had been a rash of child pornography. The sale of movies showing explicit sex acts between children and adults had been hot stuff then. The legislature had even passed a tough law on it, over the lukewarm objection from ACLU and libertarian types. Yet it had been movies that caused the uproar, not old-fashioned snapshots.

One of the photos from the middle of the pile slid toward the edge of my bed table. I caught it before it fell to the floor. Putting it back with the others, I glanced at it, then stared hard.

"Holy shit! Why the hell didn't you tell me who was in this?"

"You didn't ask," the Block answered.

I turned back to the picture. It showed a middle-aged man, wearing only his distinguished silver-gray hair, with an intense, almost pained look on his face. On her knees in front of him, an equally naked young girl of maybe eleven or twelve, I judged from her just barely formed breasts, was orally copulating him—Fred Casey, the lieutenant governor of California, strongly favored to be our next governor.

This wasn't child porn; it was a neutron bomb for the careers of those who had appeared on someone's candid camera. I recognized a few more members of our state legislature and surmised that the other men's pictures would be found among the gallery of our state assemblymen and senators. The blackmail potential of it was staggering, I thought, evaluating the pictures more closely. They appeared to have been taken from hidden cameras placed at different angles. They were all of the same location, a room with brightly colored, almost psychedelic walls, and a huge round bed. Most just contained a child and man, but some had group activities. In about five of the shots, the participants were sniffing a fine, white powder, no doubt cocaine hydrochloride.

In one, the blurred figure of a man fondling a child caught my attention. There's something familiar about him, I determined, placing the picture back on the pile, going to the next, only to turn back to it again. Without comment, Paul handed me a magnifying glass.

"Oh, my God," I moaned, "it's the Zombie. I don't believe it."

"You can believe it. That's his skinny ass, all right," the Block confirmed.

"What did he say about all this?" I asked.

"Nothing. Nobody's seen him since he took a leave of absence right after we got hurt," the Block told me.

What had Louis said not too long ago? The squad was short us, Bini, and the Zombie. I hadn't asked him about the Zombie, assuming it was routine sick time or something.

I stared numbly at the picture, the sickness of it overwhelming me. Somehow, Adolph Stone was behind this. I hardly noticed the Battle-Ax surging into the room.

"Well, well. I see you're recovered, not that I thought you were really anything more than lazy and just putting on an act. O.K., let's go," she said, starting to lift me from the bed again.

Paul and the Block were smiling.

"Leave me alone, you witch!" I yelled at her.

As usual, nothing deterred this madwoman. Once again she wrestled her arm around my waist. "It will do you a world of good, you know," she gushed, looking down at the pictures as she pulled me out of bed.

"My lord," she gasped, letting me fall back onto the bed so hard that it sent all kinds of new pains shooting through me.

"The filth of it! I can't believe it. You, a policeman! You're a pervert. I knew all along that there was something wrong with you." She turned, glaring at the Block and English, bent double with laughter, then stormed out of the room.

I lay back on the bed, totally drained, out of it.

"Why don't I do some library research on Casey and give Eric Stone a try? We'll come back tomorrow, if you can fit us in," Paul suggested.

I nodded my head weakly in agreement. I needed about two solid weeks of sleep.

"I'll go after Bosco. Do some surveillance, O.K.?" asked the Block.

"Only if you promise not to try to take him by yourself."

"Sure, no problem," he agreed.

I didn't like his agreement. He might be smarting over getting shot, hoping for a dramatic comeback pinch to show all of us he hadn't lost anything. I cursed my helplessness.

"Block, as a favor to me, O.K.? I want to be there when we take the son of a bitch. You'd feel the same way, wouldn't you?"

I could almost hear the wheels clicking as he pondered that.

"I said, 'O.K.,' " he muttered.

But this time I believed him. He had been looking forward to producing Bosco for us with a touch of bravado.

The phone jarred me out of a restless, drugged sleep.

"Hello," I grumbled.

"I'm sorry," the hospital operator said, "it's against hospital rules to put any calls through after ten-thirty P.M." I looked at my watch. It was 0330 hours. "But the man said it was life or death, and he's one of your team of policemen," she hesitated.

"Put him on, please."

"Fraleigh?"

"No, Dr. Kildare. Who the hell did you ask for?"

"Grouch, grouch, grouch. Here I been breaking my ass while you sleep and you give me a hard time."

"I'm sorry, Block, it was nice of you to call to see how I was doing."

"Very funny. Listen, I got Bosco under surveillance. He's holed up near the railroad yards. I already called Paul. He's gonna pick you up in ten minutes outside the emergency room entrance. The rest of the joint is locked up."

I was wide awake now. "Hey, Block. Wait for us, O.K.? If he splits, follow him if you can, but don't worry about it if he loses you. We know where we can find him," I invented.

"You do? Then what the hell have I been knocking myself out for? You're lying, Fraleigh. You just want to take him yourself 'cause he tried to snuff you. I already told you I'd wait."

"I appreciate it, Block. I really do. I'll see you soon."

I quickly dressed in my street clothes. One of the nurses at the hall station gasped as she saw me walking toward the elevators. Battle-Ax, bent over her reports, looked up and shrieked.

"See you at breakfast, sweetheart," I leered, watching closely to see if she was going to have a stroke. The elevator arrived before it came to pass.

Paul was waiting outside the emergency room. I fought off some dizziness opening the car door. Sliding into the seat, I urged, "Let's step on it, Paul. The Block is thick. I don't want him taking on Bosco without us. I'm not sure he's completely recovered from being shot in the ambush."

"You won't be of much help, Fraleigh. My advice is to let us handle it."

"Just get us there, dammit."

The Block met us some distance from a wooden paint-peeled boardinghouse that couldn't have been any closer to the tracks without getting hit by a locomotive. We talked it over. The consensus was that Paul would take the back and the Block and I the room itself. I retrieved my magnum from the Block, who had reclaimed it from the hospital people. While we waited for English to get into position in the rear, I checked to see if it was loaded, like they do on television. I had just gotten it back into the holster when Bosco suddenly emerged from the front door.

For a moment he looked at us, then ran toward the tracks. The Block took off after him. I yelled for Paul and joined the chase. Within five steps, I was clinging to a lamppost, trying to stop the world from swinging wildly around. Paul was so fast that he was there, grabbing me before I slumped down.

"Help the Block, you idiot."

He turned and sprinted. Bosco had crossed the tracks and was running along a footbridge spanning the main yards one hundred feet below. I couldn't believe my eyes. A freight train almost took the Block as he jumped past it, following Bosco onto the bridge. By the time Paul got there, he had no place to go—the train blocked him.

Desperately, I looked around. The boardinghouse had an outside staircase leading to a second-story porch. Pulling myself together, I managed to climb the stairs. I could see over the train onto the bridge.

A false dawn illuminated Bosco, turning back, stalking the Block. He had realized Paul and I were cut off by the train. What the hell was wrong with the Block? "Shoot him! Shoot him!" I screamed, but the train drowned out my voice. The Block didn't know what a killer he was dealing with. I whipped out my magnum and tried to brace into a firing position, but I just couldn't steady myself enough to get any kind of a decent sight picture. Paul was beside me. He gently took my arm down.

"It's too late. You might hit the Block."

I sagged a bit and Paul put his arm around me, half holding me up. We watched. Bosco led with the same ponderous right hand I remembered. The Block had at least a half an hour to get out of the way, but he had his own style, as I knew. At the last second, he simply turned his head sharply downward, letting Bosco break his hand on top of an iron skull. I could almost hear Bosco's groans over the freight train noise. Then the Block unleashed his own right. I couldn't explain it scientifically. His punches seemed so ponderous and slow that they couldn't possibly land, and even if they did, they shouldn't have had any umph. But this punch hit Bosco full in the face like a pile driver. Although he was over two hundred pounds, he was propelled backward with such force that he hit the bridge railing and, before our stunned eyes, toppled over, going down a hundred feet. Almost in slow motion, another freight train approached his prone, unmoving body sprawled across the tracks.

I felt the breath go out of Paul as he looked away at the last instant. I sat down on the steps, unable to move.

The Block looked over the rail, then walked slowly toward us. The freight train had passed. "It wasn't my fault, Fraleigh. I know you wanted a piece of him yourself. But you saw it. It wasn't my fault."

"You did good, Block. Don't worry about it. But help me up, would you? I got to get back to the hospital in time for breakfast."

I used the next day in the hospital to rest and plan. It seemed to me that the one chance we had to break through in the case was Casey. Stone wasn't about to even see us. Not that the lieutenant governor would, either, unless we found a way. About 1000 hours, the light bulb lit up. I made a call to Sacramento and by 1400 hours, when English and the Block checked in, I was able to offhandedly tell them we were going to see the lieutenant governor in the morning. As usual, my brilliance was wasted on them. You would have thought there was nothing to arranging an interview to question the second-highest executive in California about various felonies he had committed.

English started to tell me about some of his research findings on Casey. My eyelids were fluttering. "I can brief you on the drive tomorrow," he decided. I didn't argue.

Someone was holding my hand. It wasn't unpleasant. In fact, just before I came fully awake, I realized that it felt pretty good.

"You have the deepest blue eyes."

Dr. Brown-Eyes was taking my pulse. It wasn't quite holding hands, but why quibble? It was nice.

"Yours are a lovely brown," I tried out on her. The sparkle of our dialogue left me groping for something to say.

"Did you really disappear in the middle of the night to visit a girl friend? It's strictly prohibited to leave the hospital, you know." Somehow, her teasing smile undermined the reprimand.

"No, it was nothing like that."

Her raised eyebrows mocked me.

"Really, we went out to arrest a hood. He resisted and got knocked off."

"I bet," she said, scribbling something on my chart. "Take care of yourself, Fraleigh. You're the most interesting specimen . . . er, I mean patient, we have around here. I'm going to have to come back and monitor your progress," she purred, checking over her shoulder to make sure I was monitoring her swishing departure.

I didn't have the heart to tell her that she wouldn't see me again. I planned to leave for Sacramento with the Block and English at 0700 hours and stay healthy for the rest of my life.

Twenty-four

MY HEALTH WASN'T ALL THAT GREAT WHEN I MET THEM
outside the emergency room promptly at 0705. I felt more
aches and pains than were possible for one person. English's
monologue wasn't exactly morale-building, either.

His research showed Casey to be an outstanding former
military man. Before entering politics he had been an officer
in the Korean and Vietnam wars, piling up wounds and a
hero's medals. His refusal to make statements after being
taken prisoner in Vietnam had been widely publicized. It
had made him a hot ticket politically.

He had come up fast and was rumored to be the next governor. The incumbent was believed to be a sure thing to ap-
point himself to the United States Senate seat held by
George Barney. Senator Barney had cancer. He was in a
coma and expected to shuffle off within a few months. Under the state constitution Casey would automatically become
governor.

Looking into Casey's background seemed to have
touched some old problem areas for Paul. His usual cynical

good humor, if that's what it was, had given way to a kind of gloomy despair that we hadn't seen before.

The Block had produced two rap sheets that were very interesting. Raoul Chavez had gone back over the routine name checks that were supposed to have been done by the Zombie. It turned out that Don Fortune had been busted in Santa Cruz two years before on a child-molesting beef. The record didn't show any court disposition. Raoul's telephone digging indicated that some hush money had changed hands and the parents of the child had declined to allow her to testify. It wasn't all that unusual to lose children as witnesses in this type of case. But the investigating dick had implied to Raoul that some big names were involved in what had been described as a groupie drug and sex orgy. The Block had reported the final piece of information without change of expression, but I had turned and looked at him. The parents had mentioned that a female psychologist by the name of Jacoby had advised them that forcing the child to testify might cause irreparable mental damage.

The image of Sandra's doctoral degree hanging proudly on the den wall flashed into my mind with such blinding force that I almost missed what the Block was saying about Phillips.

"What was that about Phillips?"

"Yeah, it's hot shit, if it's the same guy. It seems he did two years in the federal joint for selling defective computer components to the Defense Department and charging them three times for the same crap. But get this. He was chief executive officer of Stone's electronic company. He was the only one charged. The company claimed he was acting on his own, and his lawyers never let him testify or make a statement. So he took the fall. His name then was Bertram Phillips, but it sure sounds like the same asshole running the MRG." I had plenty to think about on our trip to Sacramento.

I wasn't exactly chipper myself, watching the Block maintain his steady sixty to the fury of early-morning commuters rushing to arrive at their electronic company cubbyholes to begin another exciting day's adventure.

"Why don't I go over to the Department of Justice to see what I can find out about the attempt to abort Bini's computer query?" Paul suggested.

"No deal. I want you there when we take on Casey."

Neither the Block nor English was nervous. They had complete faith in me. I was nervous for all of us. It was lunacy. Three lowly dicks, not even on duty, taking on the lieutenant governor of California. The subterfuge necessary to even get us in was weak, preposterous, really, but it was the best I could come up with after racking my brains for days.

Jason Stead was a journalist working for one of the national wire services in Sacramento. After two years in journalism, Jason and everyone else realized he would never win a Pulitzer. Thirty years later, he was still plodding along, steady, dependable, nonthreatening to anyone.

Four years ago, I had risked my job to do him a favor on a homicide case we were working on. His son, Richard, was within two weeks of ordination after divinity school when he had the misfortune to try a last fling. Two hours after he left her, the prostitute he had been with was murdered in a sensational razor-slashing case. I had rather quickly ID'd Richard Stead as the hooker's next-to-last John. Within a few hours and a short interview with him, I knew he played no role in the case.

The D.A., however, who ultimately prosecuted the case, would never have agreed with me, and the boy's life and career would have been ruined. I knew Jason fairly well from when he had been a police reporter with the local newspaper. Without a word to him or anyone, I pulled the material from the case file. It was risky. Sometimes cases blow up.

Preliminary evidence and conclusions turn out to be wrong. I didn't think it would happen in the razor-murder case, but the risk was there, and I would have been hanged for falsifying evidence. Fortunately, the killer copped out and the case faded quickly from view.

A few weeks later, Jason called and insisted on taking me to lunch. The boy had told him everything. The father had been a police reporter long enough to know what I had done. He only mentioned it once on the way back from lunch, telling me that he owed me a big one and not to hesitate to call for it when the time came. I told him to forget it.

I hadn't exactly felt like a champ when I swallowed my own "forget it."

Without cluing him in, I let him know we needed to interview the lieutenant governor and didn't stand a chance unless it was a surprise visit. He got the message quickly but didn't like it when I told him how we needed him.

With his above-reproach reputation from years in the capital, I knew he could set us up as visiting journalists from some nonexistent publication. Had we tried to do it ourselves, we would have been shuffled off to some press secretary, who just might have made verifying phone calls or done something else to shoot down the whole flimsy scheme.

Ironically, the reason Jason didn't like it was what made him perfect. He was a decent, honest guy. Politicians loved him. He never tried for exposés, and they could count on getting good press out of him, since he usually just repeated whatever they told him. As I said, no one ever expected him to win a Pulitzer.

So it was that we appeared at Fred Casey's impressive office. The Block, somewhere, had come up with a camera outfit, which he slung over his shoulder. It looked like an ancient Press Graphic to me, but most people are so intimidated by technology of any kind, I assumed we'd get by.

And he certainly wouldn't be taking any pictures with the thing.

We had a hairy moment when I spotted the state cop on guard as security in the outside office.

"I know him. Try to block his view of me," I whispered to Paul. I needn't have bothered. He was deeply engrossed in a *Playboy* magazine, barely looking up, as I, with my back to him, gave the secretary the information about our appointment.

"The lieutenant governor will see you now. He has a conference in an hour, so he's taking you right on time. Do you know how long your interview will take?"

"That's entirely up to him, ma'am," I replied truthfully.

She ushered us in. The office was huge, lined with handsome mahogany paneling and bookshelves stacked with expensively bound, virginal law books.

Casey, behind the desk, was as recognizable with his clothes on. He looked a little haggard, but managed a statesmanlike greeting. He must have been just over fifty. His expensive suit did well in minimizing some of the ravages of expense-account meals in good restaurants. It was uncanny how like Stone he was. Not physically, but in the cloak of affluence, power, assurance; yet there was the slightest trace of fear there, lurking deep behind his smiling blue eyes, and a touch of uncertainty that I had never sensed in Stone.

"It was a little tight fitting you in, but Jason Stead is a hard guy to say no to. That's an odd-looking camera." He smiled at the Block, who ignored him. "Well," he asked, a little uncertainly, looking away from the Block toward me, "do you plan on using a lot of pictures?"

"Just these, Governor," I said, casually tossing several snapshots of him and the children on the desk.

He picked them up, looked, and dropped them as if they were hot.

"I don't understand," he said, eyes narrowing.

"Governor, we're police officers. You have the right to remain silent, the right to an attorney," I intoned, conspicuously placing the pocket recorder in front of him on the desk as I finished the Miranda warnings.

He swiveled in his chair and for a long moment stared silently at the lush greenery outside his window. Then he turned back to us.

"I'm aware of my legal rights. I don't really have to answer your questions. I wasn't so fortunate in Vietnam. There, the questions had to be answered one way or another." The lieutenant governor was trying to decide whether or not to talk to us.

"I remember you at the Nang Compound, Colonel. You gave all of us something to live for," Paul said.

Casey, for the first time, looked closely at Paul. "You were there? Yes, you were. I can see it in your eyes," he sighed.

English continued, but pain was evident in his voice. "They caught me trying to escape too. I know what you must have gone through."

Paul's comment had stirred Casey. He and Paul sat silently, oblivious now to the Block and myself. It was eerie. Mentally, they were both reliving a period of evil hell, sharing a rapport that left us on the outside. A chill swept through me as I imagined the memories of torture and suffering flowing through them.

"And I became a politician and you a policeman." He was looking at Paul with sympathy. "Once more your sense of duty is causing you pain. This time because you are required to confront me with my disgrace."

"I'll be in the parking lot." I had never seen Paul so agitated. I nodded my agreement and he left. He hadn't wanted to be here for this. I felt lousy about insisting, but he had done his job. Casey was ready to talk. I was in a cold sweat.

It hadn't been pleasant watching, but I needed Casey's information.

"I came into the business late, you know."

We omitted telling him that we did. Paul's research had been complete. Casey really didn't want to answer anyway.

"It was all so foolish, so naïve, thinking you can do something, make a difference. The most crushing thing after you get here," he mused, "is that no one really cares. The public is oblivious. It's not entirely their fault; government is so complicated, there are so many low-visibility decisions. After a while, the prison-camp syndrome begins to haunt you. Who will ever really know that you make decisions based on principle? You see many of your colleagues, and it often seems the most popular ones succeed because they are totally amoral. You learn quickly that money is the oil of the political engine. Enlightened political movements need just as much lubrication to run."

Casey stood and walked to the bookcase. Turning to face us, he continued, "That's where Stone got me. Men like him are always circling, looking for an opportunity, gradually enlarging their sphere of influence until you have to deal with them or not do business at all. Have you ever thought what it takes to get a piece of legislation passed? People think that we find out what the public wants and do it. Actually that rarely is a factor. Even when it is, the backers of a particular piece of legislation have to deal with the committee controlling the bill, then the assembly and house leaders, not to mention the governor, of course. And all along the way, any vested interest group can sink your bill, sometimes even where the public mandate is clear and overwhelming. Let me give you an example."

I found myself hoping that it would contain something specific about Adolph Stone. I wondered about the secretary's comment on his next appointment.

Casey went through a long-winded description of how he

had tried to help a school for retarded children avoid some of the red tape of licensing, and so on. It was then he learned that his colleagues only played ball when you had something to offer them in return. In the end, it was Adolph Stone's influence that pushed through a bill exempting the school from some regulations it couldn't comply with.

"So you see, my first meeting with Stone was delightful. He was educated, sensitive to the school's plight, and actually produced. It took a long time to realize how truly evil the man was, a genius at intrigue and manipulation."

The lieutenant governor went on, telling us how a month later, when the legislature was in a battle over authorizing oil, gas, and mineral exploration in certain reserved areas, he had put together enough opposition votes to defeat the measure. Stone had been pushing for the right to explore, and Casey had waited uneasily for his call asking him to back off in repayment for help on the school bill, but the call never came. And the exploration bill went down to defeat.

"The point of the story is that this year, I sponsored the legislation to open up the land that we had protected two years ago. That's how Stone works." He nodded toward the pictures. "Oh, he was good enough to make up some inane reasons why I had changed my position in case anyone asked. No one did, by the way. They can be quite clever around here, moving extremely profound legislation through without it attracting much attention."

"How did it happen, Governor?" I brought him gently back.

"It sounds trite, I suppose, but we get very lonely here. Almost all of us live elsewhere. Election to the state legislature is almost as famous for breaking up marriages and families as election to Washington. There's more to it, naturally. But you'd be surprised how many good men—and I have to say women, too—in the legislature get compromised simply by the socializing they get into. Some of them don't hesitate about accepting the inevitable sexual and other favors offered by lobbyists. They aren't the ones I'm talking about. I don't care about those who consciously sell out. It's the others, ensnared by Stone or someone else. Those people I have some feeling for. I ought to. I got trapped the same way.

"Stone was a master entertainer. He had ties with Hollywood. Small dinner parties, prominent people in attendance. It was easy to drift into thinking it was all right. After all, with a little too much to drink and attractive young women who were eager bed partners for important politicians . . . We lived in an adult age, don't we? What adults do is their own business, isn't it? So the rationalization went. We avoided thinking about what happened when Stone called and politely made his pitch on some legislation. You see, he was polite. People deceived themselves that they were voting their conscience. And lots of people of importance get through to us. So what was so wrong if Adolph Stone called once in a while?"

We stayed silent, and he went on, "What was wrong was that underneath Stone's offering the latest fashions in sexual liberation, he had patiently suckered key politicians into going further and further. They, in turn, were used to entrap others. For example, the Senate majority leader introduced me to Stone. The man's dead now, supposedly an accidental fall from a cliff while mountain climbing. There were rumors that he couldn't live with what happened after he was introduced to cocaine by Stone."

"I can't believe that none of this reached the news media, Governor," I interrupted.

"Oh, it did. But you understand the blackmail part wasn't known. The rest of it was merely titillating private eccentricities of politicians—subjects for reporters' enjoyment, but not for publication. That would violate the peculiar code of privacy that the media embrace when it comes to sexual practices.''

"Even sex with children was protected?'' I asked.

"Yes. Even with children,'' he finally answered, after a long, anguished pause.

"Not that it changes or excuses anything, but you have to understand that most of these incidents with children occurred after Stone had disarmed us over a long period of time. Stone was adept at providing fine-quality cocaine and other drugs after guests had already had too much alcohol. I've found that I'm not that unusual in not remembering clearly all that happened. But most important of all, everyone knew that the mere surfacing of the pictures anywhere in a politician's home district was tantamount to political oblivion and personal hell. Then, too, you seem to forget that many media people had their own little games and were quite tolerant, as a group, of what others did. Maybe they weren't that different from us in not wanting to face the evil engulfing us.

"Stone, not surprisingly, is my strongest supporter for governor,'' he told us. "You may not believe me, but even if you men hadn't come, I was going to at least cheat him out of that triumph.''

Something had been bothering me. "Governor, we're not in any way contesting your version of this, but nevertheless, it seems pretty extreme to set up something like this just to create some lobbying clout.''

"That's only because you don't know that in the next session of the legislature, Stone plans a series of bills that will net his different conglomerates six billion dollars in various mineral development rights and approval of commercial and residential coastal housing projects, along with some changes in banking statutes.''

"Six billion?'' The Block whistled.

"Six billion,'' Casey repeated. "Does that help explain

why he went through four years of elaborate development of the Moral Reaffirmation Guild? Sexy pictures of consenting adults simply wouldn't have provided enough umph to pull a rip-off like that: the most massive steal in the history of California.''

Another Stone lie. He had just about convinced us that he hated Phillips and the MRG. Now it turned out that he had founded and nourished the movement for his own sex kicks as well as its blackmail value. It came back to me what Eric Stone had told me in the hospital about his father's deviousness.

"What can you tell us about MRG, sir?'' I prodded.

"Just that Stone brought me there, under pretty strong compulsion. It was after he had allowed me a glimpse of those snapshots. I didn't have much strength left after I saw them. When he insisted I accompany him to this so-called youth project, I went. What I saw brought me back to the Vietnamese prison camps.

"They were conditioning those youngsters. You know the formula: long sessions of silence, no sleep, little food, then constant chanting, et cetera. They were taught to sit staring into each other's eyes for hours without speaking or moving. A standard disorientation technique. They became willing workers for his entertainment sessions in Sacramento and elsewhere. And the man in charge is a psychopath if I ever saw one! The whole thing was monstrous. The day I was there, he and Stone almost killed each other. I wish to God that they had.''

"Could you tell us more about that, Governor?'' I asked, hiding my eagerness.

"Yes. It seemed, incredibly, that Guy Phillips had actually been providing young children to Stone's assistant to attack sexually while he filmed the events. When he showed us one of the films, Stone became furious. He actually hit Phillips with a hammer. Phillips screamed that he would destroy him. Then Stone said a strange thing. He threatened Phillips with the police. Something to the effect that he would put the cops on him. It seemed to have an astonishing impact on the man. He calmed down, apologizing to Stone, but there was no mistaking the hatred between them.''

''The man in the film, what did he look like, Governor?''

''Rugged, handsome in a way, Sergeant. Phillips called him by name. I don't remember''—he frowned—''but Stone told Phillips he'd kill him if he didn't leave Don alone.''

''Could the last name have been Fortune, Governor?''

''Yes, that was it, Don Fortune.''

''What else do you remember about the commune?'' I encouraged when he drifted into a deep silence.

''What?'' he started. ''Oh, yes, of course, you men need information.''

''How many kids did you see in camp that day?''

''There must have been about thirty youngsters and as many adults. Probably some were parents of the children. They were all lethargic, zombielike. They weren't . . .'' He hesitated.

''Engaged in any sexual activities,'' I helped out.

''Correct. As I mentioned, I recognized that what was going on was an exercise in mind control. When I put two and two together, Stone's use of them for sex and blackmail, the man's evil hit me like a sledgehammer. I haven't been the same since.''

''One question, sir. No offense, but it seems a little preposterous that Stone could entrap the whole legislature—the mere numbers, the turnover in office and all . . .'' I prompted.

''I didn't make myself clear. Stone probably didn't actually use the children against more than a half dozen or so, but they were people in key positions of influence in the legislature to help him with his legislative schemes. They could indicate to him who needed more lobbying. You see, he had a wide range of influence by utilizing the standard lobbying techniques. In addition, he sometimes used outright bribery or other illegal methods. Remember, the process itself is one in which, if you are perceived to have power, you have it."

"I don't get it," I interrupted.

"Well, think about the example I gave you with the school. Stone was known as someone who could help move legislation. In turn, you would be expected to support his measures. The public may be shocked by this, but it's routine. Government would halt tomorrow if these techniques weren't used."

That might not be so bad at that, I thought, asking him, "Why so many kids in the camp? It must have been an expensive operation for the relatively sparse use of the kids that you're describing."

"I'm not sure I know the answer to that, although there is some indication that they also supplied children to the Hollywood and Las Vegas markets. It's apparently a thriving business. It may explain why Stone was always able to arrange that celebrities be present at his parties, the subtle threat of disclosure. And I'm sure the fees more than made up for any expenses. They treated the children very poorly, from what I saw at the camp. It couldn't have cost them much."

Exhaustion and strain were evident on his face. "Governor, one last thing, you wrote a letter for Stone to our city asking for police assistance in locating his daughter. How did that happen?"

"Wrote? Signed, you mean. We returned to Stone's home from camp. He was still incensed over Phillips. I think Stone was scared of him. It's logical. Stone is an intelligent man. No doubt he recognized that Phillips was a psychopath and consequently dangerous and uncontrollable. He wrote the letter and asked me to sign it. Not that I had much choice, of course, but Stone is clever in not directly wielding his power over people."

"For example? With the letter, I mean?" I needed more on this. Something was missing.

"Well, instead of just telling me to sign it, he explained that Phillips was unbalanced, dangerous to the children in camp, but had a pathological fear of the police because of a past criminal record of child molesting. If we sent officers to question him, it would keep him in line."

Incredible. Stone had reported his daughter missing, knowing that when we went to the MRG camp we might well find her and Judy Fortune present. He knew we would ultimately learn of Phillips's record, not for child abuse as he had told Casey, but for theft. He knew Phillips was vulnerable and scared of cops because he had been in the joint. Stone would probably have been delighted to have seen Phillips pull a gun and get blown away or even busted by us for drugs, kidnapping, sex offenses, or whatever. But just our appearance and grilling of Phillips would have made him putty in Stone's hands thereafter. Adolph couldn't lose, or so he figured.

"Can you tell me how you came into possession of those pictures?" Casey was asking.

"As a result of your letter and Adolph Stone's report that his daughter was missing, we were assigned to the case. We never actually got to Phillips for a variety of reasons, the most important of which being that someone tried to knock us off in an ambush. We ended up in a hospital."

"Good God!" he said with a sick look on his face. "I was almost responsible for your being killed."

Casey was in enough trouble. I let him off the hook.

"Not really, Governor."

"But who actually tried to kill you?"

"That we haven't completely figured out yet," I told him. "Oh, we know who the hit men were—mob button men of no importance and, fortunately for us, of not much skill, either. But they're both dead, so we can't question them to find out for sure who put out the contract. Although we suspect Stone, we can't figure his motive. And another puzzle is why would the mob start hitting cops? It's not their M.O.''

He stroked his chin thoughtfully. ''Has it ever occurred to you that they didn't realize you were police officers?''

I looked at him. ''What?''

He continued, ''You have to know Adolph Stone to know how devious he can be. It's quite possible that he lied to them, told them you were rival gangsters or something . . .'' Casey paused. ''Not that I'm in any way implying that you men look the type.''

Not much, but I guess it was no worse than being mistaken for terrorists. Casey had provided an intriguing explanation. Instinctively, I found myself accepting it. Yet there was a problem with it. ''But what would happen when they found out they had rubbed out cops? The boys can get a little angry at being fooled.''

Casey didn't answer me immediately. ''Knowing Stone, he probably assumed they wouldn't be that unhappy as long as they weren't traced to it, and he was their goose laying golden eggs. They had a major share in the six-billion-dollar windfall. They couldn't afford to retaliate against him.''

Not right away, maybe, but Stone would have learned the hard way that the mob eventually cut people out with their own unique gusto. On the other hand, he hadn't been successful in hitting us. More important, his whole scheme with the legislature was as dead as the hoods, now that we had exposed it.

Casey's thoughts must have been running along the same lines.

''He may well be in some jeopardy when they come to realize that the scheme has been exposed,'' he speculated.

"As far as we know, they're still in blissful ignorance, and Stone won't be in any hurry to tell them," I said.

"No. I'm sure he won't be." He stroked his chin.

"Anyway, Governor, the pictures were in the possession of a muscle man. He's no longer with us, as I mentioned, so we don't know why he had them."

There was an awkward quiet. We had run out of questions and Casey was far, far away.

"I'm sorry, Colonel," I told him as we got up to leave. He showed no sign of noticing our departure.

Twenty-five

"LET'S EAT. IT'S A LONG DRIVE BACK."

If the Block had said it, I would have regarded it as strictly routine. But it was English.

We avoided the Capitol Mall with its unsavory cast of characters. They were almost a match for the politicians. We selected a quiet sandwich shop a few streets from the freeway entrance.

The Block ordered two beers and three hamburgers with "everything." The waitress wrote the order and started to walk away.

"Hey, ain't you going to take their orders?" he asked.

"You're each having a hamburger, right?" she answered.

"Naw. Those are for me. These guys can order their own food."

"You're gonna eat three jumbo burgers by yourself?" she asked.

Shaking her head, she turned to me.

"Just coffee."

"Fraleigh, you got to eat something; you didn't even have breakfast," the Block complained.

I tried to remember. We had stopped on the road early. The Block had ordered corned beef hash and poached eggs. Along with that, he devoured two baskets of muffins and toast, much to the disgust of the waitress. I had managed some orange juice and coffee. Now I didn't even want coffee. It was just something to occupy myself with while the Block did his thing.

"You better have something, Fraleigh. You've lost about ten pounds since that last trip to the hospital," Paul said.

I was used to the Block's criticisms leveled against Paul and myself for our unhealthy eating habits, but English, the health nut, urging consumption of high-caloric, high-cholesterol food was strange. Very strange. Rather than argue, I ordered a hamburger and picked at it. English slowly consumed a tuna fish salad concoction, while we both tried without success to ignore the noises the Block was making and the curious stares from other customers.

"What will you do, Fraleigh?" Paul asked.

"I don't know. I guess the first thing we do is brief Louis. Then take it to Judge Leary. There's no doubt we have probable cause against Stone and the politicians on sex charges."

"That's not what I was asking. I meant afterward. Have you thought about it?"

It was the same old thing. Trying to keep these guys focused on a case was impossible. We had a whole shitload of work to do on this case, and English was wondering about the next assignment.

"Maybe I'll take some vacation," I told him, impatient to get back to the case.

"You're forgetting what I told you about Ibsen's Dr. Stockman. This one is an open sewer. We are going to be persona non grata."

"What the hell do you mean? We didn't kill anyone, bribe any politicians, or sodomize any kids."

He shook his head from side to side. ''You're missing it, Fraleigh. This one is so sick, so disgusting that you're going to become the enemy of the people, sort of like the news media after Watergate.''

''Well, what do you suggest we do, Paul, destroy the evidence and take disability pensions?''

''Don't get angry. I'm merely pointing out that we will not be permitted to continue on in the department. That means a lot more to you than to the two of us.''

''Shit!''

''Your usual eloquence has deserted you,'' he observed, ''but the ugly truth is that you, Don Quixote, have exposed some truths about the workings of California democracy that the folks will not appreciate. It could be worse. In days of old, when knights were bold, the runners, braving all sorts of dangers and agonies to carry news of the battle to the king, were beheaded when they told of a defeat.''

''Sometimes you sould like you've already been beheaded, English. We worked a homicide case. The chips fall where they may. They won't dare touch us with all the media publicity.''

''What makes you think the media will give it that much coverage or be very concerned about us?''

I tried to recall what Casey had said about the media. Paul supplied it for me.

''Remember what you told me Casey said. The news media *know*. They won't be that scandalized, and it's only speculation that votes were changed. Remember ABSCAM. Some of the crooked politicians who were charged kept screaming that no one was safe when law-enforcement agents could entrap legislators. That wasn't surprising. They were caught. The surprise was that some other real big shots defended them and tried, with some success, to put pressure on the FBI and Justice Department. The danger of you and a police state may scare them worse than what they really don't want to know about life in the capital.''

''Why do you put all the emphasis on me? It seems to me that you two are in this case, too.''

''Neither the Block nor I have field marshals' batons in our knapsacks. Nor are we consumed with your compulsion to right wrongs and to instill justice in a society more interested in winning the football games than knowing about recruitment violations.''

''Yeah! No one gives a shit about how much they pay the jocks as long as the team gets to the Rose Bowl,'' the Block added.

''Do you want to call Louis?'' English asked before we got into the car.

''No. We might as well leave him out of this for now. At least until I can think it out,'' I added in response to their raised eyebrows and amused looks at each other. They were right, dammit.

''So congratulations, my dear Fraleigh, it appears that your initial intuitive deduction that Adolph Stone spoke with forked tongue turned out to be quite correct.''

''Gee, thanks, Paul. Is it O.K. if I make a note of your compliment in my scrapbook?''

''Feel free to do so, Sergeant,'' he answered generously.

But my head was occupied with Fred Casey. In the back of my mind, some thoughts about his future were forming, despite my determination to prevent them. He would not suffer the disgrace of exposure. Somehow I didn't want to think what alternative he would choose. I went over his narrative again.

We whizzed by the fleet of old mothballed navy ships, bypassed Benecia along with the rest of the cars, and rocked across Carquinez Bridge in fairly high winds.

I thought out loud, ''Fred Casey isn't your average politician. A guy survives prison camps, then goes under in politics. I don't get it. Some of the others, well, nothing could surprise me, but the prison camps didn't break him. How did he cave in, in the legislature? Where did it start?''

"In the first century before Christ, Publilius Syrus wrote, 'Money alone sets all the world in motion.' ''

"That's great, Paul. I'll write it down in case I ever need it on the witness stand.''

"I don't get how they kept kids that young in line for all that sex stuff,'' the Block said. "I guess kids grow up faster nowadays.''

"Those kids never grew up at all,'' Paul told him. "I'm an expert on radical therapies, awareness alterations, and personality snapping. I was educated, or reeducated as they put it, by the masters in Nam.''

"Shit, Paul,'' the Block interrupted. "What's that got to do with those kids orally copulating politicians and stuff like that?''

"It's not that different,'' he answered. "They depersonalized us by destroying our self-identities. They were good at it, I'll say that for them. One day they would starve you, sometimes actually pretend to shoot you, letting the hammer fall on an empty cylinder. The next day they would be warm, friendly, all-forgiving if you would just open your mind, confess, promise cooperation. They were patient. If you weren't ready by then, they could keep you in total darkness for a couple of weeks, with no human contact. Sensory deprivation, followed by induced stress on the central nervous system.''

"But that was war,'' the Block scoffed. "A prison camp in a foreign country where they could do anything they wanted. These kids were right over in good old Santa Cruz County. They didn't threaten to shoot them or anything.''

"No. What I was describing was earlier, primitive, I guess, compared to the present personality-altering techniques. No force is necessary here. They just follow some basic psychological, communication techniques and lure people in. By the time they've realized what's happening, if they ever do, it's usually too late. When I was at Stanford, I spent a lot of time with one of the faculty members who was studying the phenomenon. He was interested in my experiences. In return, he explained to me the common personality-altering techniques of the new unorthodox religions—the Krishnas, Moonies, Church of Scientology, and so forth. Two things are surprising. One, there are a lot more of these movements than you realize. And two, they are remarkably similar in methodology and exploitiveness of the people they indoctrinate."

"Was the professor able to help you?" I couldn't help asking.

"I'm still here," Paul said dryly. "But," he added, "you have to remember the incredible expansion of the cult and mass therapies in this country over the past decade. They have been enormously successful in recruiting and programming hundreds of thousands of adults. It's infinitely easier to affect youngsters of the age we saw in the pictures. For children, what is, is normal. Remember, they were either without parents or their parents had brought them to the camp. In some cases, just like Jonestown, the juvenile courts made them wards of the wonderful Moral Reaffirmation Guild."

"Is that really true? How could that be, a judge assigning a kid to a kooky movement like that?" I questioned Paul.

"It wasn't presented as kooky. I'm sure Stone was able to produce glowing comments from prominent people, including elected officials in high office, along with smiling pictures of them visiting the camp. Then too, the jargon of 'increased awareness and fulfillment' is polished enough to sound catchy to well-meaning people."

Neither the Block nor I had anything to say to that for a while.

"Their eyes all looked funny in the pictures," I observed.

"Yes, that's the famous thousand-mile stare, symptomatic of disorientation and delusion, resulting from the physiological stress and group pressure utilized by self-awareness groups. They usually entice people in, initially establishing a friendly, loving environment, gradually convincing the individual to cut off from family, friends, and the outside world. By the time they finish, they don't need physical coercion. Chanting, diet, sensory deprivation, hours of staring into someone else's eyes without moving, and so forth, destroy the mind's ability to think. Gradually, people perform as directed. Emotions and feelings vanish, along with anything resembling formerly held value systems. Believe me, they have conditioned adults to do a lot stranger things than what they had those kids doing. Look at the Zombie. He was actually their man in the police department," Paul finished.

"It's unbelievable that the law don't crack down," the Block commented.

English responded, "Crack down on what? Religious activities protected by the First Amendment? Or self-awareness therapies people join voluntarily? Or just emotional fascism generally?"

"I can't figure Stone," the Block complained. "With all that bread, his mansion, swimming pool, all the broads he wants, why does he do all that conniving? He has more money than he can spend."

"As the Hunt brothers put it after their silver buying surfaced, 'Money is just the way to keep score,' " I answered. "Power is the game. We can figure from what Casey said why Stone might have sent us to pressure Phillips. On the other hand, we really don't know what happened to his daughter, Lisa."

"Still, it makes you wonder," Paul put in. "It seems like a pretty elaborate scheme to use three police officers as strong-arm goons. How did he think he could maintain control over us?''

''Yeah, even the department can't,'' the Block chuckled.

''Stone is accustomed to buying politicians like we buy newspapers,'' I said, disregarding the Block's oblique comments on my supervisory abilities. ''He didn't anticipate any trouble with us. After all, he apparently had already lined up Tweedledum and his brother's law firm. Hell, he almost got us retired after they failed to kill us.

''The more interesting question is why he got so furious. He had Casey lined up, the mob supporting him, and the state legislature under control. He even had the Zombie spying on us. He was in the catbird seat.''

Twenty-six

WE STOPPED IN GORDON'S, DEMORALIZED. I DIDN'T BE-
lieve the booze or fellowship was going to snap us out of it,
but I hoped some plans of what to do next would crystallize.
Before I had swallowed the first sip of my beer, Raoul Chavez touched my elbow, motioning me to one side. "I'm glad
I just happened to stop in on the way home. Just before I left
the office, Moon called."

Moon was one of my snitches. I wondered absently what
he wanted.

"Fraleigh, Moon said it's a must that you call him within
an hour," Raoul said.

"Within an hour? You're kidding. Who the hell does he
think he is, Deep Throat?" But both Moon and I knew I'd
call. Once, information he provided had enabled us to stake
out a bank armored-truck robbery just fifteen minutes before
the crooks showed up.

Someone had heaved in the phone booth recently. The
management had done its usual mediocre job of cleaning up.
Dialing Moon's number, I tried not to breathe.

"What's up?" I asked.

"Got to see you right away, pal."

Neither Moon nor I used any names nor too many words either. I protested. "You sure?"

"Surer than I've ever been in my life, pal. I got a package for you. By the way, leave the two ghouls home."

"O.K. The usual location?" I asked.

"Fifteen minutes," the talkative informant said, hanging up.

"You two ghouls stay here until I see what Moon wants."

The Block, on his third beer, beefed, "What do you mean, ghouls?"

"Moon's words. Not mine. I just passed them on in case you were interested in how the world sees you. It's part of my educational duty as your supervisor."

"Et tu, Brute?" Paul said.

We blended with the bums more and more each year, I thought, watching Moon cautiously approach. St. John's Park had seen better days. But the winos were docile, and occasional foot patrol and cruiser sweeps kept the rat packs off-balance enough to make the place reasonably safe until dark. We had a couple of hours of margin. I had never been with Moon more than fifteen minutes at a time since we first established a relationship a year ago, so we were probably safe.

Studying him meander toward me with all the techniques of a CIA man, I recalled our first meeting. Bull Hansen, regarded by Foley as the best investigator in the bureau and by the other dicks as a dumb sadist, had beaten Moon badly in the squad room after picking him up on suspicion of burglary of a stationery store. I had wandered in and told him to knock it off. Bull had a lot more brawn than brains and took a swing at me. For five minutes, I gave him a boxing lesson while Moon looked on silently, but undoubtedly wildly approving.

Foley had wanted to prefer charges against me for conduct unbecoming, but wiser heads prevailed. About two weeks later I spotted Moon as I drove through the downtown area. He hadn't made any charges against Hansen, but I drove up next to him to let him know that even if he did, he was clean as far as the squad was concerned.

Moon had jumped about two feet when I pulled the unmarked car into the curb. In the best Cagney tradition, he whispered from the side of his mouth, "In the park—ten minutes." It had been the start of a profitable relationship. I never fed Moon much money for information, mostly because we never had much. Money was a mistake anyway. The FBI always outbid us. They had all the money. We needed other incentives. With Moon, mine was his protection from what he feared—cops like Bull. I never could have convinced him that people like Bull only last so long. Not that I ever tried to enlighten him. Whatever motivated Moon to toss me some information now and then, I appreciated.

I was sitting at a dilapidated concrete checkers table. My ass was chilled from the cold concrete seat when Moon slid down opposite me.

"Jeez, you look bad, Fraleigh. I heard you was hurt, but I didn't know it was so bad. You lost a lot of weight."

"I'm going to start drinking malteds, Moon, not to worry. Did you have anything else on your mind other than my health?"

"I was just askin'. Don't get sore." He bared his yellow-green, broken teeth at me in what he undoubtedly considered a winning smile. He was so dishonest that I occasionally found myself liking the little runt. Anyone with his conniving character who had stayed alive forty to sixty years had to be admired. His whiskered chin, red-veined face, and scrawny body made it impossible to guess his age any closer.

"Some people you know and I know sent this to you." He peered around, then slipped a white envelope across the table.

I emulated him looking around. Not seeing any Russian spies, good-looking broads, or anything else of interest, I took the envelope and opened it.

It was a letter addressed to me, handwritten, and on paper bearing the seal of the lieutenant governor's office. I glanced down to the end of the page without reading it. The signature was scribbled in blue ink across the bottom. It was signed by Fred Casey.

"Where did you get this, you little prick?" I had grabbed Moon by the shirt so quickly that he was helpless.

"Please, Fraleigh," he whined, "just read it. Then I'll tell you everything. Look, I never held out on you before, did I?" he whispered, his eyes shifting in rapid motion.

I released him and read the letter.

Dear Sergeant Fraleigh,

I know this is a surprise. As a result of our meeting, I flew here by private plane. You see, I knew Lisa and Judy were alive. I didn't tell you about it because I believe that I have more of a chance to save them than you do. Please listen to the bearer of this note and give his offer a fair hearing, not for my sake, but for Lisa and Judy.

He had signed it in an unsteady scrawl.

Moon had been watching me intently as I read the letter. Now as I looked up, he said, "It's for real, Fraleigh. But I want you to know I'm just a messenger. I don't have nothing to do with this. Whatever you want to do is O.K. with me," he said.

"How did they know you're my snitch?"

"There ain't much they don't know, Fraleigh," he said, avoiding my eyes.

Now I remembered wondering a couple of times how this nothing-looking guy had come by such heavy info. The mob had sneaky ways of its own. It never acknowledged that snitching people to the cops was permissible. Instead it constantly preached that it called for the death penalty. Yet we knew double and triple crosses were going on all the time. Using a front like Moon to leak stuff sometimes served their purposes in stopping unauthorized jobs or sinking rivals.

"They told me to show you these, Fraleigh."

He handed me two Polaroid snapshots. I held them by the edges so my fingerprints wouldn't be on them. Not that I didn't trust the boys. It was just that boys will be boys. The first print wasn't exactly of a family picnic. Five people were sitting behind a table. Adolph Stone sat stiff and somber. His usual confidence seemed absent, but his eyes were alert and clear. Not so Fred Casey sitting next to him. His eyes were pain-filled and cloudy and he sagged backward in the chair like he had been injured. His face was white. On his left, a balding man in his mid-fifties stared angrily at the camera. His brown eyes had an intensity to them. His clothes and what remained of his hair were disheveled. His hands weren't visible. I wondered if they were handcuffed under the table. On his left, I recognized the terrified faces of Judy Fortune and Lisa Stone from their snapshots.

The other picture was of the Zombie. A thick rope knotted around his neck was strung over a beam, and he was hanging, with his eyes popped out.

I felt a chill, half of apprehension and half of anger at myself for being set up so easily. I didn't have to look over my shoulder or around the park to know we were covered. "Leave the ghouls," he had said, and I walked into it. The mob didn't casually hand this kind of evidence to cops. I kept my voice even.

"Who's the man next to Casey?"

"That's Phillips, the guy who runs that commune. He's not playing with a full deck. The pictures and the note are for real, Fraleigh. The cop was a suicide. He hung himself."

"Yeah, so what? I ain't in the market for letters from politicians or pictures of stiffs."

"I told them you was hard, Fraleigh, that you wouldn't buy the deal that easy, but they made me come. You know that, don't you? I ain't in on any of this."

"What's their proposal, Moon?"

"They said this can all be kept quiet. No need for a big fuss. You guys go back to work— Wait!" he squeaked, as I grabbed him again by the shirt.

"Do you mean those sons of bitches are trying to bargain our jobs?" I snarled, remembering Tweedledum's retirement pitch.

Moon could hardly speak. "Don't be mad at me. I don't know except what they told me to say. They said everyone would hate you guys for showing up a popular war hero like Casey and some of the other politicians and for dragging the kids through the publicity."

"Those slimy bastards," I muttered, releasing him. "You can tell them I don't care if I ever work again or about publicity for any of them. They did it, and that's that."

"Yeah, yeah," he said. "I told them you would say that, but they made me come."

"I'll get you a certificate from the police department for bravery. You're so noble, Moon."

"Don't take it out on me, Fraleigh. I can tell you I sure didn't want to bring you this stuff."

"Where are those kids now? And don't talk to me about deals, or I'll wring your neck off right here in the park."

"I don't know! I swear it! I don't know!" he shrieked. "I only know what they told me. Phillips's assistant, who's nuttier than a fruitcake, has them, but the parties who sent me here made me write this down to say to you."

He pulled a dirty envelope from his pocket. I could see it was his chicken scratching, or I would have grabbed it away from him. Haltingly, he read:

> "We know he's straight, so if he gives his word, we'll see the girls are saved. We never knew Stone was using our people to hit cops. Fraleigh shouldn't lose any sleep over Stone or Phillips being taken out. Stone never got any phone calls. He made up the kidnap story because he knew the two kids were camping near the commune and figured the cops would grill Phillips at the commune. Phillips was scared of both Fortune and Stone. He only grabbed the two girls for protection after he killed Fortune. He figured Stone would set him up next. But Phillips was nuts. He had killed two kids who wandered into the camp. It was one of those bodies that Stone lied about, saying it was his daughter Lisa. He wanted you guys to go after Phillips to scare him into line. Then Stone would protect him, and he would have to go along with the scheme. . . ."

I brooded over that, but couldn't pick any holes in it yet. Moon continued reading:

> "No bodies are going to turn up one way or the other, so the cops don't have anything to investigate anyway."

That was the misstatement of the year, but I didn't interrupt Moon's performance.

He read on:

"The scheme is dead. All of the politicians in the pictures will resign and the Moral Camp will close. We're doing all this because the heat for us isn't worth it. . . ."

Moon had paused for breath. He was having a tough day. He was especially nervous about the next part. Glancing at me, he turned his eyes down to the envelope, mumbling,

"If he says no, we feel no responsibility for the girls after the way Stone treated us. If the deal is on, we'll talk to Fraleigh on the phone about where he can find the girls."

Moon came to a halt.

"What else are they angling for, Moon? Heat ain't enough for them to do all this."

"That's all I got," he said miserably.

"Then no deal. I know those bastards. There's something else here they want and I'm not agreeing to anything until I understand what they're after."

"They figured you might be stubborn. They made me promise not to tell you unless I had to. If this story comes out, they'll be the laughingstock of the eastern families. They been bragging for years how they were going to lock up the California action, how they were wired right into the governor's office and the legislature. That's why they sent me to make you an offer."

I leaned back. Months of violence, crime, human misery, and now some hoods wanted to erase the record to protect their egos. I began to laugh and couldn't stop.

Moon almost crumbled. "You're crazy, crazy! Jeez,

what are you laughing at? I can't believe it.'' His eyes were wide with fear.

His reaction started me laughing more, but I stopped. The image of Lisa Stone came to mind—reading to a blind woman, helping out other kids, and all the while living with a bastard like her father. I looked up through the palm trees into the darkening sky.

My cards weren't much. I had very carefully made no movement as Moon stuck the pictures and Casey's letter into his dirty Windbreaker. I could almost feel the cross hairs of the high-powered rifle scope on my chest. They weren't about to let me take that kind of evidence out of the park. Moon was as scared as I was. He knew that if they took me out he would keep me company. The boys didn't believe in leaving witnesses.

So all they wanted was that I pretend nothing had happened. The case was over. The dead are the dead. May they rest in peace. He was watching me.

"Tell them O.K., Moon.''

We went to the public phone booth on the corner. Moon got in and dialed a number. When it was answered he mumbled a few words that I couldn't catch and hung up.

"They said we got to wait here a few minutes, Fraleigh.''

"What the hell for, Moon?''

"I don't know. I just do what they tell me.''

"You would have been the life of the party at the Nuremberg trials, Moon.''

"Noor-what trials? What are you talking about?'' He frowned.

"Forget it. I'll wait with you, Moon. Nothing better go wrong!''

"It's gonna be O.K. They said it would.'' But he chewed his lower lip.

The two of us stood there for fifteen minutes. We rejected sixteen appeals for a quarter and four for lewd acts. The requests came from various males, aged between sixteen and seventy. I was just about to tell Moon to call his number again when the phone in the booth rang. I jumped. My nerves were raw.

"It's for you." Moon handed me the phone.

"Hello."

"Are you in agreement with our arrangement?" a gravelly voice asked. The only thing I was in agreement with was the need to get myself out of the area alive and to try to get a handle on where those two kids were being held. The mob was right. I didn't give a shit what they did with Stone, Casey, and Phillips.

"How do I know I can trust you guys to turn over those two girls?" I wondered if my stalling was obvious.

He laughed. "Hey, you know something, copper? You're funny. We can blow everyone away as easy as me hanging up this phone and walk away clean, and you're asking how do you know you can trust us. It's the other way around. How do we know we can trust you if we release the kids?"

He had a good point. I was trying to think of the most clever dishonesty I could come up with when a clock in the background chimed eight o'clock. My heart skipped a beat in fear that he would realize that I recognized that rich melodious sound, which had reminded me of Big Ben.

"Moon knows me. He can tell you I play straight. And you're right. I don't give a shit for the others, only the girls." I had said the first thing that came into my head to keep him from thinking.

"How about at least letting me talk to Lisa to make sure she's O.K.?"

"She's O.K. I'm looking at her now. She's bare-ass naked. Just for security reasons, you know." He chuckled.

I hoped that he would be there when I got to Stone's place. When I didn't say anything he continued: "We been careful not to let them see anyone who they might be able to recognize later just in case you should double-cross us. But I guess for now, we got to take a chance on your word. Just remember we don't forget. Put Moon on. I'll tell him how it will go down.''

Moon stepped back into the booth. I watched him closely with one eye and the car traffic with the other. As soon as he hung up I cuffed one of his wrists and hooked the other cuff to the telephone-booth door handle.

''You're crazy! You know they got us covered. They'll kill us right here. What are you doing?''

I had started to dial the emergency number, but I dropped the phone and pulled my magnum as three men emerged from the shadows with that too-careful casualness. I brought the magnum to bear on the lead man. The bulge under his coat was probably a sawed-off shotgun. I would shoot him first. Then follow the slight recoil of my weapon to take out the guy on the right and swing back, hoping for a lucky hit on the guy to the far left. It was dreaming, of course.

Bright light flooded the three people. Casually, they changed direction, walking slowly away from us. The loudspeaker that went along with the cruiser spotlight blared at me, ''Who are your friends, Fraleigh?''

It was Bruno, the young blond who had been at Tricia's crime scene. She was now riding solo. I could see that she had gained a couple of pounds, but her Remington shotgun, held in full shoulder position, was very steadily following the three retreating pedestrians.

''It's O.K.!'' I yelled to her.

I stuffed Moon handcuffed and whining into the caged backseat of the patrol car.

''You have strange friends, Fraleigh. What gives?'' Bruno asked.

''I can't tell it all to you now. Just get this car as fast as it goes up to Balsa Drive. The mob is holding two young girls there.''

She looked me full in the face, rookie uncertainty gone. ''Christ, you look ten years older.''

I looked down at her ring finger. It was bare. We had both aged.

She flipped on the red lights and siren and made a U-turn. We were up to forty miles an hour in heavy downtown traffic before I had a chance to reconsider the wisdom of my order. I ignored a tractor-trailer truck bearing down on my side of the car and called communications on the radio asking for the Block's call number. I hoped they had taken possession of Raoul Chavez's police cruiser outside Gordon's.

''Where are you? We started toward the park to look for you.'' The Block's voice grated across the airwaves.

''We're code three to Stone's house. They've got Lisa and Judy. They're still alive.''

''Ten-four. We're right behind you.''

Bruno cut the light and siren but not the speed during the last mile to Stone's house. Moon's anger at me had been replaced by white-faced fear over Bruno's driving. He had bounced all over the rear seat. His handcuffed hands were useless to him.

We screeched into Stone's driveway and came to a halt right in front of the handsome double doors. They opened and two goons came out before we had gotten to the front steps. The one in front was big. Very big. About six four and 240 pounds. The second guy was slightly under six feet tall and probably weighed 200. He looked small by comparison.

''This is private property,'' the lead giant snarled at us. ''So unless you got a warrant, I suggest you get the fuck out of here.''

I wasn't terribly happy about trying to defend myself against these two. In my condition Moon would have been plenty to handle. Bruno unbuckled her baton and strode forward. "Out of the way, asshole, before you get hurt," she told the big guy.

"Hey, Louie, did you hear what this cunt said? She—" Bruno had moved so quickly that I almost didn't see what had sent him down in agony. Her baton caught him squarely on the right kneecap. He would remember her for the rest of his life. The other guy had closed on her before she could get the baton back in position, and he was using his superior weight to push her into the police cruiser. I started toward them, but had to jump back when the Block almost ran me over, pulling his car right up into the brawl. He stepped calmly to where the smaller hood was still trying to take out Bruno. The Block punched him in the back of the head. No finesse. Just a six-inch straight right that landed with a bone-crunching thud.

"Jesus! You killed him," Bruno gasped. He had sunk to the pavement and lay motionless.

"Fuck him," the Block said. "Any more of them around, Fraleigh?"

We left Paul to help Bruno secure the prisoners. I heard her calling for fill units and an ambulance. I hoped one ambulance would be enough as the Block and I, guns drawn carefully, edged past the huge grandfather clock and Stone's other trappings of wealth. We searched the kitchen after crossing the spacious living room. I opened a door on the master bedroom suite. It was empty. I turned away, then came back into the room to look at a picture window that faced inward, not out toward the open pool area the way it should have.

"Jesus Christ!" I said. The Block had moved next to me and looked through the window into the room beyond. The young naked bodies of Lisa Stone and Judy Fortune were strapped to the room's opposite wall. They sagged in the chains binding them. We bumped into each other trying to open the door. I got in first and immediately fell over a body just inside the wall. Stunned, I shook my head and started to get up. I was looking almost face-to-face with Fred Casey, whose eyes stared lifelessly upward.

The Block helped me to my feet. The characteristics of the room were beginning to force their way into my consciousness. The mirrors, racks, whips, leather fittings, vibrators positioned into the floor and the walls. White nurses' and doctors' uniforms. A huge screen, video tape cameras, and the round bed that had been in the damning sex pictures. Gym equipment of different kinds. It was a room for bizarre sex, and Adolph Stone had sat in his expensive bedroom and watched through a one-way mirror. His own daughter. It had been high-tech incest. My stomach rose.

Lisa Stone moaned, "Please . . . Please." Her eyes pleaded. Then she fainted, slipping forward into her bindings. I went toward her. The movement behind what looked like an electric chair caught my eye. There was another body, but this one was moving.

"Careful, Fraleigh," the Block cautioned from the other side of the room.

I went behind the chair. Adolph Stone, gutshot, was crawling toward a .45 automatic just beyond his straining fingers. His slate-gray eyes looked up at me. The events of the last month washed over me. His eyes watched expressionlessly as I raised the magnum so that the sights lined up on his nose. For ten seconds we looked at each other. Paul English stepped in front of me. I hadn't heard him come in. Gently he moved my gun hand sideways, at the same time kicking the .45 away from Stone. Stone turned his head ponderously to stare at Paul. It was his last act. A shudder ran through him and his head dropped to the floor and was still.

The Block and T. Bruno had freed Lisa and Judy, wrapping them in blankets. He carried them into the bedroom, where she helped them into bed. Both kids appeared weak and in shock. I felt sure that they would respond to medical care. But mentally? Adolph Stone's oppressive spirit closed over me. I went into the bathroom and retched until Paul came and helped me into a chair.

"Children. His own daughter. How could he? He didn't grow up ten in a shack, abused and starving. We see those cases. But Stone had enough money for anything he wanted."

"Yes. Maybe that was his problem," Paul sighed. "Unlike most people he was able to gratify each new fantasy, until the only ones left . . ."

"Phillips is in the den. He was handcuffed and beaten to death. It looks like Casey died of a heart attack. The hoods probably figured the game was up. We were just lucky to get here before those punks outside finished the girls off. You made a good guess, Fraleigh," the Block said.

"You'll be interested in this file from Stone's den." Paul handed me some papers. They had to do with the Washington Housing Project. Another Stone lie was exposed. It was clear from records in the file that Stone's company did indeed own the project. He had purchased the property from the city under the subterfuge that it would be improved. Yet, it was clear that the plans called for it to be made into an electronic industrial park. Its location was too valuable for low-income housing, so concluded his consultant.

Raising rents and evicting people whenever possible would lower resistance to the eventual razing of the structures so that new development could occur. This last analysis came from the very prestigious law firm in which Captain McCarthy's brother served as a senior partner.

Their letter contained all sorts of sagacity. They pointed out that the developer might well be frightened off by the area's high crime rate. Solution? Their firm would use its contacts in city government and the police department to "address" the problem. The letter made it clear why Foley had "lost" the missing persons report on the children from the project. Finally, they said that although investments by two members of the city planning staff, three elected council members, and a state assemblyman did not in their legal opinion constitute a conflict of interest, it would be just as well not to publicize their participation until the project was completed.

Bruno came in and took the file with one hand and pulled me to my feet with the other. "We got a doctor here to examine the two girls. I asked him to take a look at you too. Come on."

"I'm O.K."

Nevertheless I allowed myself to be led into a small bedroom on the other side of the house. Paul English came along. A small man with close-cropped gray hair pulled a stethoscope and a gadget for taking blood pressure measurements from his black medical bag. "They told me something of your recent medical history, young man," he said, frowning at me from behind plain no-nonsense spectacles. He roamed around my chest and back with the stethoscope. Paul had helped strip my shirt off. Bruno kept her eyes on the doctor as if she were expecting an important announcement or something. He took my blood pressure, then my pulse. "Amazing."

"That I'm in such good shape, huh?"

"No." He had taken a hypodermic needle from his bag and was loading it up. "Amazing that a policeman would be so stupid to do this to his body."

Bruno smiled. Her maternal instincts had been vindicated.

"I don't want you to put me out, Doc."

He had already rubbed my arm with a cotton ball swabbed in alcohol and was easing the needle in. "This will help you sleep for the next hour or two. After that, see your doctor.

He'll prescribe a couple of weeks rest. And he'll also tell you to get another doctor if you don't do what he says.''

I stretched out on the bed. Bruno threw a blanket on me. "Here, don't catch pneumonia.''

I fumbled with the blanket and she impatiently reached over and firmly tucked me in.

"Hey! What does the 'T' stand for?''

"Theresa.'' She was frowning. Then she opened up and smiled. "Terry is better.''

"You did a hell of a job today, Terry. I'm not even going to comment in my report on your driving.''

"My God! That poor guy is still locked in the backseat.'' She rushed out.

So I slept through two hours of bedlam as tech crews pored over the crime scene. Actually, the whole house was a crime scene. I awoke with a headache and went into a bathroom adjacent to the bedroom to wash up. I went into the living room and saw Louis Robinson arguing heatedly with Captain McCarthy. It struck me that I had never seen McCarthy in the field before.

English approached me. "How do you feel?''

"What's going on, Paul?''

"Tweedledum is trying to take charge of the crime scene, and Louis threatened to knock him on his ass if he interferes. But Louis is going to lose. Here comes Deputy Chief Stein.''

Paul's prediction was correct. Tweedledum grabbed Stein's ear. A minute later Stein walked over to Louis and whispered something. Louis had been conferring with Barney Fuller. He turned angrily on Stein. I couldn't hear what was being said, but Louis's expression left no doubt.

"Get the Block and let's get out of here with whatever evidence we have. I don't trust these clowns. Do you have the folder on the Washington Project?'' I asked.

"I put it in our car when I saw McCarthy arrive.''

We were getting into our car when Louis came stalking up. "I've been ordered to tell you guys that you've been put on administrative leave." He was steaming.

"Shit. We're already on administrative leave, Captain," the Block said.

"What's happening, Louis?" I asked.

"I'm just about on administrative leave myself. Stein took command of the crime scene and ordered me to go back to headquarters to prepare a press release for his approval. Press release! The goddamn press is all over here even now. Look."

I turned and saw two television crews and three newspaper reporters arguing with a uniformed cop, who was trying to keep them behind a rope strung between two marked cruisers.

"Can you tell us anything, Louis? I've been out for two hours."

"I know. You should be back in the hospital. The girls are all right physically. The guy the Block clobbered recovered consciousness in the hospital, but he's mob. He's clamming. We got lucky on the big guy. Bruno broke his kneecap. He'll be limping from now on. But he's spilling his guts out. It turned out they were in too much of a hurry for muscle and got careless. The guy's not connected at all. He's a lightweight. A bouncer from a Hollywood nude-dancing joint. He's desperately trying to sing himself out of a murder rap."

"Yeah, I helped interrogate the asshole myself," the Block laughed, tripling my headache pain.

"We all better clear the scene," Louis said, looking over his shoulder at the floodlit house entrance. "You guys come to my office tomorrow morning. We'll tie up the loose ends."

I looked at my watch. It was 0130 hours. "0900? O.K."

"Better make it 1000 hours. I have to be at a promotion ceremony in the chief's office at 0900."

"Promotion? Who's getting promoted?" I asked.

He frowned. "Foley's making captain."

"Louis, Jesus Christ! I don't believe it! You're pulling my leg. You were on the promotion committee."

"Get off my back, Fraleigh." He was furious. "You know how civil service works. Foley was next on the list. Unless he can be skipped for cause he gets promoted."

"Cause? There's plenty of fucking cause, and you know it."

"Lower your voice." He looked again at the house. "The chief personally decided that Foley deserved promotion."

"Yeah, no doubt after Tweedledum told him so." I turned and got into our car.

"What happened in the park? We were getting worried when we didn't hear from you," Paul asked, pulling out of the driveway.

"Moon was a messenger. They had me covered. I couldn't figure out what was behind the bullshit deal they were talking. I knew they weren't going to let me take the note from Casey and the pictures Moon showed me. I was lucky I heard Stone's clock over the phone and that Bruno came along when she did. They were moving in."

"Where to, Fraleigh?"

"Where to?" the Block protested. "It's almost 0200. What the fuck do you mean, where to?"

"There's one more stop, Paul."

"Rio Del Mar?"

"Right. They had to be stalling me for some reason. There's no way they could have believed that I would license a couple of murders and stay quiet. And they knew I'd say anything to negotiate for the girls' safety."

"The bouncer told us they were flying in a torch from Las

Vegas. Stone's house and all the bodies and records were going to go up like the Fourth of July.''

"I think the Block has answered your question. Zombie's body was in the garage. Those two hoods were on the way to bring it into the main house when you and Bruno surprised them. They were hoping to keep us strung out negotiating with them until the funeral pyre was set. All the evidence would have been in ashes.''

"They probably didn't want to kill me if they could avoid it. I guess they figured they could squash anything I'd say internally, like they did on the Tricia Greene case. It would only have been my word on what happened in the park. I sure wouldn't have had much credibility if I had let Moon disappear with the letter and pictures.''

Twenty-seven

THERE WAS A ROUND, FULL MOON. WE PULLED UP IN front of the Fortune place. The house was dark. Approaching the entrance alone, I wondered if she would answer the door.

I rang the bell for a good fifteen seconds, hearing it sound inside. Then I rang again. A light went on in the bedroom. I heard her steps. My heart was beating way too fast. She paused, looking through the peephole. I found myself hoping that she would refuse to open the door, sending us back over the mountain. She thought it over. Then the door opened.

I perched uneasily on the couch. She sat opposite me in a straight chair. She had on a light blue robe. It swung open when she sat. I glimpsed her long white thigh through the sheer negligee, one that I had eagerly peeled off her on a number of occasions in happier days past.

"Why are you here, Fraleigh?"

"Lisa and Judy are safe. Adolph Stone lied. Physically they're all right, but they've been sexually abused and they'll need treatment."

297

She blinked and looked down at the floor. When she glanced up, her eyes met mine. "You could have told me that on the phone. Why are you here?"

"Tell me about you and Adolph Stone, Sandra."

"Ah, yes, you're the detective now, not the lover. I know you won't believe me, but I was going to tell you about it when you were fully recovered. I have nothing to be ashamed of."

"Start with Stone," I said when it became clear that she was waiting for me to comment.

"Yes, Officer." Her eyes had misted slightly. "Adolph Stone was my patient. I don't feel justified in discussing his medical history with the police."

"I don't want his medical history. I want his personal history. His history with you."

"Very well. I suspect I'm telling you what you already know, but for a period of six months I was very close to him. We were intimate. It was six years ago. I've known for some time he was using me, just as viciously as he does everyone else."

"Yeah. How did your husband feel about all this?"

"Don?" She laughed. "I guess I overrated you as a detective. Did you know that Don was Adolph's son by his first marriage?"

Jesus! Just when I thought all of Stone's evil had been exposed, something else always seemed to come out. First he had pushed Fortune into sex crimes against kids, then set him up to be hit by warning Phillips that he was on the way to camp. His son.

"Your expression answers my question. Yes, Don too was too my patient. His father had made me a successful psychologist. His wealthy friends flocked to my office on his recommendations. I knew it was professionally wrong to take Don as a patient, but Dolph pressured me."

Dolph—that cut into me like a knife. So that was what she

called him. I wondered what had been his intimate name for her.

"Start with Stone," I repeated, hating myself.

Her glance came back to me. "Yes, Officer." She spoke so softly that I had to lean forward to hear. "I was just about ready to give up the idea of starting my own practice. I had only two patients during the first four months. Then Adolph Stone presented himself as a patient. He caught me at the lowest period of my life. I was ripe for him. He was wealthy, cultured, charming. After a couple of months we became lovers."

She took a deep breath. "Three months later, Don came into my office for counseling. By this time I was becoming uneasy over the depth of my involvement with Dolph. But I only began to learn how brutal he was as I treated his son. Don was a borderline schizophrenic. I was crushed to see what cruelties his father had lavished on him."

She stopped now, and I watched the mental debate. Candor won.

"Everything was patient-therapist with me, or so I thought until one day Don's darker side took over. I suppose I should have realized what was happening. Don was ruggedly good-looking, fun loving, young, very physical, and vulnerable. I was attracted. I should have known that I was sending some mixed signals to a disturbed young man."

"What happened?" I asked when she paused.

"All right, damn you," she glared. "When Don came in that day he had liquor on his breath. He, he . . . raped me. There's no other way to describe it. He was a brute, and so strong that he totally terrified me." Her eyes were haunted now, roaming around the room as she continued in a hushed voice.

"It was a warm day. I was wearing a blouse, skirt, and sandals."

I looked at her now. Her negligee was pale green, and

through it I could see her firm, erect nipples pointing outward through the delicate fabric. Her breasts were rising slightly faster than normal and a slight flush, spreading upward from her neck to her throat, was evident. As she continued, I realized with dismay that I had an erection.

"There was no warning. I was in midsentence when he ripped my blouse off. He dragged me to the floor. I struggled, but he ripped my skirt and panties off and forced himself into me.

"He was so rough that he was hurting me, and I cried. Suddenly, he came with a rush and an animal cry, and I realized that I had climaxed also. I felt dirty and ashamed."

I fumed at her honesty. Why the hell couldn't she have skipped the explanation and just said that she had been raped?

"It was so degrading. I suppose if it had been a stranger, it would have been more frightening, and I wouldn't have experienced it the same way. I found myself rationalizing that he was disturbed, unable to control himself, and that I had sent out female signals triggering his violence. I didn't know what to do."

I got up and went to the kitchen for a glass of water I didn't want. When I instructed new dicks in interrogation procedures, one of the principles I stressed was not to let the witness pause to ease the pitch of emotional tension. Those were the moments when the goodies came—the location of the bloody hatchet or the buried corpse or the real motive. Yet, now I was the one who had to move. What I really wanted was not the water but to pull out the Beefeaters and let the two of us get blotto, forget, and make love like none of it had ever happened, which was why I had the Block and English waiting outside. My chastity belts. I went back to the couch.

She hadn't moved. She was sitting hunched forward, hugging herself. Fixing on me with those big green eyes, she continued. "Two weeks passed before I could bring myself to see Don again. I was terribly nervous. He came in and we began the session without any reference to what had happened. He was in anguish. I felt helpless, without the ability to reach out and comfort him. He fell to his knees, sobbing hysterically, begging for forgiveness."

She moved forward on the chair and continued, "I held him in my arms as you would a child. I couldn't let him leave. He was so unstable that he might have hurt himself or someone else. I thought I could never bear to have him touch me again. Yet, I held him in my arms to comfort him. I was honest enough to recognize a whole rush of feelings—not just maternal instincts—shooting through me. It was blind lust too. We made love, but he wasn't quite as rough. Then he asked me to marry him."

Her eyes were focused on the wall above me. "I held off giving him an answer for three weeks, during which time we saw each other constantly. Exactly five weeks after being raped, I married my attacker. It violated all theories of psychology and common sense."

I stayed silent. She went on, "It only came apart in the last year. He became totally impotent. That drove me crazy. It wasn't long after that . . ." She trailed off into silence.

"That we arrived with our questions," I supplied.

"Yes, and something about you attracted me immediately."

"Yeah, something swinging between my legs."

She rocked back as if I had hit her.

"Let's stop the crap, Sandra. When did loving Grandpa Dolph give you me as an assignment?"

"He called before you arrived. We knew you were coming."

"You should get an Oscar. The comments about graffiti and the reaction when you learned we were from Homicide were professional."

"They were real. Adolph spoke to Don. I didn't pay much attention. Don never told me why you were coming."

"And your bitterness about Stone?"

"He had threatened me!"

"What?"

"Yes, a day earlier, he called and told me not to continue to counsel Don against helping him in his legislative efforts. He said anyone getting in his way would be 'crushed.' That even a nonentity like me would be removed. He was furious that I had told Don to avoid him. He warned me that he would have me declared unfit and take the children from me, as he did with Don's mother."

She touched a tissue to her eyes. "The terrible thing was that I knew he could do it. I had seen that he wielded enormous power over politicians. Can you imagine? That evil man taking my babies? Are you enjoying your pound of flesh, Fraleigh?"

"No."

"But you won't stop, will you?"

"You're the one making this tougher. I'm not interested in every last detail of your libido. Just tell me how Stone sicced you on me."

"You bastard. You're just like them. You manipulate people. You don't care about pain. What difference is there between you and them?"

"Well, for one thing, I didn't murder or rape anyone or blackmail any politicians or . . ."

"Oh, no, you're so goddamned righteous." She was near hysteria. I wanted to comfort her, but I didn't dare touch her.

"You have to remember the state I was in. Don rushed out. I was alone with the children, frightened. Who could I turn to? I called Adolph," she whispered.

"And?"

"He was sympathetic. He told me not to worry, he would

send men to find Don. Everything would be fine. It was what I wanted to hear. I took a sedative and went to bed. The sheriff's deputies woke me in the morning asking that I identify Don's torn shirt. It was horrible. I collapsed. Mrs. Smith took care of the children for two days."

So that was how Stone had been able to alert Phillips that Don Fortune was on his way to the commune.

"Sandra, did Stone talk about us?"

"Yes. He exploded when I told him Don had showed your assistants the computer while you spoke to me in the kitchen. He actually cursed Don."

The computer. My God! That was the cause of the Block being shot, English slugged, and me cut and beaten, the reason why we had almost died that Saturday afternoon. Stone knew the whole scheme had been written in just one place—in the brain of his son's computer. When he heard Don had shown it to us, it never occurred to him that it was only for innocent games. He assumed his mentally ill son had, for some reason, displayed the program to three cops. What had he said earlier to Sandra? "Anyone getting in the way would be crushed."

"Do you want me to continue?"

"Yes. Tell me how Stone sent you to me."

"You make it sound so calculated, so . . . so dirty."

"Wasn't it calculated?"

"No. I mean, at least, not as far as I was concerned. Stone . . . I don't know."

"Don't you, Sandra?"

She put her head in her hands. "Yes, yes, I confess. It was whatever you think it was. Can't you leave me alone?"

"What did he say?"

"It sounds silly now, but he said he was worried about you."

It wasn't silly at all. He was so worried that he ordered us knocked off. When it failed he had to know what was happening. What better way than Sandra?

"You believed him, Sandra?"

"Yes . . . No. Oh, God, I don't really know what I believed."

"Who suggested bringing me back here?"

She sagged. "I can't take much more of this. What happened between us just happened. Can't you accept that?"

"I'd like to. It's just that even now, you're holding out on me."

"I've told you everything," she protested.

"Yeah? Do you deny you got my home address from Stone and that once you got me over here you fed him information about what I was doing?"

"He gave me your address, but . . . I guess I should have known better, but I'm not a detective, a cop. The information was harmless. And I was afraid to antagonize him. He made it clear that the house, all of the investments, were in his name."

"Yeah. It's the same old message. Bucks count more than anything, even lives."

"I don't say I'm without some blame, some fault, but I wasn't part of any crooked conspiracy."

"No. You weren't part of it. You just lived off it. When they threatened to pull out the golden rug, you weren't about to rock the boat by asking too many questions.

"And when you told the parents of the young girl whom Don took to Adolph's sex orgy not to let her testify, that wasn't because they told you to do it or anything. It was just professional, right?"

"It was true. It would have destroyed the child and Don."

"Or were you in Adolph's special fun room with them, Sandra?" She shook her head from side to side and waited stiffly for my next question. "But you've been there, I bet.

Maybe even helped the old boy to equip it. And did you and he stay together hand in hand by the bedroom window getting turned on by watching the games through the one-way glass?''

For a moment I thought she wasn't going to answer. When she spoke she picked her words carefully. ''I'm a doctor. I refuse to let myself fall into the sexual guilt traps that plague so many of my patients. Adolph needed stimulation. Viewing others from the bedroom worked for him. There were never any children involved when I was with him. You'd be surprised how common this kind of thing is in the executive circles of the high-tech and entertainment worlds. But it didn't mean anything to me.''

She was slightly flushed. Her mouth opened and her tongue flicked across her lips. I remembered that it was the way she controlled her breathing when aroused. Like hell, the sex room hadn't done anything for her. Just thinking of it now had gotten her hot. I thought of the way her nipples would have hardened under the negligee. How she would be moist, ready to receive me. And I cursed her silently because her excitement had aroused me. And she knew it.

''It was the children, not the money,'' she answered, but even she could hear some of the doubt in her voice. ''I still didn't know anything for sure about Adolph, and I never gave him any real information on you,'' she said more firmly.

''I guess you never happened to mention to him that I took the kids to the beach in the mornings, then?''

She paled. ''I mentioned that. It was perfectly natural.''

''Or that we would be staying in the St. Francis Hotel in San Francisco?''

Her face was coming apart, trembling. I looked away.

''Naturally, it never occurred to you that there had to be some motive for him to want that kind of information.''

"He told me we were in danger, someone would watch us," she mumbled.

"Sure, we were in danger, all right. If Bosco hadn't been so inept, the little tidbits you supplied would have provided my obituary. How did you sleep after you knew you set up Bini, Sandra?"

"Oh, please, please don't. Just go."

"It was on the pad, wasn't it? It took me a long time to figure that out. You repeated the car license number, my scribbling on Bosco, and Bini's name and extension number, didn't you? For once, Stone was efficient. Bini probably helped out a bit by drinking his lunch at Gordon's, and the Zombie was typically helpful to his pals."

"These are terrible things, Fraleigh. Maybe I should have added everything up sooner, but I didn't. I couldn't cope with the threats about the children. What else could I do?

"Tell the Block and English to go. Stay and hold me. With your strength, we can erase the scars, let it heal. We have our whole lives together. I know you love me as much as I love you . . ."

She trailed off as I stood glaring at her. "I can forgive and forget everything, Sandra. I'm not as rigid as you suppose. I can even understand that you set us up because of fear that you would lose your children. Even the attack on me in San Francisco, I could forgive; after all, I survived. But every time I'd look at you, I'd think that you helped kill Bini."

She was unmoving as I walked to the door and let myself out. I took a deep breath, then another. The air had a touch of fish in it, along with the purifying salt. I walked to the car and got in.

Paul, behind the wheel, made no move to start the car. I looked at him. His brown eyes were unblinking. "You sure, Fraleigh? We can come by and pick you up tomorrow."

"Let's go," I grated.

He started the engine and drove slowly upward toward the

highway. We stopped for a red light above the house. I looked down. A light was on in the kids' bedroom. Beyond the house, the bright moon was dancing on the sea's darkness. Tomorrow would be a good beach day. We headed back into Silicon Valley.

ABOUT THE AUTHOR

Joseph D. McNamara is chief of police in San Jose, California. He has published articles in the *New York Times*, the *Washington Post*, the *Los Angeles Times*, *Cosmopolitan*, and many other journals. He was born in New York City and, like his father, walked a beat in Harlem for the New York Police Department. He is the author of SAFE AND SANE, a guide to protecting yourself and your family, and is currently at work on a new novel.